THE ELEVENTH COMMANDMENT
A DYSTOPIAN ROMANCE

NORAH WILSON &
HEATHER DOHERTY

Published by

SOMETHING SHINY
PRESS

Norah Wilson / Something Shiny Press
P.O. Box 30046, Fredericton, NB, E3B 0H8

Cover by Kim Killion, The Killion Group Inc.
Edited by Lori Gallagher
Book Design by IRONHORSE Formatting

ISBN-13: 9781927651223

PROLOGUE

Late Summer, 2063

THE PAIN throbbed through him with every breath he drew, but still the Prophet studied the soldier carefully.

This was the one. The one they called Kallem.

Those eyes! He remembered them now. They'd been so fierce, so intelligent. Indomitable, even. But that was before the Prophet's Holy New Order had converted this man before him.

The soldier—this Kallem—stood at attention, his eyes forward, chest out, shoulders back, feet together, hands fisted at his sides, every line of his body taut and ready. And he was blindly obedient as he awaited his Prophet's command.

"At ease, soldier."

Some of the tautness went out of the man's posture as he clasped his hands behind his back and shifted his feet further apart, to shoulders' width.

There had been no file to look through on this one. No chip in his shoulder to be activated. No record or badges or medals of honor. He was one of the originals, for whom there were no records. And he had the tattoo to prove it. They were the first of his soldiers, ten years ago. The hand-picked and chosen ones. The first to change with the Prophet's Ending Testament. To trample the non-conformists, and to move the cogs of the wheels for his new society.

Kallem would have been hardly more than a boy then. Twenty-one, twenty-two at most.

They'd all been that young, his One Hundred and One First Guard. Powerfully built, muscular, quick. Natural born combatants. They'd been shaped into elite soldiers, trained to carry out the Prophet's command and that of his few generals. Swagg himself had seen to it. And those soldiers had killed for him, each and every one of them. Killed on command, without question. That had been part of the price of admission to the First Guard. But by that time, not such a one on their souls.

This was *His* new world. The Holy New Order. The only one there could be.

The Prophet shifted on his throne—an ornate mahogany monstrosity of a chair padded with an exquisite embroidered cushion—trying to ease his discomfort. His medic, Graham, had helped him out of his bed, fretting all the way. A man with a collapsed lung and a chest tube ought not to be ambulating, he'd protested. Even now, Graham waited— nervously no doubt— outside the chamber, ready to put his patient back to bed. But this matter had to be attended to, and the Prophet refused to give his charge to the soldier Kallem from anywhere but the true throne, his rightful place.

The Prophet opened the smoking jacket Graham had helped him into and withdrew a long rectangular box. From it, he removed three needles, one by one, and laid them on the table to the right of his throne—thin syringes filled with a dark red liquid, almost black now in the low light of his chamber. He always dwelled in the low light, and not just for fear of the cancer brought on by the relentless sun outside. The dimness suited him. It pleased him, too, to sit in the shadows while his visitor stood illuminated by a small but bright spotlight.

He watched Kallem standing there in the pool of light, eyes forward still. His shoulders were massive. It occurred to the Prophet how easily this trained killer could bridge the gap between them, if he chose to. The larger man could snap his neck in an instant if he wanted to. Yet the Prophet wasn't afraid, even in his weakened condition. For he could end life so easily for this young man, as easily as he'd started it for all of them in his Holy New Order. And he could do it with just one command: *"Inject yourself with this needle."* The soldier would obey. Of that, the Prophet had no doubt. Then he would almost assuredly drop dead. Yet the Prophet could inject himself with the same dose and live. No, not just live. He'd be transported to that place where God talked to him and only him! It was as Swagg said—he was so much stronger even than this strapping young soldier. Holier than them all!

The Prophet leaned back in his throne, as much to ease the pain in his chest and shoulder as anything, but knowing, too, that the casual pose helped project his comfort and confidence with the authority he wielded. He played with the needle. Rolling it on the table with his right hand, back and forth, back and forth, as Kallem waited for his command.

"Do you know why I called you here?" the Prophet finally asked from the shadows.

"No, sir."

"You've heard the rumors? The rumors of what happened here earlier tonight?" This was a test. *Would he answer truthfully, no matter what the cost?* The sirens had stopped barely an hour ago. Yet no floodgates had been opened, no forces had been sent along. Of course Kallem had heard the rumors.

"We have runners."

"Yes," the Prophet answered, tightly. "Two of them. Females. One a common whore, and one a prize."

"A bleeder, sir?"

Ah, he was smart. A bleeder had never before escaped. They were heavily guarded. Kept always in their compound except when being bred or attended to medically. Kept away from the general population so that only the select, fittest men could attempt insemination. But the guards had not thought to question the Prophet's whore when she'd presented herself with written orders, marked with the Prophet's personal seal, to release the bleeder for transport to the Prophet.

How dare she!

His chest and shoulder throbbed with pain, but his heart—the heart his own whore had so narrowly missed with that blade—throbbed still harder with fury. The slaying of two of the fool guards had done little to assuage his wrath.

"Yes, she's a bleeder. But not just any bleeder. We've run the tests. This one is special, capable of breeding many times. Full ovaries. Completely *healthy* ovaries. We've not seen one like her in decades."

"You want me to bring her back, sir?"

Anxious to start. That was good. And no mention of the other one—his whore. This one knew the rules and apparently had no qualms with them. Runners were to be executed; no delay, no hesitation. Only their heads were ever brought back, to be displayed permanently for all the other females to see—their eyes pecked out by birds, the flesh left to rot and mummify. The oldest of the runners' heads were just skulls now, gleaming white in the burning sunlight. There were dozens of such trophies—such warnings to the women—in the compound. But the Prophet knew, the soldiers knew, and the females knew—there were a few who had gotten away. And legend had it they'd found their sanctuary.

That they'd found Society Three.

4

"I want you to bring them *both* back," he ordered. "The bleeder and the other. But Kallem," he whispered, leaning forward. "Not right away. First...see where they go."

The soldier's eyes shot to him. Good. He was understanding. Figuring out now why no floodgates had been opened, why no soldiers had rushed into the woods that buffered the compound. This wasn't just a mission to retrieve and punish. This wasn't about setting fear into the hearts of all other females. This was more.

"The whore is clever," the Prophet said. "Brave, for a woman. But still, I want her alive. That one I'll kill myself." But only after he'd dealt with her. And struck his blows deep into her heart. Into her unclaimed soul! And the Prophet knew just how to hurt her. Through the bleeder, Zophia, the one Maree had so foolishly forfeited her life to free. How deep did her affection run for that girl? Why? Or perhaps Maree only wanted to deal the Prophet yet another blow by taking such a priceless commodity.

Either way, he would see to it the bleeder was never reprieved, even after her time was done. And if the mythical Society Three truly existed, he'd find it and destroy it. It and all rumors of it—all *hope* of it. And he'd do that in Maree's name too. "Yes," he said slowly. "Leave the whore to me."

For the first time since he'd entered the chamber, Kallem's eyes met the Prophet's, though only for a moment.

Interesting.

The solider had seemed to react at the mention of Maree's name. Why? Had Kallem known her also? No. Impossible. The Prophet had taken her as a virgin, called her to him frequently. And as often as he'd punished her, he'd never sent her to the soldiers, and no woman went there willingly.

Maybe it was only the name that had caught the soldier's attention. For everyone knew Maree was his and his alone.

The needle broke under the Prophet's fist. He snatched his hand back, wiped it on his robe. No splinters, no blood.

"Leave at once. Track them well," he ordered. "Don't let them escape, but *do* let them lead you to where it is they would go. And once they've revealed their destination, take control, Kallem. Bring the females back."

Kallem nodded, gave a deep bow, and whirled to execute his orders.

The Prophet pulled his robe away from his left shoulder and looked down at the covered wounds. Blood was soaking through the bandage over the stab wound on his shoulder. The chest tube, he didn't dare look at. The medic would examine it and give him something more for the pain.

Maree would pay. For these injuries to his flesh, yes, but more so for the wound to his dignity. After she'd stabbed him, he'd played dead like a weak and fearful woman. The memory shamed him. Through cracked eyelids, he'd watched her scurry to his desk, draw out paper, write something. Finally, she'd applied his seal to the papers and folded them. He'd planned to raise the alarm the moment she left the room, but she'd lingered over the papers. By the time she'd tucked the document into her skirt pocket at last, his left lung had collapsed. He'd risen to summon the guard, but pitched forward into unconsciousness. She was long gone by the time one of his generals had come hours later and discovered him.

And to add insult to injury, she'd taken his knife—his *sacred* knife. The one she thought she'd slain him with.

"And Kallem?" The Prophet's words arrested the soldier just before he reached the door.

Kallem turned, came again to rigid attention. "Sir?"

"Do you remember the Eleventh Commandment?"

"Yes, sir," the soldier answered.

Yet, as he said it, the Prophet almost felt the cold shift in the room. Just the flicker of it in the pause. Had he really paused? Had there been a trace of hesitation in him?

Kallem put his hand to his heart and dipped his head. His voice rang out clearly in the chamber. "Thou shalt not disbelieve."

The Prophet again was satisfied. "Very good, Kallem. Don't fail me in this."

"I won't, sir." With another deep bow, the soldier hurried off to do his bidding.

CHAPTER 1

THEY FELL to the ground in exhaustion. And it was only then, when they stopped running—stopped panting and steadied their breaths—that Maree realized she could no longer hear the sirens. Had they traveled that far? Had they traveled that straight? She'd kept track of the moon as they'd run. The select stars she'd seen at the tip of the crescent.

Please let me be right, she silently prayed, though she knew not to whom.

Maree lifted her face from the earth and looked around the darkened clearing. Now that they weren't racing through the field and crashing through brush, she heard the night noises start up, crickets and katydids. But the natural sounds did little to calm her terror.

God help her, what had she done?

What needed doing, that's what.

It was a steadying thought, and she pulled in a deep lungful of air. Her bare arms prickled with goose bumps, as much from the chill of the August night on her cooling flesh as from the fear. But they needed to rest. Needed these few minutes. To think. To regroup.

She sat up and pushed herself backward until she could lean against the strong flare of the birch tree. With a prompting arm, she pulled Zophia closer. The younger woman went easily to her, folding to rest her head on Maree's lap and closing her eyes. Maree rubbed the other girl's exposed arm to warm it, and the younger one took the comfort she offered. Then again, why shouldn't she? They were sisters. Maree smoothed Zophia's worried forehead just as she'd done when Zophia was a child. Incredibly, almost instantly, Zophia was breathing deeply in her arms. Resting. Maree smiled.

Sisters. A word seldom heard anymore, at least not in this true sense.

Maree and Zophia were two of the rare ones who knew they were biologically related. It was a miracle, blind luck, or providence that they'd stayed together. When the Holy New Order was declared, kin were torn apart; shipped to various colonies. Though most didn't realize it, dazed as they were by the stupor of that first inoculation and the indoctrination that had followed.

Maree and Zophia had wound up in the same village only because Maree had lied.

Zophia was young enough that she hadn't had to have the shot. The population had been told that the pandemic threatening the entire globe affected only adults. There had been earlier pandemics, deadly ones. Devastating scourges that had left their mark on humankind. But the one of a decade ago, Maree now knew to have been a ruse. They'd used the population's fear of yet another pandemic to round everyone up and give them the injection. They hadn't bothered with the young ones, since, supposedly, their minds could be reshaped without the pharmaceutical reboot.

Maree had been "inoculated," but by whatever grace, she'd been spared the drug's effects. Though just shy of eighteen, she'd known to fake her way through the transition period. She'd screamed when the others had. Feigned confusion like the rest of them. Obedience. Passiveness. She'd stuck two fingers down her throat so she could throw up like the others did during those first few dark days. And when the "re-integration of knowledge" had started, she'd pretended along with the others that she was a blessed blank slate—looked up with the other empty faces at the video screens relaying the Prophet's message for hours upon hours those first few weeks. Until the messages, the "sermons" as they were called, had come to be played only every other day. Now there were twice-weekly addresses. At least, that's how it was in the Principal Compound—the one from which they'd escaped. Maree presumed it was the same in other compounds. And she'd continued to feign rapt attention to those sermons. She'd done it for herself. But too, she had done it for Zophia. Both of their parents had resisted the wave of the Holy New Order. Her father had been killed; her mother had disappeared one night, never to be seen again. Rumor had it she was dead, and Maree believed it.

Of course, Maree wasn't the only one who hadn't responded to the drug's mind-clearing effects. But those who admitted it, or who inadvertently gave themselves away, were killed. Horribly. The men, right away with a bullet to the head; the women, after they'd been given to the soldiers. Unless they happened to be bleeders—one of the rare ones, still potentially fertile after the environmental disasters. In that case, even the cardinal sin of disbelief took a back seat to procreation. Among the women, it was universally agreed that death would be a better fate than what lay before them. Those unfortunate "disbelieving" women were kept isolated even from other bleeders lest their corruption rub off. They were removed from their madness-inducing solitary confinement only to be bred. Once impregnated, the only reprieve they received from their isolation was the monthly pre-natal checks dispensed by cold and judgmental clinicians.

Maree heard a crack in the woods beside her. Immediately her body tensed, and her hand went to the handle of the knife hidden down her tall boot. A porcupine lumbered out, took one look at the two women and disappeared back into the bushes again. She eased her grip on the blade's handle, tucking it firmly back into its hiding spot.

She'd used this knife—the Prophet's own knife—against her tormentor. Yes, she'd killed him. Her first strike had hit his shoulder, just a flesh wound. But the second one... Dear God, the second blow had sunk deep into his chest. Into his black heart. Maree would do it all over again—use the knife on whomever she needed to—to protect herself or her sister.

And she'd do it without missing a heartbeat.

"The dogs aren't following."

Maree looked down at her sister, whose open eyes now glittered in the moonlight. "I know."

"And where are the soldiers?"

Silence.

"Why aren't they chasing us with the dogs?" Zophia sat up and stared at Maree, waiting for an answer.

Maree had none.

Perhaps no one had found him yet.

If they had, would they not be out in full force? Swagg— the Prophet's second in command—would stop at nothing to find her.

Or maybe they searched for another.

Her stomach lurched. Maybe one of the other females of the compound had run when Maree had left the fence open. Dear God, Liz! If her friend saw the fence opened, she'd make a run for it in those unguarded minutes. Liz knew the things Maree knew. She'd seen what Maree had seen. Felt that fury.

The inoculation had failed on her too.

"I don't know why the dogs aren't following," she finally answered her sister. "But...but we can't assume they're not still after us. Can you go on, Zophia?"

In answer, she stood. "Where are we going?"

Maree's heart leapt in her chest. She looked to the waning moon in the clear sky. Looked to the stars that surrounded it. "North," she said. "We're going north. We're going to find it."

"What?" Zophia's voice was a whisper, and yet a hopeful one. "To find what?"

She swallowed hard and spoke with as much conviction as she dared. "We're going to find Society Three."

As if suddenly weak, Zophia sagged against the birch. "That's...a myth. A legend. Society Three is just a—"

"Hope. And it's the only one we have."

Maree grabbed her sister by the hand and led her as they ran.

CHAPTER 2

MAREE SET a hand on Zophia's back, conveying her meaning without words: *Lie very still.*

Obediently, Zophia lowered her head to the damp earth. Still facing Maree, she closed her eyes, but not in exhaustion this time. In fact, the sisters had gained a few hours' sleep as the burning sun had risen, taking respite by a small, reasonably uncontaminated stream. They'd even found enough berries to quench their hunger. No, this time Zophia closed her eyes as she closed in on herself. Maree had seen this display, this behavior, many times in females. Sometimes the only way for them to find their souls' reprieves was inside themselves. Sometimes that was the only harbor that felt safe at all. Still at all. And Zophia had gone there now as her sister bade her lie still. To go deep, down, still.

And it broke Maree's heart to recognize Zophia knew how to get there.

Maree kept watch.

They were lying on the ground behind a little knoll, under the grey and green cover of leafy alder branches. Maree would've liked to have led them deeper into the thick growth, but there'd been no time. The man had come upon them that quickly.

"Where are ya, whores?" He grabbed at his crotch as he bellowed. "Come out before I have to come find ya! Before ya make me mad." He was a huge man, at least six-two with a scraped head and face. Broad shoulders, and the unmistakable alphanumerical brand running down the side of his filthy neck.

A Reprobate. The stuff of nightmares.

This too she could thank the Prophet for.

At the coming of the New Holy Order, no attempt had been made to inoculate and retrain the hardened criminals. Rather, the prisons had been commanded to throw wide their gates and disgorge their prisoners into the wild where they scrounged the broken earth for food. Maree had seen them often; all the women had. They snarled and fought by the compound fences while the soldiers—laughing—fed them scraps meant for the dogs.

The Prophet had painted the prisoners' release as a punishment. No more being fed and sheltered at the state's expense. Maree had no doubt that was part of it. Nor did she doubt that thousands of them had died. Most had died within months, living in the harsh reality of the outside world, the sun blazing through a depleted ozone layer, toxins, a scarcity of food. Only the strongest and most hardened had survived. And for those who survived, it was a mean, hardscrabble life they eked out. But she also knew the Prophet had had another motive in turning out those prisoners. These hardest, cruellest criminals had been released as a threat. A further incentive to stay within the walls and fences, to serve the Holy New Order.

The soldiers sometimes paraded the younger girls by the fences, ostensibly to torment the men, but Maree knew it was also to send the girls a message: *See what awaits if you try to escape? Or when you are of no more use, and we turn you out? Serve well.*

And yet, no matter how dutifully she might serve The Order, it was every woman's destiny to leave the compound eventually. For when they were too old and broken to be of use, they were turned out to scrounge for themselves. It was a sick ritual, a game. The soldiers would slice the woman's face on one side, ear to chin—a "hag" scar, they called it, the worst insult that could be given—then set her loose beyond the gates. She'd have a head start of two hours; no more, and no less. The soldiers would drink for those two hours, then stumble out after her. No dogs were allowed, not on this chase. The women had till sunup—if they made it to dawn, they were free. But still, almost always the women were caught. Then with a cry of victory from the soldiers, they'd slice her again with the knife, this time across the throat. If the hag got away from the soldiers, there was the threat of Reprobates always present outside the Compound fences.

A threat that was very real right now.

Beside her, Zophia did not move. Maree tucked further down, but her eyes did not leave the man as he raked the bushes, his frustration and anger growing. His burning gaze swept right past them, then he turned, and with his makeshift machete he began swinging at the low bushes. Further and further away, he went.

Maree's heart still hammered in her chest, but she drew a ragged breath when he moved out of sight. Only then did she release her hand-cramping grip on the knife. She wasn't skilled by any means in using this weapon, but she'd use it again if she had to. However she had to.

"Are we safe?" Zophia whispered just as the Reprobate moved completely out of Maree's sight. Zophia's timing, as always, was impeccable. Their grandmother had been an intuitive. A very skilled and sought-after one, especially as the world started to change, as the Ending Testament was whispered of, and authority had slowly shifted. People were looking for hope, security, salvation from a world gone mad. Some had sought her grandmother and those like her, but more had sought the powerful Prophet, and they'd voted him into power. Then people could vote no more. Thankfully, Zophia knew to hide her intuition from all except Maree. All others would brand her a witch for using this natural ability. "He's gone, isn't he?"

Maree's voice matched her sister's whisper. "For now. Hopefully for good."

There was a pause before Zophia lifted her head. "Now what?"

"Now we keep going. Like I told you."

"There are more of these men out here. We'll—"

"We'll be smart; we'll be careful. We'll make it."

"What if we don't find it? What if..." Zophia's voice drifted to silence, mostly out of mercy to her sister, Maree knew. They had to find Society Three. It was their only hope. She looked at Zophia.

Maree knew it had been Zophia's only hope long before they'd left the compound. Had been since the Prophet and his minions had found out Zophia's great potential as a breeder. She'd warned her sister to tell no one about her monthly bleeding when it started six months ago. But some of the other women in the compound had found out. One of them—a servant past her years of use and near to being hagged out—told the guard and the guard had informed the Prophet. Maree herself had been there with the Prophet when the news had come. Then there'd been the testing. Medical testing, a luxury reserved only for the highest-ranking males and potential breeders. Zophia's reproductive system was practically perfect, seemingly unharmed by the environment. Perfectly able to carry a child to term. Many children.

Maree herself had never experienced menses. No matter. No shock or dismay. Though more females than males were being born, a woman who actually experienced menses was a rare thing. Over the decades the population of the world had significantly shrunk, thanks largely to pandemics. But fertility had declined, too, more and more with each passing year. Thus, when a female had a menstrual cycle, it had to be reported immediately to the Powers. Tests were run. If there was potential for reproduction, they were bred with potentially fertile males, who were themselves afflicted with low sperm count. Thus a breeder was taken nightly, by many chosen as worthy, until she was shown to be pregnant. But still, the nightmare didn't end. They were held virtual prisoners, confined while the baby gestated in their wombs. When the child was born, the mother was allowed to nurse it only for a few brief weeks, after which the babe was torn from its mother's arms so that her cycles would return quickly, and she could be bred all over again. This was a breeder's life—her service to the Holy New Order—a life lived in a maternity ward, locked in for the rest of her reproductive days.

It was horrific! Maree refused to let her sister live that way. Which was why she'd killed the Prophet.

She'd overheard him say that Zophia was to be bred on the Sabbath, just two days hence. Since no woman had been put into service as a breeder before her sixteenth birthday, Maree had been shocked. She'd thought her sister had almost two months left before she needed worry about that.

Maree had acted quickly. When next she was alone with him, she'd wielded the knife on the unsuspecting Prophet. From that moment on, she'd known there was a price on her head. There would be forevermore. She'd killed the Prophet. She, a mere woman. The Prophet's whore.

"Will they kill us if they catch us?"

Once again, Zophia spoke Maree's thoughts. And Maree knew she was no longer speaking of the Reprobates. There was no question those men would kill them, when they were done with them.

"No," Maree said, "they won't kill you."

Zophia nodded. "But they'll kill you. And…and I don't think I could go on if that happened."

Maree looked at her sister.

Though the elders in the compound did nothing to shield the younger females from the horrors of their respective fates—whore, servant, or breeder—Zophia couldn't possibly know the depth of it as Maree did. The dehumanization that came with being taken over and over again. At fifteen, Zophia was still a virgin. There were rules about that.

"We won't be caught," Maree said, her voice barely above a whisper now. She couldn't see the Reprobate, but that didn't mean they were yet safe from him. "I promise you."

"Maybe… Maree, maybe I could talk to Swagg."

Maree's lips tightened at the mention of the Prophet's second in command.

"If the soldiers found us," Zophia continued. "I mean, if…if I'm so valuable. Maybe I could tell Swagg that I need you. Want you with me. That…that wouldn't be so bad would it? What if he let you stay with me? What if…what if I told him I was an intuitive? Then maybe he'd let me, let us—"

Maree placed a finger on her sister's lips to shush her. Zophia still had an innocence about her. One that would not serve her well in this jaded world. "Tell no one that you know things."

"But—"

"Knowledge from a woman, Zophia? Truth not given by a man? Not from the Prophet? You know the Eleventh Commandment. If you believe in yourself, how can you believe in the Holy New Order? As much as your gift is a gift, it's one you can't share. You'd be in violation."

Zophia nodded, understanding maybe for the first time why Maree had always been so adamant that she hide her ability.

"Besides, I killed the Prophet, Zophia. Your appeal would fall on deaf ears. But no matter." She stroked her sister's hair. "We're not going to get caught. We're never going back to that compound."

Maree watched as Zophia's soft eyes suddenly widened. She knew by the fear in those smoky green orbs. The Reprobate was back.

Maree crouched down within herself. She looked out between the branches and focused as the man approached again. He walked closer, closer still, scanning the ground as he went. When he was a mere few feet away, he turned toward them and met Maree's stare with his own.

She wrapped her hand around the knife.

CHAPTER 3

KALLEM PAUSED as he reached the forest's edge, where it opened onto a small clearing. His breath came hard in his ears from the loping, ground-eating pace he'd set for himself, making it impossible to listen properly. But not for long. Years of hard training had honed both mind and body, and in under a minute, his pounding heart was under control again.

He stood there, every sense alert, and waited. He was close; he knew it. If they were here in this clearing, better they betray their presence before he betrayed his.

He'd used the Prophet's best hound to find their trail initially. He and Mac, a fellow member of the First Guard, had followed the eager hound across miles of broken cement and crumbling pavement. They'd chased on through the night until they'd reached the northern edge of the old city where it met the wilds beyond. There the women's trail veered north through the brush. A brush that encroached further and further each year. Confident he could track the women now without the dog, Kallem had ordered Mac to make camp in an empty building on the wild's edge for

20

twenty-four hours. If Kallem didn't return by then, Mac was to assume he'd found the trail and didn't need the bloodhound's nose. They were to return to the Compound. The dog had been necessary to get them this far, but Kallem needed stealth now. The dogs were apt to give voice to their excitement when they neared the end of a successful track. That worked fine when the objective was to terrify the subject. It wasn't such a good thing when the objective was to follow surreptitiously.

Mac had asked no questions. Not that he'd expected any. At least not after Kallem confirmed his charge came directly from the Prophet himself. Like a good soldier, Mac had been content to stay on a need-to-know basis. And like a smart soldier, he would also appreciate that the less one knew about situations like this, the better.

Kallem's mouth turned down on that thought. The Prophet counted him as his best soldier, and Kallem had worked hard to earn that recognition. But would His Holiness hold him in such esteem if he knew the cold slide of dread that had gripped his best soldier's bowels as he'd stood at attention to receive this charge?

Maree...

Just thinking her name made his gut tighten.

He'd been unable to get her out of his mind since the first day he'd seen her, herded into the encampment with fifty or sixty other girls. She'd looked more or less like the rest, until their eyes had met for a moment too long as she'd passed by the Guard. For a second, he'd thought her a heretic, a Disbeliever, but when he looked harder, the expression was gone, and her eyes seemed as placid and accepting as the rest of them. It was over in a split second, yet he'd been left shaken.

She'd gone on, of course, to become a favorite of the Prophet's. Kallem had even been called upon once or twice to escort her to and from His Holiness's quarters. And on those occasions, he'd had to viciously suppress the rawness he'd felt on seeing the bruises on her wrists and elsewhere. He'd put it down to envy. Beautiful young women like Maree were not meant for a soldier such as himself—First Guard or not. Not until their youth and beauty were used up, or in some cases, until they were so broken all they could do was cry.

But the knowledge that he would likely be dead in the line of duty long before she ever fell to his level hadn't stopped him from fantasizing about her.

And as he'd stood before the Prophet to receive his charge, his heart had pounded as he'd waited for the command to kill her, to bring back her head. He'd been shamefully relieved when the Prophet had instructed that she be returned intact, so he could kill her himself.

A woman's shout and a man's coarse laughter ripped him from his reverie. The bleeder! It was his life if anything happened to the young one.

He was already off, racing across the clearing in the direction of the commotion.

He emerged from a small stand of fir trees and was greeted by the sight of Maree facing down a giant of a man, her hand wrapped around a blade. He was about to shout a warning to the Reprobate to stand down when Maree yelled at the younger one.

"Run, Zophia! Now! Just keep running!"

With a sob, the bleeder turned and fled. Torn, Kallem followed the path of her flight with his eyes for a few seconds, then glanced back to Maree in time to see the man strike at her. She leapt back, but not quite quickly enough, taking a glancing blow to the head. But she didn't go down.

Rage exploded like a fireball of energy in his veins. He wanted nothing more than to rush up to the bastard and smash his head in with the butt of his rifle. And keep smashing.

But no...the breeder. His priority had to be the young one. There could be other men about. Men who had no idea of her value. Men who would slit her throat if the screaming bothered them, then proceed to rape her dead body. And if they liked the screaming, it would go even worse for her.

He cast a last look back toward Maree. She grappled with the Reprobate now and he couldn't see who had possession of the knife. He lifted his rifle and sighted on the Reprobate briefly before lowering it with a frustrated curse. No possibility of taking him out with a bullet. Not without risking her life too. She fought in silence, and he knew she stifled herself so her screams of rage and pain would not bring the young one back.

Gritting his teeth to suppress the savage snarl that rose within him, Kallem turned and raced after the bleeder.

She moved faster than he would have credited for one so young, and one who must be bone-weary from having traveled so far. But terror must have leant her feet wings. She was pelting headlong downhill through rough terrain, and heading for an even steeper slope. Kallem feared she would trip and break her neck if she didn't check her speed. Normally, he would have shouted to her, identifying himself and commanding her to stop, but he didn't dare. He didn't want to alert the Reprobate back there to his presence in case he decided to flee with Maree. So he ran on.

Just as she started to descend the steeper part of the slope, he surged forward on a burst of adrenaline and caught the breeder's arm.

She shrieked. And shrieked and shrieked.

"Be quiet," he ordered in low, urgent tones as he fought to subdue her squirming body. "I won't hurt you, child. And the sooner you get that through your head, the sooner I can go back to save Maree."

At the mention of the other girl's name, she left off with the screaming and fighting. And as the fight went out of her, so apparently did her ability to stand up. She just sank to the grass like a stone.

"Go," she said. "Help her."

"Not without you," he said. "It's not safe to leave you. There could be other men...a whole party of them..."

He watched the terror flash in her eyes, but instead of galvanizing her to run again, it seemed to flip a switch in her head. She sank down even further into the earth, shrinking down into herself. Shutting down with the overload. Cursing, he dragged her to her feet and slung her unresisting body across his shoulder in a fireman's lift. Heart working overtime with the added burden, he retraced his path up the hill as quickly as he could. By the time he reached the top of the clearing, his breath came in harsh pants and his muscles screamed for oxygen.

The bastard had obviously disarmed Maree, for he'd forced her to her knees before him. The bodice of her dress had been torn open and he clearly saw a splash of crimson on her neck. Her blood or his?

Through the haze of fury, Kallem forced himself to scan the clearing. Seeing no other human presence, he carried the bleeder to the concealment of a nearby patch of alder bushes and lowered her to the ground. "Stay here," he ordered, though he doubted she had the strength or will left to move.

Then, his body and brain on fire with rage, he stepped back into the meadow to see the brute had her on the ground beneath him, her arms pinned over her head as he fumbled with her skirts. Kallem raced toward them, his blood singing with the anticipation of clubbing the bastard in the head with the butt of his rifle. The need to beat the Reprobate bloody with his bare hands was stronger than anything he'd ever known. Then the Reprobate howled with pain and rolled off her, clutching his crotch. She must have used her knee on him. *Good.* Except the Reprobate was getting to his feet now. And, oh shit, he had Maree's knife in his massive hand!

He could never reach the Reprobate in time to stop his blade. But a bullet could.

Kallem jacked the rifle up, took aim and squeezed. The bullet struck the Reprobate in the back, spinning him around. Steadier now, Kallem aimed and squeezed the trigger again, putting another bullet right between the bastard's startled eyes. This time, he went down, hitting the ground like a felled oak. Kallem lowered his rifle and jogged up to the scene. A quick look confirmed the Reprobate was dead. He also had a few slashes and nicks from Maree's blade, he noted. When he turned to check on Maree, she was already scrambling to her feet. And she'd reclaimed the knife.

"Stay back!" she ordered, waving the blade at him with a trembling hand, the other hand trying to hold together the torn bodice of her dress.

Kallem held the rifle out to his side with his right arm and extended his left hand, palm up. "Are you all right?" He gestured to his own neck and upper chest. "You've got quite a bit of blood there..."

She lifted her chin and he saw her hand tighten on the blade. "None of it's mine, soldier."

"It's okay." Kallem showed his palms again in a gesture of peace. "You're safe now. So's the other one. The breeder."

"Safe?" She made a strangled sound, half laugh, half sob. "How do you figure that, Soldier of the First Guard? You're here to take Zophia back. And to kill me."

Now that his rage had cooled, Kallem realized how badly his mission had been compromised. Dammit! Now that he'd revealed his presence, there was no way he could back off and let them lead him to Society Three. Unless...

She cocked her head. "So if you've orders to kill me, why didn't you just let the Reprobate do it? Unless you wanted to use me yourself before dispatching me." She watched the blush crawling up his face through narrowed eyes. "God, you *disgust* me." Her voice shook, but he noticed the hand that held the knife steadied. "You're just as horrible as that...that...animal."

"No," he said coldly. "You're wrong."

"Oh? You don't want to take his place between my thighs? The Prophet's place?" She angled her head. "I've seen the way you look at me."

Her voice had gone silky, and he knew she was trying to entice him. Seducing him so she could slide that blade between his ribs. He couldn't say he blamed her.

"No, I meant I didn't come to kill you," he said. "Nor did I come after the bleeder. Yet you could say she is why I'm here."

As if on cue, Zophia came running up.

"I told you to stay put," Kallem said.

"I did, until I heard the shot." Zophia turned to Maree, her eyes taking in the torn dress and the blood. "Omigod, Maree, are you all right?"

"I'm fine. Not even a scratch." Maree lifted her left arm and Zophia slid under it, wrapping her arms around the older woman. Maree hugged back one-armed. She adjusted her grip on the knife and returned her attention to Kallem. "You didn't come after us, yet we are why you're here? I don't like riddles. Speak plainly."

He was not used to a woman talking so boldly. "I've been expelled," he answered through gritted teeth. "As Captain of the First Guard, the Prophet blamed me for the loss of the—"

"You lie!" Her words cut across his, and across Zophia's gasp. "The Prophet is dead! I killed him myself, with this very blade."

"Killed him?" His eyes widened with surprise. "I can assure you, you did not. You may have injured him—I did see the medic hovering—but he's very much alive."

"But I stuck his chest!"

"Then you must have missed the heart and the major arteries and merely deflated the lung. He's alive and giving orders from his throne."

"Dammit!" Her knife hand wavered and she seemed to wilt. "So many years, I've done nothing. I thought at last I'd finally..." She swiped at her cheek. "Dammit all to hell!"

"If your intent was to strike a blow against the Prophet, this will sting much more than if you'd succeeded in killing him."

"And how is that, soldier?"

"Because now he has to face the fallout, the humiliation of having been bested by his...um, by a woman. He was furious about the loss of the...this one," he motioned to Zophia, "make no mistake. But even that pales in comparison to his rage over your escape. I'm lucky to have gotten away with my life. I thought I'd breathed my last when I stood before him. The two soldiers who guard his chambers were not so lucky."

Something flickered in her eyes, but then they hardened again. "Right. And they let you go with a uniform on your back and a rifle in your hands."

"Hardly." *Think quick.* "I...stole them. From a soldier the Prophet sent after you. I struck him from behind, so he doesn't know it was me. Left his hands shackled behind his back, hobbled his feet, and killed his hound. When he comes to, he'll have no choice but to shuffle back. But by the time he makes it, the trail will be too cold for the hounds."

"Why would you do that? Interfere with the hunt? " The tatters of her dress fell open again, revealing a breast.

"Because I stand a considerably better chance out here with a Guard's uniform and weapons than I did naked and unarmed the way I was thrust out of the compound." He stripped off his shirt and handed it to her. "Here," he said gruffly. "Cover yourself."

Zophia stepped back so Maree could accept the shirt. Maree passed the knife from one hand to the other as she put it on. It swamped her, but it had the desired effect of shielding her nakedness.

She inclined her head. "Thank you. Though I fear I've left you shirtless again."

"No worries," he said. "I took the guard's bedroll and his rucksack. I have a change of clothes." It was his own, of course.

Her eyes sharpened as she spied the tattoo on his shoulder. The mark of the Prophet's First Guard. "I see they didn't strip you of everything."

He looked down at the offending mark, cursing himself for obeying the impulse to give her his shirt. Normally, when a soldier was dishonorably discharged, the tattoo marking him as a soldier in the Prophet's service was disfigured. "An oversight, I'm sure. The Prophet's rage was hotter than I've ever seen. I barely had time to learn why I was being expelled before I found myself outside the gates."

"Or perhaps you lie?"

He sighed. Then he shot his hand out and snatched the knife from her, drawing a yelp of surprise from both women. Maree might have lost the battle with the Reprobate, but not surprisingly had snatched the blade back up as soon as she was on her feet again. She was more than a survivor. Keeping his eyes locked on hers, he drew the knife diagonally across the tattoo, making a line of blood appear on his skin. Then he adjusted his grip and drew another line, creating an X. He wiped the blade on his pants and handed it back to her, hilt first. She took it, her hand shaking harder than ever.

"I have no love left for the Prophet." Kallem heard his own voice, and marveled at how true it sounded. How true the words felt. "I am an outlaw now. But I am an outlaw with skills. I can keep you safe out here in this lawless wild. You and the breeder."

"Her name is Zophia and she's my sister," Maree said coldly. "And that is the last time you will call her breeder."

"Your sister?" He gaped at her, then looked between the two women, studying their green eyes. "But how is that possible? I mean, how could you possibly know that?"

She clutched his shirt tighter about herself. "How do you think? I remember how it was before the Prophet imposed the Holy New Order on us."

"That's impossible." But even as he said the words, he had a flash of the first time he'd met her eyes, as the girls were being marched into the compound. It was true. She was a Disbeliever, and somehow she'd managed to conceal that fact all these years.

"I remember my parents opposing the coming of the New Order and dying for it. I remember the needle and pretending that it worked, emulating the histrionics of the other girls. Repeating the vows of obedience to the Prophet and The Order as I looked up at the screens and you and the other soldiers moved through the crowd. I remember my sister, Zophia, who was too young to require the needle. And I remember *you*, Kallem Marsh."

CHAPTER 4

MAREE'S EYES locked with Kallem's.

Then a shout sounded, followed by the thrashing of men through the undergrowth. She whirled toward the sound, but there was no motion to be seen yet. They were still too far off.

Eyes wide, she turned back to Kallem. "More Reprobates?"

"No doubt about it. They tend to travel in loose packs for security. They're sure to have heard the gunshots." He shouldered his bag and hefted the rifle. "Let's go. We have to find cover."

They moved quietly but quickly, beyond the thin alders and into the increasingly dense forest beyond. On and on they moved, Kallem leading the way and Maree bringing up the rear, with Zophia between them. Finally, in deep brush, he brought them to a stop. They hunkered down and listened, waited. Eventually, when no sounds of pursuit followed them, Kellem relaxed slightly.

"We should eat something," he said, keeping his voice down. He dropped his bag and started rummaging through it.

Then he stood with a handful of small packets. Maree watched as he handed Zophia two of them.

Military rations, she knew. Reserved for the soldiers alone under the Prophet's command. Had Kallem appropriated them from the soldier he'd allegedly that uniform and rifle from? She eyed the fit of his jacket across broad shoulders. If so, he'd been fortunate indeed that the soldier had shared his height and breadth so closely. Or was the whole tale of being cast out in disgrace a fiction designed to ingratiate him into their trust? Yet he'd drawn the knife through his tattoo, marked himself as an outcast...

Her stomach growled and hunger gnawed her insides as he held two packets out to her.

She didn't trust him for a minute; she couldn't afford to. But neither could she afford to refuse the high-calorie sustenance he offered. She took the rations.

As hungry as she was, it was the energy drink she opened first. One of the rules of survival she'd learned along the way was that charity was fleeting. Often false. And often revoked at the giver's whim and delight. This liquid nutrition was the most valuable, so she drank it down quickly.

"Drink up," she whispered to Zophia, and watched as her sister obeyed.

Zophia had been quick to obey Kallem too, when he'd commanded them to follow him. Maree fully believed that the pursuers were Reprobates, and that their small party was in grave danger. She'd been ready to follow Kallem too. But she hadn't been as quick as Zophia. Her sister had immediately fallen in behind him—this guard, this boy from long ago.

Yet he couldn't be further from the boy Maree had known. His eyes...not just the way he looked at her, the Prophet's whore, but the steeled intelligence there, the hardness. The man was a killer. A former soldier. Perhaps a soldier still.

And what had Kallem seen when he looked into those smoky green eyes she shared with her sister?

Nothing. She knew it. She demanded it of herself. She'd long ago learned to bury the humiliation, the pain, and the anger. Though the latter had risen hot inside as she'd held the knife in her hand.

Zophia could feel it, though. No matter how well Maree hid it from the rest of the world, she had little doubt her intuitive sister felt very keenly the pain she kept crushed down inside.

Yet in this, she wasn't alone. All the whores learned to bury their humiliation and anger. So many women did—had had to even before the Order had come into power, when the rumblings of the new ways had started. When many had started blaming women and their *evil ways* for God's terrible anger that was supposedly showing itself in the world's decay and decline. Never mind that it was men and their wars and their greed and their need—*their professed right*—to dominate every living creature that had destroyed the earth. Maree's hands fisted at the thought.

But God's punishment fell on the women's shoulders. That's who was responsible—or so many voices had clamored—for the changing world, the tornados, the floods and famine, and most of all, the disease. Two pandemics had swept the globe, each taking proportionally more men than women. Women carried the virus, and most suffered with it, but not to the extent males did. Before the outbreaks, there was already a movement afoot to blame women for the state of the world. Women who didn't know their place under God's plan. When men started dying at such an alarming rate, those misogynistic sentiments swelled. As significantly more females were born into the population than males, the people began attributing that to female disobedience to man, shunning of their rightful role to produce male heirs! The public bought into what the Prophet was selling, lock, stock and barrel.

The result? The vast majority of women were relegated to a life of servitude and slave labor, while some—the prettiest—were made into whores, and others—those with reproductive potential—became breeders. And finally, when they'd outlived their usefulness as servants, women were forced outside the gates to fend on their own. To be used, raped. A fate she'd come so close to at the hands of that Reprobate.

Tears burned her eyes but did not fall. She would push them down too.

"Thank you, soldier," Zophia said to Kallem. She gestured to the meal on her lap, already more than half gulped down. "For this...and for saving my sister from that horrible Repro—"

"We're not saved yet, Zophia." Maree glared at Kallem, making sure there was no mistaking the hardness in her voice, or the suspicion she felt. "And I doubt this one offers us any such safety."

Kallem met her rigid gaze. "Eat," he said. "Finish up quickly. We have to go."

His words, spoken with a soldier's authority, were like a punch in the gut to Maree. Suddenly she was sure he was taking them back to the compound after all. Her body tensed, her stomach tightening and threatening to expel the little she'd been able to consume.

"To go back to the compound, you mean?" she spat. "What makes you think I'll go back alive? I can imagine the fate the Prophet has in store after I humiliated him—"

"Not back to the compound. I told you, I can't go back any more than you can." He gestured to his still-bleeding arm and the ruined tattoo beneath the bandage he'd so hastily improvised. "I'm no longer one of them. You know the mark of a disgraced soldier."

"Then where is it you think we're going?" Maree watched his face carefully.

Kallem set his empty ration packet down. "I don't know. But I do know that you'd not have left the compound without a plan. You're too smart for that, Maree."

"You think you know so much!"

"I know you've survived."

"Yeah. For all of what—thirty-six hours?"

"That's not what I meant." He folded his emptied packet tightly, carefully packed it into his rucksack so as to not leave any trace behind. "I can help you. I will help you find your destination. I feel I owe it to you both. But I'll help you only till you're safe, then I'm gone. You think you're the only ones with a price on your heads? I may have been thrown out of the compound, but once I disarmed that soldier and stole his supplies, I signed my own death warrant with The Order. I'll get you two to safety, then I have to find my own."

She eyed him suspiciously. "How can we trust you?"

"What choice do you have?"

Where are ya, whores? The Reprobate's words rang in her mind. She closed her eyes against the horror of the attack, against the thought of what he would have done to her. Or, oh God, to Zophia! When she opened them, Kallem was staring at her.

"I'm going with you," he said, in that flat voice.

"Is that a threat, soldier?"

Tense silence stretched between them as they eyed each other, until Zophia suddenly spoke. "North! We're heading north, sol—Kallem."

"Zophia!" Maree hissed. "What are you doing?"

"I'm trusting him, Maree. Like he said, what choice do we have? Do we just wait around for more Reprobates to come again? We know nothing of this outside wor—"

"I'll keep you safe," Maree said. "I'd give my life to it."

"And who will keep *you* safe?" Zophia let out a breath, visibly softening as she sighed. "Maree, I'd give my life for you too. We escaped that compound to be together. To find a different life. And we may actually have a chance to do that now that we're outside the gate. But we'll have a better chance if we trust this one. If we let him help us."

Maree wet her lips, weighing her sister's words and balancing them with her own fear. She knew so much more than Zophia of the ways of men. And yet, the look in her wise sister's eyes...

"Yes, north," Maree finally said. She'd tell him little, as little as possible for now.

"Where?"

"To So—"

"Just north!" Maree's tone was sharp and warning as she interrupted her sister. "We travel by night, by the north star."

"And pray the sky's clear." Biting her lip, Zophia glanced upward.

Maree followed her gaze. Already the sky was covered with clouds. The cover might blow over by nightfall, but chances were not good.

Kallem reached into the rucksack on the ground. From a small side pocket, he pulled out a circular metal disc. "This will help," he said. "This will lead the way. It's a—"

"Compass." Maree let out a long breath. The Prophet had showed her one once. Another time when he'd been on one of his needle binges and hadn't watched so very closely what he was doing. Hadn't realized the woman he'd just torn into was truly observing all that he did. Stocking the information away. A compass was a powerful instrument. One they could use.

"I'll get you north," Kallem said. "Let me take you in that direction, at least today."

"Give me the compass," Maree stated. "If you really want to help us—"

"And wander around in these woods myself? Hoping for cloudless nights so I can find my own way by the stars? I don't think so."

Maree sat silently. Thinking. Deciding. Her stomach churned with the reality that she had little choice.

"It'll be fine," Zophia said. "Remember, there's security in numbers. We'll just let Kallem lead us north for a while. Just till...just till we're safer. Just until we're past the worst of it."

She looked at her sister. Violence sickened Zophia. It always had. She was still shaken from the Reprobate's attack on Maree. If the soldier could offer her some sense of comfort, at least for a short time, maybe she should allow it. Slowly, Maree nodded. "All right. Just until we're past the worst of it, Kallem. Then you leave us."

He snapped the compass closed, nodded, and began packing up their makeshift camp.

Silently, Maree finished her meal. Yes, she'd let Kallem go with them, but only for a little while. She wouldn't lead him anywhere near Society Three. Most soldiers didn't believe in it—a place where women could be safe. Could rule. Could live. But she believed. She had to. And dammit, she'd seen the map.

Though kind-hearted Zophia might trust him, Maree was a harder sell.

Maree bent to collect the empty ration wrappers—hers and Zophia's—and turned to hand them to Kallem to store in his rucksack. But when she looked up, Zophia was helping Kallem wind a piece of clean gauze bandage around his powerful bicep. As she secured the bandage, she laid her hand upon the gauze-covered wound as if trying to somehow heal the gashes the knife had made, and Maree's stomach lurched at the sight.

"Zophia!"

Zophia dropped her hand and turned to Maree, her eyes questioning.

An innocent, Zophia would have no idea what cruelty her touch, her kindness, might be met with. Maree would have to speak to her. For now, she handed Zophia the empty ration packages. "Put these in the rucksack with the others."

Zophia turned to do as her sister bid her, and Maree met Kallem's eyes over her gracefully bent back. His grey eyes were flat and inscrutable.

She'd kill him if he hurt Zophia. Kill him if he took her as soldiers were known to take everything they wanted. *Somehow*, she would kill him if he crossed them. And she let that promise shine from her eyes.

Something flickered in his stare—something almost like admiration—but then it was gone. "We have to go," he announced.

Zophia had finished with his rucksack, and he shrugged the heavy weight of it onto his back, then shouldered the rifle. With a glance at his compass, he nodded toward a large birch tree. "This way's north," he said, and started out.

Maree held back, putting a restraining hand on Zophia's arm. Kallem could not have failed to notice they weren't following, but he didn't break stride. Not until Maree called out the final question she couldn't help but ask.

"Why? Why are you doing this, Kallem Marsh? You say you were kicked out of the First Guard because we escaped. Why are you helping us now?"

He paused then and turned to face her. "Because I can no longer uphold the Eleventh Commandment. Which makes me the worst of sinners in the Holy New Order. A disbeliever, like you."

"But why are you helping us?"

He looked away, for the first time not being able to meet her eyes. "Redemption. For my other sins." When he swung his head around again, his glare was hard. "I have many."

CHAPTER 5

HE HAD taken a needle for the pain, and so the Prophet sat both silently and calmly as the medic changed the dressing on his wound. He could have taken something also for the humiliation, the anger rising over what Maree had done to him. But no. He wanted to feel that. Needed to feel that.

He would use it.

The chest tube had come out this morning, his lung having reinflated uneventfully. And though the site of the puncture still hurt, it was no more bothersome than the shoulder wound. It was the latter that Graham, the medic, worked on now. Carefully, tenderly.

Graham was an older man, mid-sixties. His grey hair was shaved short against his scalp as was the rule for all of his discipline. The Prophet watched him closely—not the work, but the man's face. Instilling the fear of God with that silent stare. And it was a stare that said it all: *Do this right, or else*. The medic nodded, and the young female assistant at his side wiped the sweat from his brow.

Good. He fears me. Still, the Prophet was not unaware of what was going on in the compound. Wasn't immune to the murmuring. He saw the looks passed between the others as they came and went from his quarters. Glances in the doorways. And too, Swagg had been in to inform him of how badly things were going.

The people were wondering. How could their Prophet be wounded so grievously? Nearly killed! How could he have been so wrong as to be wronged? And by a mere female! A whore!

And then there was the most dangerous question of all. The Prophet knew they muttered an unfinished, *what if she'd succeeded?*

He winced. Not at anything the attentive medic was doing, but at the thought. Still the grey-haired man looked up, startled. But Graham held the Prophet's glance a fraction of a second too long.

"Do you disbelieve, Graham?" the Prophet asked.

Beside the medic, his female assistant lowered her head and cringed, as if expecting a blow to come with the question.

"No, sir. Thou shalt not disbelieve," the medic answered dutifully. "It's the Eleventh Commandment."

He nodded slowly, continuing to stare at the man until the poor fellow lowered his own eyes. "What about the others in the compound?"

"The others, Prophet? I...I cannot speak for—"

"What have you heard, Graham?" The medic had finished wrapping the wound, but the Prophet did not glance down at his shoulder to inspect the work. It would be perfect. As was the binding about his chest. "Tell me, what are the whispers? What are the others saying about their Prophet being so injured? Stabbed by one of the whores. By Maree."

The man paused long enough that the Prophet couldn't help but know his reluctance to answer. He rubbed the thumb of his left hand over the medic tattoo on his right hand. The sign of his trade: the Caduceus—the staff and the snakes. On a whim, the Prophet could slice through that tattoo, cast him out of the trade, and out of the compound.

"There…there are rumors, Prophet."

"Tell me."

"Most people think it's terrible, just terrible, what Maree did. They don't understand why she—"

The Prophet threw up a hand to cut him off. "I'm not interested in those people. Tell me what the rest are saying." The Prophet felt his heart beat harder as he waited for an answer from this man bound to tell him the truth.

Graham sighed, lowering his head some more. "There are those…" He swallowed, his Adam's apple bobbing. "There are those who don't understand how it happened. Some say you…you're slipping in your judgments. I've heard talk of how perhaps this is a sign in itself. And then there are those…"

"Those who what?" His heart hammered all the harder. "Go on, Graham."

"Those who wonder if maybe you've been wrong all along. That they've been wrong all along, about you. Maree wounded you. She got away with Zophia—and that one a bleeder. The people…some of the people…just cannot understand how this could be."

A chink in the armor.

So it had begun.

"I…I don't think they know… I…can't understand it, Your Holiness." The fool of a medic was blubbering now, obviously in fear that being the messenger, he would bear the brunt of the Prophet's anger. "I'm sure it'll blow over once the soldiers come back with Maree's head. But…but they weren't sent out, Prophet. Not right away, and not in great numbers. Yet, you know best and, well, there are some that say…I've heard them say you were growing soft, but I—"

"Leave!" the Prophet commanded. "Leave at once!"

"I said no such things, Prophet. I only report—"

"Get the hell out of here!"

Graham hastened to gather his supplies, but dropped them in his nervousness. His trembling assistant helped him pick them up again, and they both exited as fast as they could, bowing their way humbly out of the chamber.

The Prophet rose, crossed the room to a set of large, dark cabinets. He pulled a key out from his robe and opened the locked doors. He chose a vial—clear liquid—and with smooth and practiced motions, drew up the narcotic and injected himself. The pain had started throbbing again at the twin sites where Maree had injured him. But he'd carefully chosen this vial. Yes, he wanted the anger to remain. It would serve him.

Perhaps he should have sent more than Kallem out for the two women...

No. He'd made the right decision. As hot as he was to have Maree's throat beneath his hands, he had to know once and for all about the existence of Society Three. That would strengthen his position! That would redeem him! If anyone could lead one of his men to the society, it was Maree. Her fierceness, he'd seen. That was why he'd taken such great pleasure in defeating her in his bed time and time again. Even if it was only her body he took...

What was her attachment to the younger girl?

Relations? It did not seem likely. All sibling groups were torn asunder when the Holy New Order came in. Loyalty had to belong to the Prophet alone. Yet the two females did share the same eye color... Perhaps there *was* a blood connection there. Or perhaps in her barrenness, the shared eye color had caused Maree to seize on the idea that Zophia was her child. That happened sometimes. Not usually with the whores, but with the wet nurses employed in the nursery. Barren they might be, but lactation could still be induced, freeing the breeders to be bred again sooner. Sometimes those barren women became deluded that the child they nursed was theirs.

Whatever the reason, Maree felt enough attachment to the bleeder to risk running with her. And yet, the Prophet could tell no one what he suspected—that the abhorrent Society Three did exist. There was a risk if others knew. Risk in knowledge. Danger in hope. No, until the Society was destroyed, he said nothing. The rumors…would be quashed in time.

Meanwhile, the masses were wondering why he'd not sent a whole contingent of soldiers. Second-guessing him! Suggesting he was going soft!

He smashed the syringe against the cabinet door, then smashed the door itself closed.

"Guard!" he hollered. Immediately, the door swung open. Gomez, a young and loyal guard, stepped inside.

"Your Holiness?"

"Bring me Liz."

The guard hesitated. *Hesitated!*

"That one lies in the clinic, Prophet, from last night's—"

"Bring her!" he roared.

"Yes, Prophet." Gomez closed the door behind him.

The Prophet sat. Already his pain was abating. The physical pain, at least. But the humiliation, the anger—the fucking rage!—scored his brain like a demon's claws as he waited for Liz, who served him now in Maree's stead.

And in Maree's stead, her friend would pay.

CHAPTER 6

KALLEM CAME awake suddenly, but without moving a muscle. His ears strained to catch the sound that had pulled him from his light slumber. There was another scraping sound, but from within their small shelter. Just one of the women stirring. He relaxed. Or as close as he could come to relaxing while propped in a sitting position at the mouth of a cave.

Actually, it was more of a niche in the rocks near the base of a cliff than a cave, barely big enough for the three of them to fit into. But it was the safest, most defensible campsite he was able to find, and it gave them shelter from the brutal midday sun. Despite the heat of the day, it was cool in the cave. Between them, the two women had only the one small blanket they'd been traveling with, so he'd insisted they use his bedroll. He'd dug his jacket out of the rucksack for himself. *His* rucksack, of course. He'd taken it off no soldier. All part of the lies he was weaving.

Another noise from inside. He turned to see the young one crawling toward him.

"Zophia?" he called softly. "What is it? Do you need to relieve yourself?"

"No. I just can't sleep, and I didn't want to disturb Maree." She positioned herself next to him, drawing her legs up for warmth.

"I think your sister would be more disturbed to find you here talking to me."

"She's very protective of me, and she still doesn't trust you."

"But you do?"

"I do."

His gut twisted at her simple declaration. "You shouldn't, Zophia. Maree is right," he said. "You should trust no man."

She did not shrink away or show any inclination to return to her sister's side. Rather, she just tipped her face up to him. "You will protect us, Kallem. I'm sure of it. You will see us safely through these wilds until we reach—"

She broke off quickly and looked away.

"Reach what, Zophia?"

"A better place."

He would have pressed her, but Maree started to whimper piteously in her sleep. The noise tore at him. He nudged Zophia. "Shouldn't you...I don't know...go back to her or something?"

"Not until it passes."

"Would it not comfort her to have you at her side?"

"No doubt. But if I go to her, she'll waken, and it would pain her to know we witnessed her distress." Zophia turned her head toward him. "She pushes it down, Kallem. The pain and humiliation, the anger, that comes from being taken again and again. Most women in the Compounds do. They bury it so deep inside, it can only come out when the conscious mind shuts off."

"You're a wise girl."

She shrugged. "Just an observant one."

Kallem blinked, thinking of his own nightmares. As Captain of the Guard, he'd had his own private quarters now for two years, but prior to that, he'd always hated sleeping in the barracks lest he betray himself as Maree had just done when the nightmares came. He was a loyal servant of the Holy New Order, and he always did as he was commanded, but in his heart of hearts, he feared he *wasn't* the soldier the Prophet thought him. A good soldier, a true soldier, would have a stronger stomach for soldier's work.

Could it be the same for the whores? Were there some among them who couldn't stomach their jobs? He'd assumed that they just accepted their role. After all, relatively speaking, they enjoyed more privileges than other women and moved more freely about the compound.

"You sister has a hard lot, I know," he said. "I've seen the bruises when I've escorted her back to her quarters. But what of the others? The Prophet doesn't suffer them to be harmed, unless with his permission. How then do they suffer?"

"He doesn't permit them to be *physically injured*," Zophia pointed out. "I imagine there's a lot of potential for pain before you hit that threshold. But more than that, it's that they have no control. They must submit to any man, provided he's on the Prophet's approved list, any time they wish."

Zophia fell silent, and it was then Kallem realized that Maree had stopped thrashing.

"I must go back to bed now," she said. "Get some sleep, Kallem."

He watched as Zophia lifted the bedroll and crawled in with her sister. Maree must have woken, or at least sensed her, for she made a welcoming sound and pulled her young sister into her embrace. For a second, he let himself imagine her warmth and softness, but banished the thought immediately. He had enough aches from dozing in an upright position; he didn't have to add another one.

He thought again of Zophia's words. She'd given him much to think on as the scorching sun moved across the sky.

CHAPTER 7

MAREE BRACED herself as Kallem threw her to the ground. Or rather threw her to the ground *again*. She lifted her head for protection from the hard blow; braced her whole body. She slapped her left palm down. Then she looked up at the man who towered over her, squinting into the sun that came from behind his shoulder, darkening his silhouette as he took a step toward her. She waited for Kallem to speak. He extended a hand as he locked eyes with her, an offer of a lift up.

Still on her back, Maree raised herself up onto her elbows. "Well?"

"Not bad." Kallem's face was grim, determined. His posture serious. "We'll do it again."

"Not bad?" Ignoring his hand, she pushed herself to her feet. "What do you mean *not bad*? That was a perfect breakfall."

"Perfect? Hardly. I told you to breathe out. That'll—"

"Yes, I know. Keep the body more relaxed, and so less vulnerable to injury." Dammit! She would have to do it again.

Zophia giggled. "Want me to show you how it's done again, big sister? Who's head of the class now?" She giggled all the more as Maree shot her an acrid glare.

The basic aggressive techniques that Kallem had taught the two women—a couple short, hard strikes to be aimed at a man's most vulnerable regions—Maree had readily picked up. Easily and quickly. She'd wanted to learn more offensive skills, and right away. More aggressive moves. Debilitating and painful strikes. Death blows. But Kallem had insisted she needed to know basic self-defense also. He was right, and she knew it.

But in truth, Maree had to work on the conceptualization of it. The anger in her, the rage, was fierce and righteous. She was determined to strike blows, but never to receive them. Never, ever again.

Zophia, of course, had read her mind. Eased her mind. "We'll get there," she'd whispered, laying an easy hand on her sister's shoulder. She drew herself even closer. "Yes, *there*. And then we'll fear no more. Never need to cower and take a strike. But until then, we do need to know how to survive."

Confronted by such wisdom from her little sister, she settled her emotions. She could do this.

She *would* do this.

"Fine," she said to Kallem. "But this time I—"

He flipped her before she could finish the sentence. Maree protected her head, slapped down her palm to absorb the shock of the fall, and breathed out as she did. Kallem was right! The exhale made her whole body less tense as she hit. She jumped up to her feet like a cat.

Yes! That was a—

"Damn good breakfall." Kallem gave an authoritative nod.

Zophia laughed. Kallem even looked like he might break into a grin too.

Almost.

48

With the back of her hand, Maree wiped the sweat from her brow, only then realizing the exertion she'd been putting forward in Kallem's fighting lessons. He'd been a reluctant teacher, at first. And though Maree had no experience asserting any kind of authority with men, she had insisted he show them how to fight. At least a few moves of offense. "For when you leave us, *soldier*," she had said, emphasizing disdainfully the position he had claimed to have abandoned. It was a test, of course; they'd all known it.

"The knife," Maree now said. "Show me how to use my knife."

"And yet this, you already know," Kallem said.

Maree tensed. There was a hardness to Kallem's tone. He was speaking about the Prophet—about her attempt to kill him. And it was, after all, his ornately carved knife that she now called her own. He'd had it specially made when he'd come into power, by the finest craftsman. It bore the symbol of his testament.

"That's enough for today," Kallem said. Maree's knife remained in his rucksack. She'd awoken this morning to find it missing, and had known that Kallem had taken it. For his own protection, he'd assured her. So he didn't trust her either. Though she now knew the few moves he'd taught her, Maree wasn't foolish enough to imagine she could overpower the man to retrieve the blade. Not even with Zophia's help.

At least not yet.

No, she did not trust him. She never would. But she needed his knowledge. Needed the skills he could teach her. And the sooner she acquired them, the sooner she and Zophia could ditch him.

They'd traveled a good deal this day by Kallem's compass. Finding the small cave a few hours ago had been a Godsend, allowing them to rest unseen. Maree's dreams had been troubled, but her body had greedily taken those needed hours of sleep. Zophia too had slept. And though Kallem had kept vigil at the cave's opening, he too had rested, if not quite so well.

But it was now early evening. They'd had that short rest and a dinner of cold rabbit and some greens Kallem had gathered. And of course, the self-defense lessons. Now it was time to move, on. Maree had insisted they travel the way the map had shown them—at night—for many reasons. Not the least of which involved eventually leaving this soldier behind. And though she'd heard no dogs and seen no smoke, and Zophia had felt no air of warning—at least not one she'd expressed to Maree—they had to be wary of what lay behind them. More soldiers could be coming.

Soldiers. She hated the very word.

A shiver shuddered through her and she hugged herself. "We should get going."

"Not just yet," Zophia said softly, calmly. "Can't we rest for a little while? I'm still so tired."

Maree looked at Zophia, seeing the exhaustion written on her face. Maybe something else—she just didn't look very well.

"Kallem?" Zophia said.

"It's a good shelter. Better to sleep here for a bit and travel later. That way, I'll have morning twilight to help me find the next suitable campsite."

That made sense, she supposed. Plus Zophia would never suggest they linger if she had any inklings of danger...

"You're right, Zophia," she said, walking over to put her arm around the younger girl. "We need our rest."

It was good to see the smile on her sister's face. The two of them went back into the cave and lay down together on the cool ground. But Maree leapt up again quickly as Kallem approached with the quilt. Her heart beating wildly, she snatched it from his hands with such force the blanket would have torn had it not been so strongly sewn. "Never touch my quilt! Never!"

Kallem stared back at her, his eyes stormy with anger and confusion.

Zophia put a hand on his arm. "It's all we have," she said simply.

That was true enough. Females were allowed pitifully few possessions, but their own quilts the Prophet allowed. Hags on the outside of those fences made them for the females—gathered scraps, stitched them with strong twine then brought them to trade at the compounds' fences for small bits of food, or clothing, or scraps of cloth to make more such quilts with their simple and plain patterns. The Prophet allowed this meager exchange between the taunting soldiers and the hags who'd gotten away.

"Yes," Maree said, not by way of apology but by way of explanation. "It's all we have."

Wordlessly, Kallem returned to the mouth of the cave and resumed his earlier position. After five minutes, Maree knew he'd fallen into a light sleep. Soon Zophia was breathing easily in her own much deeper sleep. But Maree lay wide awake looking at the dozing man, and more so, beyond him as the stars came to light in the darkening sky.

Maree pulled the quilt closer around herself.

CHAPTER 8

IT WAS Zophia who spotted the pond. Well, Maree had to admit, she hadn't really *spotted* it. She'd found it. Led them to this place of such value, just a ways beyond the northbound path they'd traveled for most of the night. Dawn was approaching; they would soon be resting again, but Zophia had begged them to travel this short ways with her off the path. "I feel it," she'd told Maree. And Maree had trusted her. Her sister's feelings seemed to be growing stronger, more urgent, the further they got from the compound.

And the water she'd led them to was pure. Spring-fed, Kallem had explained excitedly, though she could see that for herself. Places like this were rare. But nature was slowly taking over again. Rising once more, little by little. She'd seen it even in the city as they'd escaped, in the encroaching grass and strong weeds that poked through the concrete and rubble of the abandoned streets. Dead trees had supported new green vines, which snaked up them. And the evidence had grown more abundant as they traveled through the wilds.

Even the crows—those beautiful birds—seemed more plentiful the further they went.

Crows had flown over the compound, too. The Prophet had told the people that that was the *only* place they still flew. That there was no sustenance elsewhere, beyond the compound walls and the precious nearby lands the women tilled and sowed and harvested. Beyond that, there was nothing but vast stretches of desolation separating one compound from another, or so the Order said. It was another teaching lesson. Death, destruction, decay—that was all that remained after the wrath of God had swept through the world. Ah, but the Prophet had offered hope. And perhaps even more importantly, he'd offered up a scapegoat— *women*. And sadly, so many women themselves had accepted that role even before the inoculation. Hope had been abandoned beyond the walls of the Prophet's Order— his Holy New Testament. And that supreme, overarching commandment.

Thou shalt not disbelieve.

Zophia had been the first to the water, once Kallem had scouted the area to his satisfaction. And Maree had felt a motherly spurt of panic as her sister had bent to drink from it. But she bit it down. *Spring-fed*, she reminded herself. Perhaps not completely pure, but as close to it as they were likely to find anywhere. Maree, then Kallem, joined Zophia at the water's edge, greedily drinking.

And now, they stood back from that clear water, behind the cover of thick shrubbery very near to where Kallem had hung his clothes. The two women crouched down low and peeked through the branches, watching as Kallem, his bare backside to them, waded in.

The water went up almost to his chest. He dove in, then rose again quickly and shuddered out a profanity. It had to be cold. He gripped a bar of hard soap and quickly began washing his body.

Maree caught her sister staring. "Maybe you shouldn't be looking."

Zophia battled off Maree's only half-serious attempt to cover her younger sister's eyes. "Maybe you shouldn't be either, Maree."

Maree snorted. "Nothing I haven't seen before."

Except Kallem Marsh's naked form was nothing like anything she'd ever seen. Nothing like the Prophet's.

She'd felt the power of those muscles, of course, when he'd taught her the breakfall, and she'd seen his bare torso when he'd given her his shirt after the Reprobate's attack. So it shouldn't have come as a shock to see the whole of him exposed. Yet it did, somehow. She couldn't deny the odd flutter in her belly to see how it all came together. The way his neck flowed into wide, powerful shoulders, then nipped in to lean hips. And his buttocks... Watching those rock-solid mounds as he'd strode to the water had been strangely fascinating.

Kallem ducked under the water one final time, rinsing the last of the soap away. He raked his hair back with hard fingers, and started walking out of the frigid water. Maree could not have stopped her gaze from going to his groin if she'd wanted to. His penis swayed as he walked, but it was the ridge of muscle running from hip to groin on either side that grabbed her attention. Memory stirred. Movie stars used to look like that, in their low-slung jeans. Actors and models and athletes. When she'd been Zophia's age, she'd spent hours with her girlfriends, giggling at such pictures on the Internet.

The memory sent a tendril of dread through her. The Internet. Computers. Television and cell phones and tablets and streaming video with programming that wasn't the Prophet's propaganda. Freedom and friends and casual laughter. She hadn't thought of those things in so very long. It was too dangerous. Too easy to betray herself.

"Hmmmph. Not such a big deal."

Maree bit back a laugh at Zophia's comment. Though she doubted he had a shy bone in his body, it wouldn't do for them to be caught watching him as he'd bathed. Besides, she didn't want to laugh at her blessedly-inexperienced sister's lack of knowledge.

"No, not a big deal...*right now*," Maree felt obliged to say. "It shrinks in the cold. It can be quite different when it...um...warms up."

Despite herself, Maree tensed at the mere thought of an erect penis. *Pain. Torment. Humiliation.* That was all she'd known in the Prophet's bed. How could she tell her sister this? How could she not? But at that moment, Kallem neared and she could say nothing. She only watched him dress. And then turn to where they hid.

"You can come out now," he said. "Show's over."

Zophia groaned her embarrassment.

Maree said nothing.

Of course he'd known they were watching. Despite the slash through his tattooed arm, once a soldier, always a soldier. He'd have to know where they were at all times. He'd probably counted on it, damn him. He'd left his clothing and rucksack perfectly placed. Near enough to the shrub cover that they could spy on him, yet close enough that if they made a dash for the precious commodity of his gear, he could get to it just as quickly.

Grabbing Zophia by the hand, Maree led her out of the hiding place and over to Kallem. If he thought to embarrass her, he was wrong. And she knew the hostility was there in her eyes as she approached.

Zophia moved to take the soap from his hand. But with a squeeze of her sister's fingers, she stopped her reach.

"And where will you be, Soldier?" Maree spat. "From where will you watch us?"

Her heart was pounding, ready to rage. Some of the soldiers took pleasure, forcing the women upon each other. Watching them. She'd die before that happened.

"Near enough to be sure of your safety," he said. "But you'll have your privacy while you bathe. I give you my word. Then I'll leave you to rest, while I go in search of food."

Kallem's answer surprised her—especially the latter part. Both that he would leave them, and that they needed food so quickly. An urgency rose in her.

"What about the rations?" Zophia asked, glancing at the rucksack. "And we can fill the canteens here. The pond's a little muddied now and will be even more so after Maree and I bathe, but the spring that feeds it is still clear." She glanced to her right, automatically knowing—sensing—from which part of the dense blanket of dead trees the spring trickled into the pond.

"Our rations won't last beyond a few more days. If our journey is long..." Kallem's eyes drifted from Zophia's to Maree's as he let his words trail off.

He was waiting for one of them to answer of course. Waiting for them to betray how far they were from their destination—from Society Three.

Silence.

With a sigh, Kallem turned his back. Hands clasped behind him, feet spread shoulder-width apart. He waited.

Maree could feel Zophia's seeking eyes upon her. Maree said nothing, but nodded to her and they both began undressing. They dropped their clothes to the ground.

With a girlish whoop, Zophia dashed toward the water and dove in. Maree felt a pang of panic to see her disappear beneath the water, but reminded herself the water had gone up to Kallem's chest for quite a distance. As long as they didn't venture out any further, they wouldn't be over their heads. Maree followed more cautiously. She'd known how to swim before the mass inoculation, and assumed it was a skill she'd retained.

Zophia broke the surface with a loud gasp. Maree dove into the water herself, and echoed that shocked gasp when she came up.

"This is the coldest—" Zophia stopped mid-sentence and turned to Maree. "Do parts of us shrink up like that too?" She had an impish smile on her face, no doubt knowing full well the soldier could overhear.

Maree snorted, then glanced up at Kallem. He stood where they'd left him, his back still turned, but she could swear there was a bit more tension in his shoulders.

She splashed her sister. Zophia splashed back and soon they both were laughing. As their bodies adjusted to the cold, they ducked under and up again. Maree turned onto her back and dared a few strokes. She could still swim! Then, looking up at the sun, she simply rested there, floating these moments on her back.

"I'm going to try that," Zophia said.

Maree stood again, then crouched down in the water. Now that her body had mostly adjusted to the cold, it was warmer beneath the water's surface. "It's not that easy."

Zophia eased herself onto her back in the water. She floundered briefly, but was soon doing it—floating on her back, trusting that the water would support her. Trusting enough to let go. There she was, victorious in the water, smiling up at the sky.

Maree watched her sister's innocent enjoyment. *This is what it's like to be free, this is what hope feels like.*

She caught herself. Hope was a dangerous thing. Hadn't she always been taught that? Ever since the inoculation. Yet she was on this trek to find Society Three. There was a moment of sadness, which ached behind eyes hardened from tears that would not fall.

Lost in thought, she startled when Zophia laid a hand on her shoulder. Her intuitive sister leaned in to whisper. "Nope, nothing shrinks out here at all. Nothing shrivels in the cold. We won't let it. Especially our spirits. Right, sister?"

Maree blinked rapidly at Zophia's unexpected insight. But she shouldn't really be surprised. More and more, Zophia seemed able to read her thoughts.

"Right." Maree smiled her broadest, sunniest smile. If nothing else in this world could, her sister would keep her going. She would cling to the faith of a child. One who had so far been spared the worst of the pain of the place they'd left behind. "Come on. Time to dry off."

Though the day would be warm, right now with the early-morning breeze, gooseflesh prickled when they left the pond. Maree picked up Kallem's shirt, the one he'd given her to cover herself with when her dress had been ripped. She handed it to Zophia to dry herself with, then quickly used it to dry her own limbs as her sister dressed. She'd lay it out on the bushes, in the gentle breeze and warm sunshine. It would dry soon enough. In the meantime, her torn dress...

...was mended?

The stitching was rough, utilitarian, as a soldier's stitching would be. In fact, the long needle and coarse black thread lay on the ground still beside it, as if the chore had just been finished. Kallem must have done this while they'd been playing in the water. While they'd not been paying attention. And he had to have made a fast retreat from the spot when they'd stepped out of the water. He'd granted them privacy, after all.

Maree pulled the dress on.

"You can come out now, Kallem," Zophia called. "We're dressed."

A moment later, he walked out of the cover of trees. Maree touched a hand to the mended bodice of her dress, but said nothing. Nor did Kallem say a word. If he expected a thank you for this—for any of this—he would be sorely disappointed. And it occurred to her, not for the first time, to wonder what payment the soldier expected.

Kallem's frustrated stare broke from hers. He bent to the rucksack, then sat on the ground as he distributed 'breakfast'. Spring water would be the drink of choice as long as they had access to it—either here at the source or from their canteens. Maree suspected precious little liquid energy remained in Kallem's store of rations. They were heavier than the packets of food. He handed them each a protein bar, and took two for himself. That made sense; he had more mass to sustain. Also, they'd be resting here this morning while he went to hunt. At least that was the plan. But Maree was thinking of another plan. She looked down at the needle and thread. She chewed on the dry and tasteless food, sorting it out in her mind.

Kallem stood as he finished his breakfast. "I'll be no more than an hour. I saw some rabbit pellets back along the way we came. With any luck, we'll have meat soon."

Rabbits. Maree hadn't seen evidence of them herself as they'd trekked to this located, but then again, she wasn't trained to. Kallem was. Though all species had taken a beating from the environment's degradation, it made sense that rabbits would rebound, given their exceptional reproductive capabilities.

"How?" Maree asked, no elaboration of her question necessary. She knew Kallem carried a gun, but the sound of a shot would attract attention.

"I set out snares earlier," he said. "As we moved along this way at dawn. Rabbits are crepuscular. With any luck we'll have one or two already."

"But I didn't see you—"

"You weren't supposed to."

He'd only been a minute or two out of their sight, to relieve himself or to allow the women to do the same. It must have been then that he'd set the snares.

"Leave the knife, Kallem."

Zophia's words surprised Maree. Though of course, her sister was right. They'd need it for protection. And maybe something more. "Yes," Maree said. "Leave the knife."

He did not move.

"We may need to defend ourselves," Zophia said. "Beyond what you've taught us."

Maree watched his stone-still face, then caught his moment of decision. This wasn't just about protection. Not even close.

Kallem swung the bag around. He unzipped a side pocket, pulled out the knife and handed it to Maree. The butt of it felt warm in her hand. Welcome as her trembling fingers slid around it again. And memory slid back in too. Of how she'd used this very blade to wound the Prophet, and how she still wished she'd sunk the steel deep into his fucking heart.

"I'll be back soon. Hide in that copse of trees up there." He gestured to a stand of fat fir trees. "But keep the pond in sight—at least a glimpse of it. That way, you won't get lost, and you'll see me when I return."

"And we'll be able to see if others venture near without being seen ourselves," Zophia said.

"Exactly. In the meantime, we don't need to leave obvious proof of our visit lying around." He retrieved his still-damp shirt from the bush where Maree had spread it and drew it on.

Reprobates. She knew that was what he was thinking. That's what all of them were thinking. *Or soldiers.*

"I'll be back soon," he said.

Maree watched his retreat, then she and Zophia moved into cover, far enough away from the pond, yet still able to see it. The ground was damp and cool under the thick and tangled growth. She would have preferred the sun-warmed ground near the water's edge, but Kallem was right. They had to hide. And they should rest. However Maree had no intention of resting.

From her pocket, Maree pulled out the needle and spool of thread Kallem had used earlier to mend her dress. When she'd picked up her garment from the ground, Maree had carefully scooped these up too.

"Do we have to do this?" Zophia asked, clearly knowing where Maree was headed.

"Yes," Maree said. "We'll be safer. The more we look like men, the less danger we'll be in." Of course, that would be a harder job for Maree than for her slighter sister. But even with her more ample curves, surely at a distance, the Reprobates would see three men traveling together, not one man and two women.

Sighing, Zophia stripped off her skirt.

With the course thread and large needle, Maree set to work.

Sewing was a skill the women were allowed to develop in the compounds. Considered domestic enough by the Prophet. Harmless enough. But too, in his cunning, the Prophet knew that the acquisition of this domestic skill was a cruel warning to the women of the Holy New Order. When they were no longer of use to The Order, they would be cast out the gates. If they were lucky—if they survived the soldiers' hag hunt that first night—they would eventually sew quilts for the young females in exchange for those scraps of food.

With skilled hands, Maree turned the skirt inside out, folded it and measured it with a practiced eye. Then, with Zophia's help, she made the necessary cuts with the knife. Finally, she began to sew. Her fingers moved quickly, and the work was soothing. Around them, unseen birds sang and insects began to buzz. It was almost peaceful. When she was finished, Maree realized that Zophia had dozed off. She gave her a poke.

Zophia came awake quickly. Taking the makeshift pants Maree handed her, she pulled them on, then rolled her eyes. "A little big, aren't they?"

"I had to let the waist out so you could draw them on and off over your hips. Use the drawstring to tighten them."

Zophia found the sturdy tie Maree had fashioned from the extra material and cinched the waist tighter.

"How do I look?" She pirouetted daintily, making Maree laugh.

"Perfect. Now rest some more while I make my trousers."

"After I've helped you make the cuts."

Maree removed her dress and reached for the knife. First, with Zophia holding the bodice and Maree holding the skirt, she cut the skirt away. When they'd cut the skirt to Maree's satisfaction, Zophia curled up with the quilt and dozed off again. Suppressing a yawn, Maree set to work once more. It was a quick job, and rougher than the one she'd done for her sister, but as she drew the pants on, she decided it was effective enough. Yes. At a distance, they could pass for men. Except for their hair....

"Oh no, you don't!" Zophia sat up, rubbing the sleep from her eyes. "Pants, fine. But you're not cutting my hair."

Zophia loved her long hair, and in truth, it probably pained Maree just as much as it did Zophia to have to cut those beautiful locks.

"But we have to," Maree pleaded. "We can grow it back again when we're safe."

"We can just tuck it up. Or better still, braid it and pin it up. You do mine, then I'll do yours."

"No, Zophia. It won't be—"

"Are you going to force this? Force me? Is that the price I pay? Is this what we're seeking out here, Maree?"

Maree's heart sank with Zophia's words. How could she force her will on her sister, after the life she'd led herself? After having been forced continually to submit to the will of another?

She couldn't.

She dropped the knife, moved to where her sister sat on the ground and began separating her red hair into strands. "God, you're stubborn, Zophia."

"Family trait."

Maree worked steadily, twisting, braiding and pinning up her sister's hair. They each had little bundles of hair pins in their dresses, and Maree used both to finish Zophia's hair. She braided tightly, and though the job was nothing fancy, at a distance it would pass. Especially with the pants, she'd look like a young male at first glance.

"There are no pins left for you," Zophia said. She raised a hand, about to pull some pins from her own hair.

Maree stopped her. "No need."

She picked up her knife with a steady hand and grasped a clump of her own hair with the other. Before she could make the first cut, there was a loud snap in the woods.

Someone was coming!

Someone was close.

CHAPTER 9

KALLEM PULLED the dead rabbit from the snare, carefully coiling the twine and stowing it in a pocket of his cargo pants.

As dawn had approached and he'd started scouting for a campsite, he'd realized they were traveling through perfect rabbit habitat. So he'd set out five rudimentary snares along the way, knowing he'd be able to come back and check them. Three of them had paid off. They would eat well today. His rations, which were intended for one, were running low.

As he lashed the third carcass to the first two and fixed them to his belt, he fought the desire to head straight back to camp. The women were as safely stowed as he could make them, and their safety would be better served by him scouting further afield than by going back.

Forcing his feet to move, he started off in a south-westerly direction. Best to make sure no soldiers were on their trail before he circled all the way around to scout forward.

As he moved all but silently through the forest, his mind flashed back to his cold dip in the pond. Not that bathing in icy water was anything new. But feeling female eyes on him as he did certainly was. Despite the temperature of the water, he'd gone instantly hard. It had taken some time—and a hell of a lot of concentration—before he could safely turn and exit the pool without betraying himself.

Afterward, it had taken every bit of discipline at his disposal to keep him from likewise spying on the women as they bathed. He would have had no compunction had it been just Maree, but not with the child present. So he'd picked up Maree's dress instead and mended it with needle and thread from his kit while the girls washed each other's hair with the bar of soap he'd given them, then fell to playing in the water. The quiet sounds of their voices and the splashing of water were a torment, but one he savoured somehow.

And Maree's reaction when she saw he'd mended the bodice the Reprobate had torn.... She hadn't thanked him, as he'd expected. Instead, her eyes had raked him scathingly.

Unless...had his well-intentioned action only served to sharpen the memory of her near rape by the Reprobate? Had he handed her fresh humiliation at the reminder of her helplessness?

His throat ached with strange emotion at the thought. What a complicated creature she was!

And beautiful. God, she was beautiful. No wonder the Prophet had chosen her. Though it wasn't her beauty that kept him calling her back to his bed again and again. The Prophet could have his pick of all the women, some considerably younger and more lusciously endowed. Occasionally he did avail himself of those younger fruits. But Maree was the only constant, and Kallem knew why. It was her spirit. Her fight.

And the Prophet's determination to crush it out of her.

Gritting his teeth, Kallem consulted his compass and adjusted his direction.

Fifteen minutes later, as he was coming around to the southeasterly point on his circuit, he froze. Voices. Male voices.

Soldiers or Reprobates? Or heavily armed traders, perhaps. There was a certain amount of commerce between settlements, mainly swapping females of breeding potential. Genetic diversity had to be maintained. If only the breeders and offspring of breeders of one community bred amongst themselves, the subsequent issue became more feeble instead of stronger.

Kallem's hand automatically checked the pistol at his belt, drawing reassurance from the cold metal. But it was his knife he drew as he crept closer. The pistol he would use only if he had to. No point alerting every Reprobate within earshot to his presence unless he needed to.

As it turned out, he didn't need to.

They hadn't posted sentries. They didn't have to; they were Reprobates. They were without doubt the most frightening animals in their world. Soldiers ignored them unless threatened, and lone wolf Reprobates cut a wide berth around a pack like this. True, there were confrontations between packs occasionally, but not often. Territories had been carved out long ago and boundaries were respected, for the most part.

Kallem dropped to his belly and crept closer. The smell of cooking meat reached his nostrils, making his stomach rumble. Good. It would take the men a while to eat their meal and break camp, if indeed they planned to. Time enough to get back to the women and put some distance between them.

The women would be disappointed, he knew, that they had to move out so quickly. They'd traveled most of the night, as was Maree's preference, and they needed rest. Yet he knew they wouldn't complain when he pushed them to march again. Knew they would gather up their things and follow him. They would know as well as he that they couldn't tarry here. Not this close to a Reprobate encampment.

Kallem's passage back through the forest was faster this time, though he did complete the sweeping arc to satisfy himself that no worse threats lurked ahead. By the time he made it back to the cluster of firs in the midst of which he'd sequestered the girls, the day's heat had begun to make itself felt in the sweat that trickled down his back and made his shirt stick to him.

As he made his way through the dense thicket, he heard nothing. For a panicked moment, he thought perhaps they'd left, forging on alone. He wouldn't put it past Maree. She would get herself killed without him. Her sister too. The headstrong foo—

The prick of a blade at his back cut his thought short.

"Move and this blade goes into your spine."

Kallem smiled at the sound of Maree's voice and put up his hands in a sign of surrender. "Well done."

The blade was withdrawn and she stepped back. He turned to see her stow the knife in the waistband of her pants.

Wait a minute—*pants*? Where had she gotten them? They weren't his. Wrong color. Besides, his rucksack was on his back.

He lifted an eyebrow. "What's this? Did you assail a passing Reprobate and steal his pants?"

"Of course not." She tilted her chin. "I made them from the skirt of my dress."

Ah, yes. He could see it now. Could see also a glimpse of bare flesh between her shirt—or what used to be the bodice of her dress, he realized—and the new pants. "You're handy with a needle."

Zophia stepped out from behind her sister and Kallem's eyes widened. She too now wore trousers, and Maree had passed along to her the shirt he'd leant her. It hung loosely about her small frame, swamping her. But the real transformation was her hair. It was gone!

Zophia laughed at his expression and took off the wide band she'd tied around her head. Beneath it, her hair had been plaited and pinned close to her head in a flame-colored circlet.

"Good thought," he said. "Put some dirt on your face and you could pass for a malnourished boy. Though I wouldn't count on it putting off the Reprobates altogether. You make far too pretty a boy."

Zophia's eyes widened. "They would molest a boy?"

Maree made an exasperated sound. "Damn you, Kallem! Why'd you have to tell her that? She was just beginning to feel some measure of—"

"Safety?" He met her angry eyes. "That's a luxury she can't afford out here. Some of those Reprobates *prefer* boys. That's what landed a good number of them outside the gates of civilization." At her expression, he softened. "Still, it's much safer to travel as males than as females. It's a good idea, really. I should have thought of it myself." His eyes fastened on her own hair, a glorious mane of burnished chestnut. "You should do the same with your hair so you can tuck it up under a cap."

"I had a different plan in mind for mine."

She took the blade in hand again and he suddenly knew what she intended.

"No, don't!"

She grasped a handful of hair and began sawing through it with the blade. He watched in horror as she dropped the hank of hair to the ground.

"Maree!" Zophia's voice trembled with shock.

"Hush, Zophia."

Her beautiful hair! Kallem suppressed a moan. Now he'd never sink his hands into all that silken glory. Never gather fistfuls of it to hold her still while he ravished her mouth.

Never feel the thrill of it trailing across his chest, and lower… The pang of loss he felt stunned him.

His stomach clenched as he watched her grasp another piece and hack through it. This time, she could not suppress the grimace as the sawing motion tugged at her roots.

He held out his hand. "Give me the knife."

"Too late! There's no going back now." Despite the tears of pain in her eyes, her smile was victorious.

"I know. But if you hold the hair, I can saw through it for you without yanking half of it out by the roots."

She blinked, surprised by his offer. "You would do that for me?"

"As you pointed out, there's no other choice now. Give me the blade. Quickly. We need to get moving again."

She blanched, but passed the knife to him. "Soldiers?"

"Reprobates." He gestured for her to lift another hank of hair, and she obliged. "They're some distance off, and they were cooking a meal, so there's no immediate threat." He sawed through her hair as gently as he could and dropped the locks to the ground. "But we can't linger here. We need to put some distance between us and them before we can rest."

She nodded and glanced sideways at her sister. "Zophia, can you start packing?"

"Of course."

He was conscious of Zophia gathering their things and packing them as he cut the rest of Maree's hair, and his respect for their resilience grew. It was one thing for a soldier to endure long marches and sleep deprivation. They were hardened to it. But these females were not.

He turned his attention back to the task of cutting Maree's hair. Though it pained him, he understood perfectly what drove her to do it. It wasn't just in the hopes of passing for a male. It was a way to reject her past, to refute her role as the Prophet's whore. She was claiming herself.

When he'd finished, he had to admit it looked a lot like the knife-cut hair sported by most of the Reprobates. At least those that didn't shave their heads with a blade.

"What do you think?" she asked, running her hand through it.

He cleared his throat. "I think we need to get moving. And I think I'd better bury this before we leave."

Kallem bent and gathered up the clumps of hair. While they continued to pack up, he scouted the ground until he found a sandy spot and dug a hole into which he dropped the clippings. On an impulse he couldn't have explained, he took one lock of Maree's hair and stuffed it into his pocket. Then he quickly buried the rest and rejoined the women.

CHAPTER 10

THE PROPHET sat on the balcony beneath the wide UV screen, the pale skin of his arms gleaming white in the filtered early-morning sun as he gave himself his first shot of the day. His private chemist had mixed the concoction. Yes, the pain would be dulled—out of his reach somehow—and he would be able to sleep soon, a luxury only afforded him now by his blessed needles. But he would *not* allow his emotions to be dulled. He had to keep his anger—ready and reachable for when his whore returned.

Though he usually preferred the shadows of his offices and chambers, this morning he needed the light. The air. A different place to think. Besides, from this high balcony above the streets and buildings of the compound center, he could see his people—the watching guards and listening soldiers, the whispering servants, the wondering whores. As he watched, an old woman—a hag—came to the north gate, where she suffered the taunting of the soldiers before they exchanged scraps of bread and bits of cheese for the quilt she bore. One of the soldiers passed it off to a nursery worker, who would pass it on to one of the young females. A comfort? No, a reminder of her lowly place in the world. Warming a bed, bearing a child, or simply lying on that quilt at night before she got to up to toil from dawn to dusk in the nearby fields or in the gristmill or the laundry.

The Prophet watched as the attendants came for Liz and took her away. She'd almost given in—almost uttered the words of soul surrender—that Maree never would. Liz was one of the strong ones; Maree had been stronger. Still was stronger. Unless she'd met her demise out there beyond the gates. Surely his soldier had located her by now, and the breeder too. Kallem would not fail him. Kallem was a loyal soldier. The Prophet was sure of it.

Wasn't he?

Doubt coiled around his heart like a serpent.

What if I'm wrong? The thought was like a hot strike of that serpent's fangs. *What if I could be so wrong?*

Didn't he believe in his own righteousness? Wasn't that the commandment—the one he'd given to stand above them all? Yes. He'd seen it. Swagg had seen it too. Though that had been some time ago...

One of his domestic servants stepped out onto the flagstone patio. He knew this one—Luvanne—an older one, barely hanging onto favor enough to remain within the compound. Slowly she came to him, bearing a tray of dried meats, bread and precious juice for his breakfast.

As she approached, his mind slipped back to the audience with Kallem, when he'd given the soldier his charge. There *had* been that flash in the soldier's eyes at the mention of Maree's name. He'd seen the recognition there. But surely that was all it was, just recognition and nothing more...

Luvanne bent to place the breakfast tray on the table before him. Before she could do so, he smashed it from her hands with a fast and raging fist. Everything spilled to the floor with a clatter, and Luvanne went down almost as quickly to clean up the mess.

How far away was this Society Three—if it even existed? Had Kallem reached it already? Had the women led him there? What if they'd found him out? What if Reprobates had come upon him and killed him? Killed the women! Kallem was his most skilled soldier, but if there were enough Reprobates left out beyond the compound walls....

What if he'd decided to keep the virgin—the breeder—for himself? What if the women killed him? He lifted a hand to his injured arm as he thought of this. Maree could do it, if she caught him unsuspecting. He'd told Kallem she still had the knife. Hadn't he? Dammit, he couldn't remember. He couldn't think! He could only...

"Doubt," he whispered.

"I beg your pardon, Prophet?" Luvanne kept her eyes lowered as she spoke.

He blinked, recalling the servant. "You dropped the tray," he said coldly.

"Yes, sir. I—"

"That's what you shall tell them. You dropped the tray. You're clumsy and old and it slipped from your hands." There was a pause. "But I've...I've taken pity on you."

With a nod of understanding, Luvanne gathered the last pieces of the fallen meal, wiped up the spilled juice with the skirt of her dress, and began to back out of the room. But she dared a glance into the Prophet's eyes as she did so.

This day she was safe.

Luvanne would tell as he'd ordered—not that he'd knocked the tray flying in an angry outburst—but that it was her fault. He didn't need more voices rising to question his behavior. The servant would lie because she was old, and in a heartbeat he could order her hagged and expel her from the Holy New Order. She'd be running for her life beyond those gates. Yes, Luvanne knew this. He knew this.

But if he expelled her now, what incentive would she have to stay quiet? To stop her from crying out the things she knew as he had her forced into the wilds? This too was knowledge they shared. Luvanne closed the door behind her, but not before he bade her to send someone else to him.

He was slipping. Not just with the tray here this morning. Not just with his brutal episodes with Liz. But it was the puncture to the armour that Maree had delivered that ate at him the most. That was the open wound. This first cut was always the deepest. The most powerful. Because it was proof that it could be done.

The door opened and a shadow spilled into the sunlight before him. Robinson. His oldest soldier—his most trusted general. If anyone could be depended upon, it was this man.

There it was again. That 'if.' Could he trust *anyone*?

The Prophet shook the thought away.

"Kallem," the Prophet said. "He has not returned?" He knew he hadn't of course, but chose to lead with the question.

"No, Prophet. He has not."

"I saw you talking to the hag at the gate."

"Yes, sir."

"I assume you questioned her?"

There were always questions, veiled and unveiled threats to these old women that came. But that wasn't what the Prophet meant. Robinson knew this.

"Yes, sir. She's seen nothing of the girls. Nothing of Kallem. Mac has returned with the hound. He said he left Kallem a day ago."

The Prophet nodded, slowly. He was growing weary. The needle was having its effect and he'd need to sleep soon. Very soon. His mind was drifting back to Maree again. Her escape with the bleeder. Her insolence. Her punishment to come. He had to bring her back. Had to get her back before the wound she'd inflicted became too deep to heal.

"I want you to go after her," he said. "Take one man. No more than that, and go after Maree and Zophia, the bleeder."

"Shall I take the dogs, Prophet?"

He pictured the hounds—those sleepy, stupid-looking piles of wrinkled flesh dozing in the sun of their kennels. Yet given a scent and a command, they would run for days. Run without food or water or rest, tugging a soldier along behind them, relentlessly following a trail that was days, sometimes weeks old. And when the trail grew hot and the dogs gave voice, the hunted quailed in terror, for they knew there was no escaping the Prophet's reach.

"Yes, take the dogs."

As Robinson stood aside, the Prophet looked down at the street below. Luvanne was walking past a gathering of soldiers. They called after her, tauntingly, but this time she did not lower her head in fear of their words. This time, she did not cover her face and the tears so ready to fall. She just continued her walk to the servants' quarters and disappeared through its door. The Prophet was fading fast as the narcotic took its hold. But he gathered the strength to make one more command.

"Hurry, Robinson. There is no time to lose."

CHAPTER 11

IT WAS a bright morning, and even though the sunlight that reached them filtered through the leaves of the surrounding poplars, Maree enjoyed the play of it over her face.

They'd been on the move almost constantly for two solid days. But this morning, they'd paused at last for a real rest. Kallem had found this clearing just before dawn, and after scouting the surrounding area, had declared it a suitable place to camp. When he'd come back, Maree had already set out the snares as he had taught her. And now, having grabbed a few hours of blessed sleep, they were enjoying the bounty Maree had found in those snares when she'd checked them. And oh, dear God, what a luxury! To rest, to fill their bellies with a hearty breakfast.

But to Maree it was more a celebratory breakfast than one of respite, and she'd whispered as much to Zophia while Kallem had tended the fires for their tea. A sign—just as the map had said there would be! She'd found it this morning as she'd unstrung the last rabbit.

Three crescent moons carved into the trunks of several thick oaks. So small, almost unnoticeable. She had to look twice, and then a third time, to be sure when she'd spotted the first set. But then as she looked around, she saw the same subtle marking on several more trees. Giddily, she'd run from tree to tree, like a child finally freed to play. Or a woman finally freed to truly hope. *They were getting closer*. The map was right. She was right! Society Three was a reality! And she and her sister would reach it. The crescents were a welcome fortification. A blessed promise.

Kallem's compass had let them travel so much faster than they otherwise would have done. They traveled both by night and day, resting when they could, and taking shelter from the punishing sun at midday, when the UV radiation was at its worst. Of course, Maree had studied the position of the stars in the night sky, the twists in the ground, the shifts in the earth, comparing them to the map to assure herself that Kallem wasn't leading them astray. She knew that they really had been bearing north. But finding the signs had still come as a dizzying relief.

She glanced at Zophia, who was concentrating on a rabbit's haunch. "Good?" she asked, sinking her teeth into her own portion. Though she already knew the answer. Compared to what they were used to back at the compound, this was a feast.

Zophia smiled, and Maree was glad to see it. Her sister had seemed distracted, almost uneasy this morning, though she'd not shared any concerns.

"Very good," she said. "Thanks, Maree."

"Don't thank me. You're the one who did such a fine job cooking it, Zophia." For something cooked simply on a spit over a low fire, it was amazingly tender and juicy.

"But we eat because of you."

That was true enough. Maree took another bite of the juicy meat, and it tasted all the richer knowing she'd caught it herself.

Yes, Kallem was teaching her to hunt. Well, to snare small animals, anyway. Still, even that small transference of knowledge would be condemned by the Prophet and the Order.

And yes, Maree'd felt a pang of sorrow—guilt even—when she'd found her first dead rabbit, dangling from the low tree branch. In truth, she had felt more for their entrapment than their deaths. But the pang in her belly had been stronger than any qualms she'd had about eating the meat.

Meat. Protein like she'd never tasted it before, even before the Prophet rushed in his Holy New Order. Nature's supplies had been running out for some time, and the gods of technology and chemicals hadn't been able to keep up. The world had been starving in so many ways. That was when the Prophet had risen to power.

He'd been a mere man before the inoculations. Just Marcus Will Montag. Charismatic preacher. One-term senator. Then vice-president to a one-term president. One term because Marcus Will Montag had convinced the world that *he* was the rightful leader. The *true* world leader. The then-president had been assassinated—some whispered that Montag had done it himself. Then had come the hurricanes. The torrential rains and floods in some areas of the country; drought and creeping desertification in other areas. Worldwide crop failures like never before. Two tsunamis in a six-week period. The bees were almost completely gone, and birds fell from the sky.

With the world's near total environmental crash, a disaster long in the making and long denied, and with people praying desperately for salvation, Montag had risen to become their Prophet. He'd used the mass media, the fear of the desperate people, and select words from the original testaments to produce the hope of a Holy New Order, complete with a new Ending Testament, given directly to Montag by God! The inoculations had followed quickly. Given the toll previous pandemics had taken, just the whisper of another one had people lining up voluntarily for the shot. And those who didn't queue up to get it were rooted out and forcibly inoculated. For the good of the many, they'd said. Except the "immunization" was, in fact, a pharmaceutical memory wipe.

Tabula rasa.

Thank God the needle hadn't worked on her! And thank God Maree had been smart enough to fake its effects. It left her knowledge intact. Left the memories—the sweet and the bittersweet.

She glanced sideways at Kallem.

When Maree had demanded he teach them how to hunt in addition to how to defend themselves, he'd been reluctant. He'd scowled and said hunting was a man's job in the Holy New Order, but Zophia had quietly countered that it was a woman's job to sew in the Holy New Order, yet a soldier could mend a garment.

Miraculously, he had relented. Or perhaps not so miraculously. In this world beyond the gates of the compound, beyond the eyes of the Order, he seemed prepared to listen to reason. When necessity required, he seemed able to bend. Perhaps he was realizing that things hadn't always been this way.

That they never should have been this way.

If that were so, how odd it must be for him. The inoculation had worked on Kallem Marsh; of that she had no doubt. Even if the Prophet *had* cast him out as he claimed, his attitudes and beliefs had been shaped for him and would not be easily shed.

Ah, but Maree remembered a different Kallem. One she'd grown up with. One who'd played varsity football at their school, yet hadn't been anything like the other jocks, who seemed to just cruise around on their electric boards, blasting misogynistic music. A boy who kept KillCount on pause on his tablet so he could call it up and pretend to have been blasting bad guys in case someone caught him reading books. One who'd looked at her like a little sister, until the day he started looking at her in a way she was almost-but-not-quite too young to understand. A way that she pretended not to notice, because if she did, he'd stop letting her hang out with him.

Kallem looked up from his meal, meeting Maree's eyes.

"You had a dog," she said.

He nodded. "Yes. Some soldiers are given—"

"No, not a service dog," Maree said. "I don't mean back at the compound. I mean a pet. When you were a boy back in Falmouth, where we came from." She was testing him. Not so much his memory as his reaction to her memories. Would he believe her? Would he be enraged? Or—and this thought made her more breathless than she wanted to acknowledge—would he be intrigued? "We were in the same complex in the south end," she said. "Same wing. When we were very young, our mothers took turns watching us while the other went out to the markets." She meant the underground markets, of course. Fresh fruits and vegetables were hard to get even then.

He swallowed a piece of rabbit meat. His face betrayed no reaction. "What kind of dog?"

"A mutt. Just a little one, with a long tail and stick-up ears. She was a rescue dog."

"Rescue dog?"

Zophia answered before Maree could. "That was what they called the kennel dogs back then. The ones that weren't part of a breeding program. They were kenneled, and hopefully, rescued. Adopted, I think they called it. But usually not."

Maree's eyes shot wide. "You remember that?"

Zophia grinned. "Yep."

Maree couldn't help but feel the pride in her little sister. Those under five—as Zophia had been—hadn't been inoculated because of the dangers the serum posed to their developing bodies. The weeks of illness and dehydration that followed were too much for the very young. Even among the rest of the population, many died from the effects, particularly the old and infirm. As did many of the poor, and those in areas less devoted to The Order. Most of the disadvantaged in fact. Maree had always suspected they'd been given something different than everyone else, something much more toxic. It was too coincidental. But memory of that time was forbidden. Discouraged with physical violence when it was merely mentioned. Yet Zophia remembered, apparently. And she'd been smart enough to keep quiet about it.

"I remember you talking about the kennels," Zophia said. She turned to Kallem. "And I remember that little dog. You used to let me walk her sometimes down by the beach. Well, you kind of let me walk her. You let me hold the middle of the leash while you had your hand looped around the end. It was one of the rare days when the beaches were open to the public—when the waves weren't too dangerous and there was enough cloud cover that the sun wasn't too vicious, yet not too smoggy. I'd begged my mother to let me go with you, until finally she said yes. And I never forgot that. Even when, years later..." She let her voice trail off. All children were afraid of soldiers.

Kallem did not blink. God, he looked as if he weren't even breathing. And that was the giveaway. He was more than intrigued. There was an edge of anger to the glint in his smoldering eyes. *His past.* Maybe a person could actually miss what they hadn't even realized they'd had. Maree almost felt sorry for him. How strange it must be for him—a rough and ready soldier—to learn of life when he wasn't so completely under the Prophet's command. When he'd let a little girl walk a little dog.

And how much stranger it would be for him if he only knew about the two of them!

For a year, she'd pretended not to notice the way he watched her. A year during which her own desires had begun to stir. A year to fall in love with her friend who'd grown into a handsome man. Life had been perfect then, until she'd blown it by throwing herself at him. At the time, she'd thought she had no choice; he'd gone to the movies twice with Charline Bartlett, a senior in high school. He'd shut Maree down, of course. He was nineteen and her fifteenth birthday was still a month away. But he hadn't done it right away. He'd been too shocked. Those few incredible, intoxicating minutes in his arms had fueled her fevered teenage imagination for years afterward.

Unfortunately, those same few minutes had been a source of nothing but shame for him. He'd dodged her calls and when their paths crossed, he could barely look her in the eye. Within the week, he'd enlisted in the army and left town.

Maree gave her head a mental shake. That man was gone. Both of them were gone, hardened in one way or another under the Holy New Order. And yet the curious man sitting with them now looked more like that boy than Maree cared to admit.

"Sometimes you'd bring that dog down to our apartment," Zophia continued. "My father didn't care for animals—any animals—and they weren't allowed in our place. One time you were there and we had to hide the—"

She stopped too suddenly. And the smile that had been slowly forming on Maree's face, slid away as she took in her sister's sudden pallor and complete stillness.

"Zophia, what is it?"

"They're coming."

Kallem came to his feet. "Who?"

Zophia shook her head. "I...I don't know. I just know they're close. And they...they know about us. They're looking for us."

Maree believed her sister completely. Zophia's intuition had been a curiosity within the walls of the compound, but out here, it had grown into so much more.

82

"I hear nothing," Kallem said, yet he began kicking dirt on the fire to extinguish it. "I scouted this morning before we slept and again while the meat cooked and saw nothing."

"How many?" Maree asked. Her words were clearly aimed at her sister, but the sharpness in her tone, aimed at Kallem.

"Two. I think. Maybe more..." Her brow furrowed. "No, there are definitely two people and they're getting closer. I know...I know they know about us, Maree. One feels...terribly mad."

Maree stood before Kallem. "We have to go now. Leave everything and go. Now!"

He raked a hand over his shaved head. "No," he said. "That's rash. We can't just rush off and leave our supplies behind. We don't even know—"

"Zophia knows."

"Look," Kallem said. "We're not going to—"

"Fuck you!" She stood toe to toe with him, meeting his cold stare defiantly. "My sister and I are going. You can do what you like."

In the distances, a hound gave voice, an excited drawn-out bay, and they all froze. Then the sound came again. Maree watched the widening of Kallem's eyes and knew it must match her own. Soldiers and dogs went hand in hand; they were on their trail. And they were drawing closer by the minute.

Kallem shouldered his rucksack and grabbed his knife in a white-knuckled grip.

"Belle," he said, and swallowed hard. "My dog's name was Belle."

CHAPTER 12

SWEET JESUS, soldiers within earshot. The Prophet must have sent out reinforcements. But to help Kallem or to replace him? Had the Prophet lost faith in his "best soldier?" Had he changed his mind? Perhaps his patience was not equal to his original orders. Perhaps his thirst for revenge against Maree outweighed the tantalizing possibility of finding Society Three.

And the timing couldn't be worse. Kallem's head felt like it was on fire with images—*memories?*—from before. Belle...the beach...the sound of the surf. But there was no time to think about these things now.

"Stay here," Kallem commanded, glad to hear his voice emerge with its usual authority. "I'll deal with the dogs and the soldiers. But be ready to travel when I come back."

"Right," Maree spat. "Ready to travel back to the compound in handcuffs, you mean."

"Dammit, Maree, there's no time! They'll be on us if I don't intercept them. In the open like this—I'll lose any advantage. Better I catch them unawares. Please," he pleaded, "just pack our things, take your sister into the brush and wait for me."

"Come on, Maree. Let's do as he says." Zophia laid a hand on Maree's arm. "He's protected us so far, helped us get this far. Trust him to do it again."

Maree's chest rose and fell rapidly, and Kallem read the agony of indecision in her eyes, but after a tense few seconds, she relented.

"Okay, we'll trust him," she said, but she fixed him with a fierce stare. "You'd better be speaking the truth, Kallem Marsh. If you betray us, if you betray Zophia, I swear I'll kill you."

Kallem stared back at her, his face carefully blank. "Start packing."

With that order, he turned and melted into the forest. As soon as he got out of the girls' sight, he picked up his pace, abandoning stealth for speed. He needed to cut the soldiers off before they got too close. Assuming the Prophet had sent them, he needed to persuade them he still had the situation under control.

After a few minutes' run, he paused and listened. Yes, he could hear them now, thrashing through the brush. He adjusted his course slightly and within another minute, a dog came into sight, straining powerfully at the end of a long lead. And at the other end of the leash, Aykroyd, a young soldier, held on for all he was worth. There had to be more hounds, though. One more, at least. A solitary bloodhound rarely gave voice, and never on the end of a lead.

Besides, the Prophet would never have sent Aykroyd after him alone. As good a soldier as he was, he wasn't senior enough to have gained notice.

Just then another hound lumbered into view, tugging an older man in its wake. Robinson. That made more sense. General Robinson had been in command of the First Guard since its inception. He'd made Kallem captain. The grizzled man was mentor, a friend. Almost a father.

Kallem stepped out in front of the first hound's path.

Aykroyd saw him before the dog did. Once a bloodhound got a scent, they were notoriously blind to the visual world. "Whoa, boy!" Aykroyd dug in and muscled the dog to a stop.

"Hey, Roscoe," Kallem called, waving his hands to attract the dog's notice. "C'mere, boy."

Roscoe tugged, hauling Aykroyd two stuttering steps closer.

"Kallem?" Aykroyd's voice raised in disbelief. "Shit, man, we thought the Reprobates must have gotten you."

Kallem ignored Aykroyd for the moment, sinking to his knees to scratch an ecstatic Roscoe behind his huge, soft ears.

In an instant, the second dog was beside him. Ignoring the ropes of slobber hanging from the beast's jaws, Kallem laughed and grabbed a handful of drooping jowl. "You too, Beau. You're a good boy."

"Told the kid you'd dodge trouble."

Kallem stood and offered his hand to the older man. "General."

Robinson took his hand in a firm grasp. "Now, soldier, you wanna explain why you're distracting my dogs when they're coming to the end of a long track?"

Straight to business, then. "I have my orders from the Prophet, and I'm *this* close to accomplishing my mission. And you, old man, were about to blow everything."

Robinson's old eyes sharpened. "Yeah? How's that?"

Kallem glanced pointedly at the younger soldier.

Robinson turned to Aykroyd. "Private, could you water the dogs?"

"Of course, sir." Aykroyd put his rucksack down and started digging for his canteen and a collapsible dog dish. The dogs perked up. Kallem knew that when a hound got engrossed in following a trail, it often ignored hunger and thirst for hours, refusing to be distracted. But since Kallem's scent was part of the trail Beau and Roscoe had been following, they no doubt felt their mission had been accomplished.

When the dogs were lapping noisily, Robinson instructed the young soldier to find the brook they could hear rushing somewhere to the east and refill the canteens.

A startled Aykroyd looked from one face to the other, but all he said was, "Yes, sir." Handing Roscoe's leash to Robinson, he moved off toward the sound of the rushing water.

"Okay, spill it," Robinson ordered. "What's going on here, Kallem?"

"The Prophet ordered me to follow the two women. He thinks if anyone can find Society Three, its Maree. And that's where they're going. I'm certain of it, though they won't say."

"Won't say?" Robinson's face darkened like a thundercloud. "You mean to say you're *traveling* with them? I thought your orders were to trail them."

"They were, and I did. But the Reprobates...there was nothing to be done. I had to intervene or they'd have killed the breeder."

Robinson spat. "This is madness! Why would they knowingly lead you—no, *take* you—to Society Three? If such a thing even exists."

"They trust me." Kallem grabbed his shirt sleeve and dragged it up to reveal his ruined tattoo. "Because of this."

"You were cast out? Who the hell—"

"Of course not. I did this myself."

"But why?"

"Once I betrayed my presence, I had to gain their trust somehow. So I told them the Prophet blamed me for the loss of his prize breeder and cast me out."

Robinson snorted, eyeing him. "And they believed you? Uniform, weapons and all?"

"I explained that away," he said. "I told them I was cast out naked and bloodied, as they well know is the custom for disgraced soldiers. But I told them too that I lurked in the woods until a soldier was sent after them. I explained how I ambushed the man, killed his hound and took his bedroll, rucksack, even the uniform off his body, so I could travel more safely. I also declared that while I had no love left for the Prophet who'd thrust me out, I couldn't bring myself to kill a fellow soldier. That I'd foolishly let him live to tell of my treachery, and now every soldier would be out for my head."

Robinson's eyes narrowed. "They truly trust you?"

"The breeder does," Kallem said, disliking the taste of that word on his tongue now. "But the whore...she does not trust easily."

Robinson nodded. "She's a tough customer, that one."

Of course, Robinson would have had occasion to escort her back to the whores' quarters after having visited with the Prophet. He'd have noticed the bruises, the chin held high, the glitter of tears that refused to fall.

"Yes, she's tough. But I've come to their aid more than once. I've slain Reprobates when I needed to and I've helped them avoid dozens more. I've found safe campsites and hunted and generally provided for them. They come to rely on me more every day. To *trust* me more every day. I swear it."

Beau growled and strained at his lead. A second later, Roscoe bristled as well. Dammit. Had Aykroyd stumbled on the women? Surely not. Not if he'd headed for the river as instructed. Kallem had ordered them to take cover in the brush near their campsite, a good quarter mile from the river.

"What is it, boys?" Robinson asked the dogs, and they pulled in the direction Aykroyd had disappeared.

"They scent the women," Kallem lied, keeping his voice calm. "I left them near the river."

"Really?" Robinson sent him a skeptical glance. "And you didn't protest when I sent Aykroyd off to refill the canteens?"

"They're further upstream," he improvised. "And they're well hidden. Without dogs, no one is going to stumble on them. Besides, if his feet are as tired and sore as mine, he'll have taken the shortest route to the river."

Robinson seemed to accept that explanation. "So, what now, soldier?"

"Follow us," he said. "But hang back a day. I don't want them to hear the dogs again."

The dogs surged at their leads once more and the old man shifted his weight to hold them back. "And how will you explain us away? Why did we suddenly abandon the trail?"

"Easy." Kallem forced himself to speak slowly, casually. "I'll tell them I slew you all."

Robinson lifted a grizzled eyebrow. "Two soldiers and two of the Prophet's finest hounds?"

"I'll say there was only one hound, and it was off its lead. It came to my call because it knew me, and I slew it. When young Aykroyd came upon his slaughtered dog, he fell to his knees and was easily dispatched. You, being more seasoned, were more trouble."

"Naturally."

Kallem grinned, though his stomach churned with the need to be gone. Something was definitely wrong.

"Very well, Captain. We will follow at a distance."

"Great." Kallem clapped his mentor on the back. "I'd better get back to the women before they start second-guessing their wisdom in trusting me. But first, I'll find Aykroyd and send him back."

"Much appreciated. These old bones could use the rest." The old man wound the two leads around a stout young tree to make it easier to hold the straining hounds and sat down.

Smiling, Kallem sketched a salute, then turned and ran off after Aykroyd with his heart pounding in his ears.

CHAPTER 13

STAY PUT.

Kallem's words whispered still in Maree's mind. And yes, Zophia's words—the very same ones—echoed there too. Zophia implored her to stay, to ready the rucksack as Kallem had asked. But how could she simply wait? How could she hide here in silence when danger was stalking her? Leave her fate up to a man? No, not just a man. A soldier.

"He's not like them anymore," Zophia said, her voice pleading. "You saw him slice through his insignia. He's not a soldier —"

"We've come too far, Zophia! There's too much to risk." She slid her knife into her leggings, and pulled the leg of her homemade trousers down over it. "I'm following him."

"You don't trust him."

It wasn't a question; it was an accusation. Maree had no time to debate it, and even less inclination. Despite all he had done for them, and all he claimed, in Maree's mind, Kallem Marsh was still Kallem of the Guard. Zophia didn't know the world like she did. Didn't know men like she did. And Maree prayed she never would.

She'd be hard enough for both of them.

"He saved us from the Reprobates," Zophia said, continuing to urge her sister to believe. "He saved *you* from—"

"I know." Maree squeezed Zophia's hand tightly. "But I'm still going after him. Hide. Stay low in the bushes until I come back for you."

Maree turned to leave, but her sister wouldn't let go of her hand. "What if you don't come back?" Her eyes glistened with tears.

"Look at me." Maree placed her hands on Zophia's shoulders. "I will. I promise. No matter what."

Zophia nodded. She sat, drawing herself down into the bushes. "Be careful, Maree."

"I will." Maree drew a fortifying breath and started off. As she slipped through the brush, she moved branches aside carefully, releasing them as quietly as she could. Carefully, she followed the trail Kallem had taken, her heart hammering in her chest with every step. He hadn't left an obvious trail, but she was sharp. Observant. Years of watching her back in a dangerous world had taught her to be. The habit of noticing everything in her surroundings had kept her alive on nights the Prophet had been frighteningly high. Just as she'd learned to read body language and moods, she'd learned to see the subtle changes in the physical environment when someone had tramped through.

She paused close to a small river and crouched down. Listening. Scanning her surroundings. Thinking.

Follow water. That had been one of the first lessons in survival that Kallem had taught them. When lost—follow water. Listen for the sound of running water. Rest close to the water's edge. Would the soldiers have gone to the water? God! Had Kallem's advice been a ploy to keep them—

She heard a snap beside her, and tried to whirl toward it, but an arm came around her throat, cupping a hand at her chin. Terror gripped her.

"Look at the prize I've found!" The soldier's breath was hot and sour on her face as he spoke those gleeful words. She knew this one by his voice. Aykroyd. She also knew him by reputation. Young and relatively new to the guard. Fierce in fighting. Perversely hateful of women.

The more she struggled, the tighter his grip grew. Then she remembered her training and went limp in his hold. "Let...let me go," she whimpered. She squeezed her eyes shut tightly.

The bastard laughed, and laughed all the more as his free hand roved up to her shirt. He tore it open. "You cut your hair—dressed yourself like a man. The Prophet won't be pleased."

She shook her head, as if a chastised child. *Let him think that. Let him think me weak. That I won't fight back. That he's won. Let the fucking bastard underestimate me.*

Aykroyd's grip loosened as his free hand roamed her body roughly. "He'll have you killed for this," he taunted. "Beaten at the very least. Whipped, I'd guess. And just what do you think will happen to that other one—the breeder? You think he'll let her go unscathed? Unscarred? I heard the rumors. He's got a special punishment in mind for that one." Aykroyd's hands dug lower. His body hardened against her, and he ground himself forward. "I've always wanted a piece of you. You walk around with your head so high and mighty. But no, the Prophet wouldn't send you to the soldiers, no matter how often he had to punish you. That cunt of yours must be something special, he wants it all to himself. Maybe I should find out while I've got the chance." Still groping her, Aykroyd dropped his hand to his trousers to free himself.

That's when she made her move.

She dropped her body down into a crouch so that when her elbow struck out behind her—with all the force she could muster—it hit Aykroyd square in the groin. She didn't aim at him but *through* him, as Kallem had taught. He crumpled to the ground with a guttural groan. Maree pulled her knife, and was on him in a second.

"You want a piece of me?" Again, she showed him the blade in her hand. "Well here's a piece of me you never would have expected."

He threw her. Injured as he was and half puking with pain, Aykroyd in his strength tossed her aside. Maree landed hard, but still she knew enough to break her fall and scrambled to her feet again even as she landed. The knife was still in her hands and she gripped it all the more tightly.

"You...fuckin'...bitch." Aykroyd's words were slow, pained, as he staggered to his feet.

Maree could have kicked herself. She'd had the chance to kill him. The fleeting chance. Oh God! *She'd* underestimated *him*!

Aykroyd was on his feet. "Jesus, you...you've been *trained*," he said. "A woman trained to fight is a violation." He reached down to his boot. And Maree knew he was reaching for a weapon of his own. The man was injured, but this tough soldier was far from out of the fight. She gripped her own knife tighter, expecting Aykroyd to right himself with a blade in his own hand.

But when the soldier straightened, it was a gun he held. Her heart sank.

"Orders are that you're to be returned to the Prophet," Aykroyd gagged out his words, as if every one of them pained him. "But when I tell him...when I tell him you tried to kill me—"

Maree threw the knife. Hard and fast and accurate. The blade struck him in the relatively soft belly, and Aykroyd went down. His eyes rolled to white as he fell, face down, onto the dirt. Unmoving. Unmoaning.

Dead.

But it wasn't Maree's small blade to the belly that had killed Aykroyd, and she knew it as soon as the man thumped forward to the ground and she saw who stood behind him.

Kallem. And Kallem's long blade protruded from the back of Aykroyd's neck.

Kallem glowered at Maree. "I told you to wait!" He bent to Aykroyd, pulled out the blade and checked for the non-existent pulse.

"I couldn't—"

Kallem ran a hand over his face, and Maree grimaced. He'd just killed one of his own. The import was not lost on Maree. Nor on Kallem, judging by the raggedness of his breathing.

"Go," he said. "Go back to Zophia and stay there. There's another solider. General Robinson. Desperately loyal to the Prophet. I'll deal with him. But you have to go now if there's any hope of getting you out of here alive!"

Maree did not hesitate now at Kallem's command. He'd just killed for her.

She raced as fast as she could back to Zophia.

CHAPTER 14

FUCK! KALLEM looked down at the dead soldier at his feet. The soldier he'd killed! Dammit, killed one of the *Prophet's* own. A soldier on a Prophet-given mission. But what choice had he had? Aykroyd would have shot Maree.

What now? What the hell was he going to do?

What you must. Keep the girls safe. Keep them on track to Society Three. Finish your mission.

Cursing, he turned and ran back toward the spot where he'd left Robinson. He didn't have to run far, for Robinson, having heard the commotion, had already started in his direction. Both dogs strained powerfully against their leads, tugging the general along.

"General!" Kallem called. "Thank God you're all right! Did you see them?"

The older man's brow furrowed. "The women?"

"The Reprobates." Kallem was close enough now to grab the collars of the dogs. They subsided as he did so. "They got Aykroyd. Two of them."

Robinson blanched, but his pistol was in his hand instantly. "What about you? Are you all right?"

"I'm fine. I managed to drive them off, but not before they killed Aykroyd. He was probably filling his canteens when they fell on him. He got a blade to the belly, I think, but was still fighting when I spotted them. Poor sonofabitch. I couldn't get there soon enough and didn't dare fire on them lest I kill Aykroyd. But the second Reprobate put a blade in his spine before I could stop him. Aykroyd died instantly."

Robinson, face flushed and eyes glittering, searched the woods. "Which way?" he growled.

"They went down river, thankfully. Otherwise, they might have blundered upon the breeder. I hid the females well, but these Reprobates know the woods..."

"They may know the woods, but they can't hide from Roscoe and Beau. Come on." Robinson started toward the river again. "Let's get the dogs on their trail and run the motherfuckers to the ground!"

"Wait!" Kallem grabbed the leather leads. "We can't go rushing off after the Reprobates. I have orders...a mission from the Prophet. I can't leave the women alone out here. Can't jeopardize the breeder. Dammit, we can't lose this chance to find Society Three."

"Maybe *you* can't, but I sure as hell can. That was my man they killed. Release your grip, Captain."

Dammit! Too bad there hadn't really been Reprobates. It would have been the perfect distraction, sending Robinson after them. But there'd be no hot trail for the dogs to follow. No chance of sending them off on a wild good chase.

Kallem didn't loosen his fist. "General, think about it! Revenge is a luxury we can't afford. The priority must be the Prophet's mission. I need you behind me. With you covering my back trail, I can move faster. I could focus my scouting on what's in front of me and not worry quite so much what might come from behind."

"I can kill the Reprobates and still catch up to cover your back trail," he insisted. "You're hampered by two weak women, while I am not. And the hounds' noses will guide me back to you."

"I don't doubt that you can still move quickly, General," Kallem said. "You caught up to us, after all. But the fact remains you are just *one* man. We have no idea how many Reprobates are in this band. What happens if they kill you like they killed Aykroyd? Who will have my back then?"

"I won't be alone. I'll have Roscoe and Beau."

Kallem snorted. "We both know they are all but blind to danger when they're hot on a trail. And their value is in their noses, not their fighting skills. They haven't the temperament for it. They'd be slaughtered. Or worse, they could fall into the Reprobates' hands. I wouldn't want to have to explain that to the Prophet."

"What would you have me do, then?" he demanded. "Walk away and leave a soldier's slaying unpunished? Walk away and leave Aykroyd's bones for the coyotes and crows and insects to pick clean?"

"No, sir. I would have you *delay* punishment, not forego it. We can come back to this place later, when the job is done. I can help you hunt down every last Reprobate in the area, if you like." Kallem felt no compunction about making that offer; all Reprobates were unrepentant, cold-blooded killers. And every last one of them would rape and kill his charges if they got the chance. Or take them as sex slaves to be tortured and violated. "I would have you stay here and give Aykroyd a soldier's burial. That would allow us to gain some ground on you, so the dogs don't give you away again."

"Goddammit!" The old man drew a hand down his grizzled face. "Okay, Captain. What you say makes sense. The Prophet would agree. We'll do it your way."

"Thank you." Kallem swallowed down the lump of emotion that had lodged itself in his throat. Relief that he'd persuaded the old man. Regret about Aykroyd, certainly. Though the gut wound Maree had inflicted would likely have killed him before he got back home anyway, a slow, agonizing death by sepsis. "I'm sorry about Aykroyd."

Robinson laid a hand on his shoulder. "I know, son. But there was nothing you could have done different."

That much was true. Thanks to Maree's reckless and foolhardy behavior—her *defiance,* dammit—all other choices had been stripped away.

"I'd best go," he said. "If I am too long, the women might run. I cannot lose that breeder."

"Well, at least you should have no trouble selling them that you slew your pursuers, with all the commotion of the Reprobate attack."

Kallem nodded and turned to go.

"Wait, Kallem."

He turned back to Robinson.

"Take Roscoe." He held out the dog's leather lead. "I'm too old to hold back two bloodhounds on a scent trail."

"Too old, my ass. Hell, I couldn't hold back two of 'em, and I'm considerably younger than you are."

Robinson grunted, but Kallem knew he was flattered. Not that he'd spoken anything but the truth. Two bloodhounds on a hot trail were too much for anyone.

Kallem cleared his throat. "We're covering anywhere between fifteen and twenty-five miles a day, depending on the terrain. Think you can hang back a day's travel knowing that?"

"No problem. I got half a day's work in front of me with Aykroyd."

"God rest his soul," Kallem said. *And mine.*

"So how will I know when you want me to catch up?"

"I told them I'd leave them when we got through the worst of Reprobate country, but I plan to follow them until I am certain they've found Society Three. And to make sure no harm comes to the breeder, of course. Then I'll retake them and backtrack."

"Sounds like a plan." The old man gave Roscoe's head a last scratch. "Get going, then, Soldier."

Conscious of what he'd told Robinson, Kallem strode off briskly in a direction that would intersect with the river a good distance upstream. He kept on that tack until he was sure he was out of the old man's sight. Then, his face set in grim lines, he corrected course and started jogging.

CHAPTER 15

IT WASN'T until they stopped walking—finally stopped to rest—that Maree realized how cold she was. The dampness gripped her then, chilled her right down to her bones, as she sat, leaning against the large, solid maple, catching her breath. Kallem had driven them hard since morning, keeping to their northerly course until finally leading them to this shelter in dense forest. There were no rock outcroppings here, just a thick growth of trees.

Maree wrapped her quilt around Zophia, but her sister refused it unless Maree shared the warmth with her. So Maree lay down too. Truthfully, she welcomed the warmth, and the rest. And as Zophia lay her head on her shoulder, Maree rested hers back against the solid maple. A red leaf fell down, twirling as it went. It settled on Maree's outstretched legs.

"That's a good sign," Zophia said. Her voice betrayed her exhaustion.

"Is it really?"

"As good as any."

The two sisters sat, spent beyond belief and yet knowing that soon, Kallem would edge them further. Or at least try to. He was determined to put as much distance as he could between them and the dead guards. Aykroyd and Robinson. General Robinson, Maree knew, was a particular favorite of the Prophet, a man with many years of service. When the two did not come back, the Prophet was bound to dispatch more soldiers. Many more.

And the Prophet wanted her brought back alive. The particular shiver that skittered up her spine had nothing to do with the cold. She knew why he wanted her returned intact. To punish her.

Always before, his cruelty had been somewhat mitigated by concern for public opinion. As brutal as her treatment at his hands had been, he'd always had that slight constraint. But now, if she were returned to him, he would be able to throw all of his energy into breaking the one thing he'd so far failed to break, that one thing he wanted above all—her soul. Now, he could use her as viciously as he liked and still be regarded as righteous, because of the egregiousness of the sin she'd committed against him—the attempted murder of the Prophet. Maree would be truly, utterly at his mercy.

Kallem had spoken of the need to put as much distance as possible between themselves and the soldiers that would no doubt be coming.

This time, it had been Zophia who held that look of skepticism when Kallem announced that he'd slain the whole hunting party, but for the hound. Just a hint of it, just a raised eyebrow, and she said nothing. But Zophia hadn't seen what had happened back there with the brutal soldier, Aykroyd. Kallem had killed him. Killed him to keep them safe. To keep *her* safe. Maree closed her eyes. What was she to make of this man?

He'd led them today with singular determination, like the soldier he once was. No time for lessons on self-defense and survival. But reassurances that those would come again, as soon as they were safe.

How long had it been since she'd felt safe? Maree's mind drifted back through the years, to those days in Falmouth. She dropped her defenses, and let it go there. The security of her parents' home. The room with the rainbow wallpaper that she shared with Zophia back then. And Kallem Marsh— next-door neighbor, son of her mother's best friend, and Maree's companion for so many years. The boy who'd turned man right before her eyes. The way he'd held her that one forbidden time. The way he kissed her, looked at her. The heat and hunger in him. Those nights of longing she'd felt then...

Incredibly, she felt desire stir, sweet and unsullied.

"Ten minutes! Ten minutes and we're moving out again."

Maree's eyes shot open at the command. Oh dammit, she'd been drifting off to sleep. That's why her thoughts had turned the corner to where they'd not been in years. She felt the heat rising in her cheeks and was thankful for the darkening sky.

In Maree's arms, Zophia barely stirred in her deep slumber. Not even Kallem's barked order had roused her. Maree eased away and lowered her sister to the ground, tucking the blanket around her. The moment she moved away, the big hound padded over and lay down beside Zophia, who murmured and burrowed closer to the animal's warmth. The dog did not scoot away. It was probably used to bunking down with a human for warmth.

Maree moved closer to Kallem. "We can't go on," she whispered. "At least not tonight."

"Just a little further. One more hour and—"

"Zophia needs to rest. She's younger than us, Kallem. And smaller. I've had to practically run to keep up with your strides today myself. We're not soldiers."

When he finally answered his words were grim. "You'll have to be."

Maree drew a deep breath. She knew what he meant. Out here, until they reached Society Three, the world was a dangerous place. Hadn't she seen that? Hadn't Aykroyd proven that?

Ah, but too, hadn't she proved it herself? She hadn't dealt the fatal blow; Kallem had. But if Aykroyd hadn't had a gun, she could have. She *would* have.

Gladly.

And she'd felt no remorse. Rather, she'd felt a pride. Not as the knife found its mark, nor in the minutes afterward. But as they'd eaten rations taken from the dead soldier's supply at the last stop, nothing had tasted sweeter to Maree than those high-calorie protein bars that were meant to nourish her enemy.

So this is what revenge feels like. This is the triumph of survival.

"We've double-timed it today, Kallem. We can afford a few hours' rest." She glanced back at Zophia. Her sister was lying now on the ground, spooned up close with the dog, not moving at all in the depth of her sleep. "We have to let her rest. It'll take a while for the Prophet to figure out his soldiers aren't coming back and send out more. Surely they're not a threat to us tonight."

Kallem chewed on that a moment. "The Reprobates—"

"We've seen fewer signs of the Reprobates with every passing mile." And that was true. Kallem had even commented on it himself—the lack of dilapidated shacks and rough lean-tos. But too, they were seeing more wildlife. Not an abundance, but they did hear more birds. Heard the light thrash of a small animal in the bushes. Plus there was the fact that the Reprobates traditionally didn't stray this far from the colonies. *They needed the handouts, survived on the compounds' leavings.* That was Kallem's rationale; what all the soldiers believed. He was probably right. But Maree knew of another reason those outcast men wouldn't venture this far north. The hags. That too was a sign on the intricate map: they were getting closer to where the hags survived. They were on the right path.

"And the Reprobates have no guns," Maree continued. "You do. I could have a gun, too, if you'd just give me Aykroyd's."

"No," came his immediate response. "You don't know how to shoot. It's too dark to teach you tonight."

"Tomorrow then." Another test of trust.

Kallem looked away. "Tomorrow then," he mumbled. He raked a hand through his hair as he stood there. He looked over at sleeping Zophia and then met Maree's stare. His jaw shifted. "All right. We'll stop a few hours. I'll gather wood, start a fire. You rest with your sister."

She nodded her thanks.

Darkness was slowly claiming the sky and Maree watched as Kallem so easily disappeared into the shadows of the forest. She was snuggled against Zophia's back beneath the blanket when he returned within minutes with an armful of small branches. Firewood.

"Safe enough for a fire?" she asked, her voice low.

"A small one. You can't see smoke at night like you can in the daytime. We'll need it for the warmth. And I can cook the bit of meat we have before it turns. We can have it in the morning."

Maree watched as Kallem laid the fire and set the kindling alight. Soon a small fire was crackling. She should be sleeping, snoring softly like her sister. But she could not. She was enjoying the freedom. The feeling of safety. And in the warmth of it, her mind slipped right back to where it had gone before when she'd nearly dozed off. The small flames were transfixing, enticing, but then Maree found herself looking through the dancing fire, and meeting Kallem's gaze as he looked back at her.

She crawled from beneath the covering warmth and went to him, Kallem holding her gaze all the way. She knelt on the ground beside him where he sat with his legs outstretched before the fire.

"We owe you...so much," Maree whispered. "If you hadn't killed that soldier, he'd have—"

"Don't!" He broke off eye contact, and his voice was low and rough. "I don't want to talk about it. About any of it."

Maree hurt for him. How much it must have pained him to kill one of his own. Not to mention General Robinson. Once Aykroyd was dead, Kallem's hand had been forced. At least he'd been saving her life when he'd killed the first one. The urgency of the moment, a split-second decision... But the second man he'd had to stalk and kill deliberately, to prevent him from running straight back to the Prophet. To buy them time.

But perhaps she could ease his pain...

"Then we won't talk," she said, her voice coming out husky and almost unrecognizable. Her heart thudding crazily in her chest, she placed a daring hand on his thigh.

His head came up. "Maree..."

"Shush. No talking, remember?" She came up on her knees and pressed her mouth to his. The shocked rigidity of his posture was an unwelcome echo of the last time she'd done this, but she didn't let it intimidate her. She wasn't a child anymore. Far from it.

She slid her hand up his thigh, then higher, feeling a surge of satisfaction when she encountered the rapidly growing evidence of his arousal. Smiling, she played her tongue over his lips, nipping at the lower one, but his mouth was different this time. Not slack with shock as it had been all those years ago, but hard and unyielding.

Then his hands came up to trap her head and he was finally kissing her, but oh, God, not like before back in Falmouth. Now, his mouth was punishing, crushing her lips against her teeth until she tasted blood. This, too, she should have anticipated. He was not the young man he'd been all those years ago either. He was a hardened soldier. Panic flared as she remembered the condition of the women who'd come back from the soldiers' barracks after having been sent there as punishment. Dear God, what had she invited?

Steeling herself, she reined in her fear. He was a soldier, yes, but a soldier who'd killed for her, again and again. A soldier who kept her and her sister safe.

Holding that thought in her mind, she stifled a whimper at the bite of his hands in her hair and pressed her breasts to his chest invitingly. He would soften. He had to. This was Kallem.

Then she found herself sprawled on the ground, Kallem standing over her, chest rising and falling rapidly, his face that of a fierce and dangerous stranger. Maree was stunned.

He raked a hand through his hair. "What the hell are you doing?"

She sat up, drawing the back of her hand across her mouth. "I was thanking you, or so I thought. But don't worry about it. I won't make that mistake again." Tears welled as she got to her feet, but she was too damned angry to let them fall.

"But I could have hurt you!" His gaze dropped to her swollen mouth in the firelight. "I *did* hurt you."

"Don't flatter yourself." The irony hit her then and she started laughing. The first time since she was fourteen that she'd willingly offered herself to anyone. And she'd offered herself to Kallem. *Again*. And he'd rejected her. *Again*. Oh God, how could she have expected otherwise? How could she have allowed herself to remember a world—a man—so removed from reality now? Her laughter built and built. She tried to keep it quiet, keep it in, but she felt like she was going to shake apart with it.

"Maree!" He seized her arms, shaking her. "Stop it. You'll wake Zophia. Or worse. If anyone were lurking out there—"

"But it's so funny!" She wiped tears of laughter from her eyes. "I never get a chance to choose. If I say no, I'm just forced. I'm raped. Fucked. Beaten. The Prophet did, that Reprobate tried... But this time, this *one* time in my adult life, I was choosing."

He looked stricken. "Oh, God, Maree, I didn't—"

She laughed all the harder, tears coursing down her cheeks.

Cursing, he drew her into his arms and pressed her face into his chest. Suddenly, she wasn't laughing anymore. To her horror, she realized she was crying. She tried to struggle free, but his arms just tightened.

"It's okay," he said. "I've got you."

He held her and rocked her and whispered for her to hush. She quieted beneath the soothing stroke of his hand on her hair. Incredibly, the anger and the hardness seemed to have gone out of him.

After long minutes, she pulled back reluctantly. He loosened his arms until she could lean back far enough to see his face in the firelight. The movement realigned the fit of her body against his, and she realized not quite *all* the hardness had gone out of him.

He groaned, tipped her head up and lowered his mouth to hers. She braced for the cruel crush of lips against teeth, but it never came. Instead, his lips tenderly shaped hers. Soothing. Silently apologizing. Without giving it a second's thought, she sighed and opened her mouth to him. At that, his hands dropped to rest on her backside, urging her lower body closer as he kissed her.

A moment later, he lifted his head, his eyes unfocused with desire. "Do you still choose?"

CHAPTER 16

SUDDENLY, MAREE'S heart started to pound. *Did* she still choose? "You won't hurt me." It was a statement, not a question.

"No, I swear." His hands came up to skim the outsides of her arms. "There was a devil riding me before. The events of the day...Aykroyd and Robinson...all of it going round and round in my head. I wasn't thinking about anyone but me."

She bit her lip. "I'm sorry. About those soldiers, I mean."

"So am I."

She glanced over to where Zophia slept beside Roscoe. The blanket was still securely wrapped around her little sister, exactly as Maree had left it. Zophia really was dead to the world. The dog lifted its huge head to regard them, then lowered it again with an audible sigh.

She turned back to him. "Okay."

"Okay...?"

"Okay, I choose."

His fingers tightened on her arms. "We'll need to move further away."

Maree felt a jolt of something, half fear, half excitement. She was really going to do this. "Of course."

He released her to unlash his bedroll from his rucksack. When he returned, he held out his hand. Self-consciously, she took it and allowed herself to be led across the clearing.

"Not too far," she said. "In case Zophia needs us."

"Of course, but she's safer than she's been yet, Maree. No one will get close to us without Roscoe sounding the alarm. I promise you."

"And if someone does get close? Are you armed?"

"Always."

Maree let go of her worry. Well, that particular one.

He made them a spot beneath the branches of a wild apple tree they'd noticed when they'd found this clearing. Maree had been delighted to see there were still apples on the tree. She'd planned to pick some to take with them. Now, Kallem dragged his foot across the ground, clearing fallen apples out of the way before spreading the bedroll.

Maree sat down on the blanket, feeling the squish of a soft apple beneath her. She giggled. "Your blanket is going to smell of fermented apples tomorrow."

"Yes." He settled beside her. "But it'll smell of you, too. Us."

Her stomach lurched sickly. *The smell of sex. Desperately needing to get it off her and never enough warm water and soap...*

Before she could lose her nerve, she turned to him and went for his belt. His hand closed over hers. "Whoa, there's no hurry."

"There's no reason to wait, either," she countered.

"Ummm, I'm not exactly an expert at this, but won't it go easier for you if we...you know...get you ready?"

His gruff concern caught her by surprise. "Honestly? I don't know. No one's ever tried."

"Let *me* try."

She let him ease her down onto the blanket so they were lying side by side. Then he was kissing her. But not like before. Not in anger and not in apology. Not even like the young Kallem of all those years ago, who'd kissed her with a kind of desperation. This was...nice. Drugging. Seductive.

For the longest while, their lips were the only thing touching, and as his tentative exploration deepened, she felt a definite tingle start up. Without conscious thought, she found her hands on his shirtfront, splaying to feel the layer of warm, hard muscle padding his chest. His breathing grew harsher, and he put his left hand on her hip. As they kissed, it crept higher to her waist, her side, until finally he brushed his knuckles over her breast beneath the old dress bodice. She gasped. Definitely more than a tingle! Taking her gasp for approval, he palmed her breast.

"Yes!"

He responded to her encouragement by bending to close his mouth over her nipple through the fabric. This time, a bolt of excitement snaked straight to her womb. She wanted him! She really wanted this. Wanted sex. Incredible! She surged against him, feeling the press of his erection tenting his trousers.

This time when she found his belt, he didn't stop her. His erection sprang free. Lacking any other way to learn his dimensions in the darkness, she laid her hand on him. He groaned as she traced the underside of his cock from root to tip, then encircled it with her hand. God help her, she almost moaned too! She'd seen him bathing that day, seen that he was built nothing like the Prophet, but God save her. Some of that lovely buzz that had been humming along her nerve endings dimmed. Surely there would be pain...

He fumbled with the ties of her odd pants for a moment, and she had to help him with them. He was much more adept at unbuttoning her bodice. As she sat up to shrug out of it, she heard him kicking free of his pants and pulling his shirt over his head. When she lay down again, his bare skin felt hot under her hands, dewy with perspiration despite the coolness of the evening. He drew her to him and kissed her again. Once more, that tingle of desire vibrated through her. And once more, she communicated it with approving noises and with the glide of her hands over his chest, his side, his back. Her touch seemed to set him on fire, which gave her a surge of satisfaction. But then he rolled her under him suddenly and her world shifted.

As he urged her legs apart, it wasn't Kallem anymore. It was the Reprobate above her, his weight crushing her, his breath assaulting her as he tried to force himself on her.

She went crazy beneath him, bucking and scratching, just like the last time. Silently fighting for her life.

"Jesus!" He seized her arms to stop the blows and rolled away, narrowly missing a knee to the groin. "Maree! It's me, Kallem. I'm not going to hurt you."

His words sank in and she stopped struggling.

"You won't hit me if I let go of your arms?"

She ducked her head and sucked in a breath. "No."

He released her arms and she wrapped them around herself. Oh, God, she'd fought him. After all his efforts to prepare her, the minute he'd covered her, she'd freaked and ruined it all.

"I'm so sorry."

Her misery increased when he lay back and she caught the white glint of his arm lying over his eyes.

"Just give me a minute," he grated.

"Did I hurt you?"

"No." One word, but again it was forced out.

"Are you sure?" She sat up. "You sound like you're hurt."

He laughed. "It's not that kind of hurt."

"Oh, right!" A pause while she thought. "I can help you with that." She scrambled to her knees.

He lifted his arm away from his eyes.

111

"It's true," she said. "We're all taught certain...skills. You may have noticed the men who are wealthy enough or connected enough to enjoy the services of a whore are often of an age when they need a little...help, if you know what I mean."

"Is that so?"

She smiled at the way he choked the words out, feeling in control for the first time tonight. Maybe for the first time ever. This she could do. She found him in the dark and stroked him, delighting in the way he shuddered. Adjusting her grip, she began to work him. Oddly, without visuals, his organ felt lovely under her hand. Skin so hot and velvety, stretched over such hardness.

"Good?" she asked.

"God, yesss!"

The knowledge came down from the more experienced women to the new girls, complete with tricks to make him finish fast or last and last, whatever the woman wanted. Maree never could fathom why any woman would want to prolong it, but she'd learned the technique anyway. And tonight she used that knowledge to bring Kallem to the brink and pull him back again and again, until finally he closed his hand over hers and pumped it furiously over his shaft until he came with a muffled groan.

She curled up beside him and watched as he brought his breathing under control again. Then he turned to her. "That was...amazing."

Her throat felt tight suddenly. "What's amazing is that you didn't force me after I led you to expect cooperation. No one would have blamed you." She ducked her head. "Not even me."

His hand found her chin and tipped her head up. "As long as we're free, it'll always be your choice. Okay?"

Tears burned her eyes. "Okay."

He propped himself up on an elbow. "What about you?"

"What about me?"

"If I knew how to, I'd like to do that for you. I mean, if it can be done. If women...you know..."

She felt another one of those jolts. In truth, what she'd just done had aroused her more than she would have imagined possible. At one point, she'd actually thought about putting her mouth on him. The idea that he might want to reciprocate made her heart thud faster.

On the other hand, teaching a man who didn't even know if women had orgasms how to help her have one in the dead dark...well, that might be too much for one night.

She leaned in and kissed him. "Yes, women do. Or *can*, rather. It's a tricky thing. But that's a challenge for another night. I think we need rest more than anything."

He caught her hand—the one she'd used on him—and kissed it. "But you'll teach me?"

"Yes, Kallem," she breathed. "I'll teach you."

She pulled away, found her clothes and started dressing. He followed suit, then picked up his bedroll and shook it out. They crept out from under the apple tree and made their way back toward the fire and the still sleeping girl and dog.

"I don't suppose you'd like to bunk down with me by the fire?" he asked.

"Not a chance, soldier. Zophia's my bunkmate. But I could send Roscoe over..."

His soft laughter followed her as she made her way to bed, and despite the hours of hard travel, her step was almost light.

CHAPTER 17

MAREE WOKE. Staring up through the maple branches at the sky, she figured it was almost dawn. A crisp-cold one. Zophia had been so exhausted she'd barely stirred in the night, and she still slept under the warmth of the quilt they shared. There was a peaceful look on her young face now, and Maree was glad to see it. Relieved to see it. So glad she, at least, had slept through the night.

So much had happened in those few hours of darkness, between Maree and Kallem. There had been a tenderness she hadn't even dared dream of. A longing within herself she hadn't imagined could ever be roused. Or rather, roused again.

The dog raised his head and yawned. Maree smiled. Roscoe had lain all night beside Zophia, giving her that extra bit of warmth. She'd feared this beast when she'd heard it in the woods, on their trail. And with good reason. Dogs were a soldier's companion, and once directed to follow a scent, they were relentless, absolutely pitiless in their pursuit. But now that the dog no longer sought her, she could see that

Kallem was right; there wasn't a malevolent bone in his body. And he was as affectionate as a pup.

"Stay, dog," Maree whispered. She crawled out from beneath the quilt she shared all night with her sister. With a groaning sigh, Roscoe lowered his head.

Maree felt the stiffness in her body as she stood. Though the quilt had been warm, and the embers of the fire still glowed with evidence that Kallem must have tended it through the night, the ground itself had been cold and hard beneath her. Normally, she would disappear behind some trees, relieve her bladder, then come straight back. But this morning, with Roscoe guarding Zophia, she decided to take a short walk to stretch the stiffness out and get her circulation going. And yes, to think, to just be alone in the peace of it all with her thoughts. What a luxury from what she was used to in the compound!

But too, she wanted to see if there were any more hag signs around. There should be, and she was anxious to catch every one of them.

The crescent moons had been the first. And yesterday, by yet another clean brook, she'd seen another sign, another lead from the map! Eggs, carved out in a stone. Three sets of three strategically placed by the water's edge. Though it had been harder to find, she had done it! Her heart had raced. And this time Maree had the pleasure of surreptitiously pointing it out to Zophia and watching the smile ease onto her face too. Kallem hadn't noticed anything, not the eggs nor their reaction, but it had buoyed the sisters' steps when he'd started them off again.

So much had happened in the last twenty-four hours.

She glanced down one more time at her sister before she turned to the woods.

"Take Roscoe."

Maree started at Kallem's voice. So did Roscoe, his head snapping up at Kallem's command. He trotted over to her

Maree's side, wagging his tail and licking her hand. She reached down and patted his head.

Maree turned to Kallem, her face warming with the memory of their encounter last night. "Have you been awake long?"

Kallem sat up. "Just since you stirred." His eyes met hers, smiling, yet shadowed with something else.

Her hand went to her belly, to the odd flutter there, then dropped away lest he notice. "Just going for a walk."

"Don't go too far." He sat up in his bedroll. "I'll put out the fire while you're gone. Ready the camp. We'll eat and then be on our way again."

"Of course."

She turned away, but his voice caught her again.

"Are we close to Society Three?"

She whirled, and this time she had no difficulty identifying the sensation in her core—alarm. She wet her lips. "You know?"

He shrugged, and the corner of his mouth kicked up in a wry smile. "Everyone knows the tales, the legends. What else could you be seeking so passionately?" His gaze pinned her. "Where else would you go?"

Of course he'd figured it out. Maree forced the panic down. He'd probably known it from the beginning. Yet still he'd helped them. Protected them. Trained them.

And yes, they *were* closing in. She'd seen it in the signs. While she couldn't claim intuitive abilities like Zophia, she could *feel* it in her bones. Oh, God, in her yearning heart, that organ she'd thought long dead to feeling. Yet, she found herself hesitating as she looked at Kallem. Did she trust him enough yet to answer? He'd killed for her—two soldiers. His eyes shifted as he waited for her answer.

It was Zophia who spoke up, her voice sleepy yet edged with a worry Maree didn't understand. "We've got quite a ways to go yet, Kallem."

Maree turned toward her sister. "I'm going to stretch my legs, Zophia. I'll be back in a few minutes."

"'Kay," came Zophia's sleepy response.

With that, Maree and Roscoe edged into the pre-dawn shadows of the trees.

Once she'd left the others behind, Maree began to notice birdsong, which she found both surprising and not surprising. All life on the planet had been so devastated by the effects of the environmental crash. Bees had been among the first to be affected. Then bats, and birds. Crows, of course, had been the hardiest and were now the most plentiful. And yes, she heard an unmistakeable chorus of cawing from the east. But this morning, she also heard another kind of song. An unmistakable one. First the *fee-bee, fee-bee* call, then the classic, tell-tale *chick-a-dee-dee-dee*. She searched the branches until she saw it.

A black-capped chickadee!

Beside her, Roscoe whined softly.

Maree released her breath. She hadn't seen a chickadee since she was a child, and never thought she would again. Nor hear it again. She closed her eyes to deepen her listening, and before she even realized it, she was hearing another sound. It started as a *fee-bee, fee-bee* like the bird, but as it got closer, turned into a barely-there whisper, "I see you there, I do."

Maree's eyes shot open. The dog beside her was alert, not barking, but looking off into the trees, the hair bristling along his back.

Maree dropped into a defensive crouch and turned in a complete circle, scanning wildly for potential enemies. Soldiers? Reprobates? She'd die before they took her, kill before she was hurt again! But as Maree completed her turn and came back to her original position, the intruder was there before her. Within arms' reach. And it was neither Reprobate, nor soldier. Not an enemy at all.

Maree stood face to face with a hag. *A hag!* Her heart pounded now for an entirely different reason.

"Good dog," the hag said, softly and kindly, almost hypnotically. "Good, quiet dog." She lowered a hand to Roscoe, who sniffed it. Then, with a whine, the dog lay down and settled its giant head on its front paws.

Smiling, the woman lowered the hood of her cloak. As she did so, Maree realized how the other woman had gotten so close without being spotted. The garment she wore was a swirl of browns and grays and greens blending in almost perfectly with the world around them.

The hag was taller than Maree, just a bit stockier, but there was an unmistakable gentleness about her. Her blond hair was pinned up, but loosely enough to frame her oval face, and the smile she wore reached all the way into her warm blue eyes. She bore the scar from cheekbone to chin— the mark of the outcast, the hagged—but it was well-healed now. She was quite a bit older than Maree. In fact, probably about as old as her mother had been when their family had been torn apart. It was a bittersweet thought.

"I'm Valentina," the hag said, taking Maree's hands in her own. Her hands were rough, work-worn, and so warm Maree wanted to cry. "You've come so far! You've done so well!"

Maree could hardly believe it. "I'm Maree," she whispered.

"I know. I've been watching you for the better part of a day now. Your sister is Zophia, and the man you call Kallem."

Her voice cracked with hope. "Are we...did we... Is this Society Three?"

Valentina put one of her warm, rough hands to Maree's face. "No, child. It's too soon. Think of your map. Remember it always and think of that promise. You're almost there. Almost with us."

Though there was an initial thud of disappointment, Maree immediately knew who this woman was. She did think of the map. "You're...you're one of the water bearers at the crossroads."

Valentina smiled. "You've read your map well."

"I've studied it. Every line and turn and for ages, years, and I could only hope—"

"And now you can only *do*. Keep going, Maree. Keep coming. As strong as you've had to be to get to this point, you'll have to be stronger to go on. Everything you've learned you'll need. Learn more. Teach more. Feel your way along."

"My sister, Zophia...she's the one who feels."

Valentina smiled. "Then out here where nature reclaims, no doubt she feels more, away from the Cursed New Order, where our gifts were suppressed. But you have gifts, too, Maree. Blessings. I've come to bear news at the crossroads. Keep going. We're waiting for you."

"Take me with you!" she whispered. "Take us with you now."

"I cannot. My post is here, at this place—as this sign," she said kindly. "I'm here to let you know you're on the right track." She reached into her cloak. "And here to give you this. I don't bear water; I bear something more."

Maree took the vial she'd extracted from her autumn-colored cloak. "What is it?"

"Hide it well," Valentina urged with a hand covering Maree's. Immediately Maree shifted the small container of murky liquid to the pocket of her makeshift pants. "It'll help protect you. It can stop a man in his tracks, make him desperately ill." She gestured down at the dozing dog. "I used a potion on the hound, too. It went to work the moment he sniffed my hands."

At Maree's sharp inhalation, Valentina placed a reassuring hand on her arm. "Not to worry, child. The dog will be well. I used a completely different potion than the one in that vial. This one was a soporific only, and its effects will wear off shortly."

So that's why Roscoe had sunk down so readily. "That's amazing!"

"We have our ways," Valentina allowed with quiet pride. "And we have our knowledge. Our means."

Maree blinked as it occurred to her the hag had touched her face with those same hands that had put Roscoe down for a snooze. Without conscious thought, she put a hand to her face where the hag had touched her. Why didn't she feel sleepy?

Her thoughts must have been evident, for Valentina chuckled. "The potion on my hands was just for the dog. A mix of plant roots, crushed herbs and alcohol we distilled. Works wonders on canines; doesn't do a thing for people."

Maree dropped her betraying hand. "I see."

"I expect you do," Valentina said. "We protect ourselves as we have to. However we have to. We learn. We survive. The Reprobates are now much more hesitant to attack those among our numbers. They see our scars and turn away. Contrary to what the Prophet and his men tell the females to terrify them, more often than not, the Reprobates let us hags pass because they fear us."

"So it's true! I've heard it whispered..."

"Yes, it's true. The Reprobates fear what we can do. What we *will* do to protect ourselves, and each other. The liquid in this bottle I've given you will make a man violently ill. He just has to inhale it and he's crippled with sickness. And then in those minutes a woman can run...or not."

Maree's mind spun. "Run or kill," she said.

Valentina nodded. "Yes. Run or kill. Those men—the Reprobates—learn from one another too. Just as we learn from one another."

Maree nodded. Roscoe got to his feet, only to drop down again. Maree watched as he stood a second time, yawned widely, and looked up at the hag with big, confused eyes.

Not wanting to subject the dog to any more of that particular potion's effect, Valentina tucked her hands deep inside her cloak, but not before raising the hood again and practically disappearing within it.

"Don't go," Maree whispered, wanting to beg the gentle woman yet again to take her and Zophia with her.

"I'm sorry, child. I must," she said. "I'm a sign at the crossroads between the world you left and the world you seek. A post. A marking on the map. A warrior posted here to confirm for you that you're on the right track, and that you must keep going. You will reach what you seek."

"When?"

"When you can. And you'll be ready, Maree. You'll be welcome, you and your sister."

A moment later, Valentina had once again blended in with the forest. And Maree raised her hand to touch her cheek as the beautiful hag had done.

CHAPTER 18

KALLEM FELL back into the warmth of his bedroll for a few extra minutes, knowing Maree would be safe with Roscoe. She was also learning outdoor skills as quickly as he could teach them, not to mention soaking up combat lessons like a sponge.

God knew she was good with a knife.

His mouth went dry as yesterday's scene played out in his head yet again, just as it had in his nightmares last night. Maree's knife flying straight and true, catching an astonished Aykroyd in the gut. A livid Aykroyd drawing his gun, taking a bead on Maree...

He pressed his hands to his eyes, trying to push back the memory of what happened next. It didn't work. Nothing could hold it back.

Dammit! He'd killed a fellow soldier.

Yes, Aykroyd would have died anyway, from the belly wound. No way would he have made it back to the compound, gut-stabbed like that. If Kallem hadn't killed him, Aykroyd likely would have been begging Robinson to do the job within the day. Or done it himself.

But it shouldn't have come to that. If Maree had just stayed put like he'd told her and let him handle it... But no, she had to go see for herself. If she'd only trusted him...

Ah, but can you blame her? Why should she trust you? You've lied to her all along. You're lying still.

But she trusted him now. He'd slain Aykroyd, saved her life, and now she finally trusted him.

On that thought, another mind-picture swept in, this one of Maree coming to join him at the campfire. Maree on his bedroll, naked and willing, at least until he'd pinned her beneath him. She'd fought like a wildcat. He had the scratches to prove it, too. They were going to sting later, when they got underway again and he began to sweat.

But what she'd done afterward... His cock responded instantly, tenting the blanket.

He heard Zophia sigh, reminding Kallem he was not alone, but when he lifted his head, he saw that she'd drifted back to sleep. The child had barely moved a limb since she'd lain down last night, and he felt the smallest stab of guilt for driving them so hard yesterday.

He rolled to his side, ordering his member to subside. Were he alone, he would have stroked himself to the memory of Maree's hands. Instead, he forced his mind back to other things. Other problems. And General Robinson first among them. And just a day behind.

He wanted more time. The girls had hedged when he'd asked how far they were from Society Three, but he knew they were close. Too soon this...interlude...would all be over. Then what?

God help him, he didn't know.

All he knew was he wanted things to continue the way they were. He wanted more time with Maree. And Zophia too. She was such a sweet girl. It killed him to think about returning either of them to the Prophet's clutches.

He'd never really thought their lives that hard, compared to the grinding physical work and the violence of soldiering, or the plight of the women who worked the fields in the pitiless, cancer-inducing sun. Well, apart from Maree's bruises at the hands of the Prophet, which everyone knew she could avoid if she'd just submit. And, okay, apart from the fact that the retirement plan involved being thrust outside the gates. He frowned. Compassion was for the weak. Wasn't that what he'd always been taught?

Always?

Except these days on the run, living with them, listening to them, he couldn't view things the same way anymore. He now understood something of the horror their lives entailed.

Of course, there was no going back to "normal" for either of them. If he returned them, life would be bad for Zophia. And worse for Maree. If the Prophet didn't kill her outright, she would probably wish that he had.

He pushed the thought away, just as he'd done a hundred times on this journey. Yet no sooner had he corralled his thoughts than they were off in a different direction.

They remembered, both of them. Remembered a life before the coming of the Holy New Order. Maree because the inoculation hadn't worked, a fact she'd managed to conceal from even the Prophet, and Zophia because she'd been too young for the shot, yet obviously had retained a lot. Of course, Zophia's memories were more limited, but even so, she'd remembered Belle.

Now, *he* remembered Belle. How could that be?

Images drifted into his thoughts, and suddenly Kallem remembered he'd dreamed about that little dog last night! About Belle. And about a younger brother. The name Errol came to mind, but Kallem had no idea whether he was inventing it or not. A mother and a father, too, but their names hadn't come to him. They were just Mom and Dad. He and Belle had been sitting out on a stoop and his mother had called them in for supper. But when he got inside, his parents had no faces.

No, that wasn't quite right. They did have faces, but every time he tried to look closely at them, they blurred and faded. Same with his brother. The harder he tried to see, the more unfocused they got. And the more frightened Kallem got. When he'd asked why he couldn't see them clearly, they'd looked at each other and laughed riotously.

He would ask Maree if he had a brother, and if so, what his name was. Though he was almost scared to know the answer. What if he did have a sibling, and what if his name was Errol? That would mean he was really remembering.

And what else might he remember? Maree? There was something there, back in the past. There had to be. That's why his heart had beaten faster when he'd seen her enter the encampment with the other females. And that's why her eyes had betrayed her for a few seconds when their gazes had met.

Dammit, they needed time to talk.

Even as those thoughts bombarded him, he knew it was folly. Society Three lay ahead of him, and Robinson behind. Kallem was a soldier. His mind had been steel-girded and bullet-proofed for service to the Prophet and the Holy New Order. He could be nothing else.

Suddenly, he was conscious that his fingers were playing over the scabbed slashes crisscrossing his service tattoo on his right shoulder.

Cursing, he kicked out of the bedroll. Obviously, inactivity didn't suit him. He'd ready breakfast.

CHAPTER 19

THEY WALKED on again that morning.

It was another day following the north-bound path, through the thick woods, up the slow inclines, past the cold streams. And it was getting colder as August wound down. The leaf cover would be gone in a few weeks, Maree supposed. But surely they'd have reached their destination by then. There were more signs now, and Maree was sure she saw every one as the trio moved past them. Signs set out by the hags for those who followed this path to freedom.

She had to get there. It was more than a want now; more than a hope. The desire burned deep in her soul. So she marched on with her sister, and with the former soldier who'd come so abruptly back into her life. Her gaze slid to him. Silent but always alert, eyes scanning, senses tuned to potential threats as he led the way. Maree and Zophia walked abreast in his wake, with the hound padding along behind them like a rear guard.

Maree felt the empty ache low in her belly as her gaze swept from Kallem's broad back, down to those narrow hips and improbably fascinating buttocks. The sensation—raw and undeniably physical—was at once familiar and strange. She knew exactly what that unrelenting ache was. *Desire.* Wanton lust for Kallem Marsh. A need to be filled. A desire to pick up where they'd left off two nights ago. *And that long lifetime ago, before he was a soldier, before she was forced to be the Prophet's whore...*

Maree shook her head to disperse the thoughts, her throat tight with anger. She thought again of how she'd plunged her knife into the Prophet's chest. Her only regret was that she'd missed his black heart. Now, she spent her days hunted but free, and her nights, free but coiled with desire.

Last night as they'd set up camp, desire had threatened to swamp her every time she'd looked at Kallem. It was both difficult to accept and difficult to quiet. Continuously, she had pushed the fantasies aside, but they'd kept pushing back as she'd bedded down with Zophia, lying on her side, awake. Her hands tucked under her cheek and staring wide-eyed into the small fire she herself had lit. She was lost in the flames, then lost to something equally consuming when Kallem sat up on his bedroll on the other side of the fire, staring back at her. She could see the rise and fall of his chest with the slow, deep, steady breaths he pulled. There was a comfort to the pattern, yet a need. And, oh, how his eyes had called to her.

But when she'd pulled the quilt back and tried to ease away from her sister, Zophia had protested.

"Where are you going, Maree?" She'd latched onto Maree's wrist as she started to crawl out from beneath the bedding they'd shared. "Stay with me," Zophia had whispered. "Please? I don't want to be alone. You can...speak...to Kallem another night."

Perhaps Kallem had heard Zophia's whispered plea, for he lay down then, covered himself with his own bedding and turned away from the two women.

Maree had settled back in beside her sister. She'd listened for Kallem's breathing to even out the way it did when he slept, but she was pretty sure she drifted off before he did.

No wonder. If desire could sink its claws this deep into her, how much harder it must ride him. Clearly he'd meant what he'd said, that the choice would be hers. Tears of gratitude had stung her eyes as she'd lain there waiting for sleep to claim her. Was there another man alive in this Holy New Order who would have left her and Zophia unmolested?

As she'd lain there, she'd wondered, too, how much her intuitive sister knew about her and Kallem Marsh. How much did she suspect? Though she'd not been forced to lie with a man herself, Zophia would have received the same message all the women in the compound got—women were for using. How could she know otherwise?

Except maybe it *could* be different... Maree had known only brutality. Coercion. Humiliation. Force. But every instinct—every ounce of feminine intuition—told her it could be different with Kallem. But did she really trust the man? Did she really trust the soldier?

"Oh look!" Zophia cried.

"What the hell?" Kallem's low tone was both puzzled and wary.

Maree's mind leapt back from her drifting thoughts and she stopped abruptly. Oh, God, there it was! Her heart raced as she took in the hovel in the hill. Yet another promise fulfilled!

Old Mother Hubbard lived in a house, the cupboards are far from bare...just look up above and look down below, but don't you sweep under there! That was in the legend. So carefully, cleverly, it was written as a child's rhyme, another sign hidden. And they'd found it! They'd found a safe place along the way.

Zophia knew this place for what it was, too, and Maree smiled to see her come alive, happy, for the first time in days. But Zophia's next words wiped the smile off her face.

"It's the resting spot! Oh, Maree, just like the map said! We're so close now! So very close—"

"Zophia!"

Zophia clapped her hand over her mouth, but it was too late.

"Map?" Kallem's voice was sharp. "You have a map? There's an actual, *physical* map to Society Three?"

Zophia paled. "No."

It was obvious she was lying. Cheeks reddening, Zophia ran toward the hovel before Kallem could ask anything more. And Maree knew he would ask; just not right yet. The find was too delightful.

It was almost hidden, would have been hidden completely had the sun not shone down through these trees as it did right now, lighting only the tip of a worn brass door handle.

"Wait," Kallem called to Zophia, who stood on the doorstep now. "Let me go in first."

He pulled back the hiding bushes, crouched down to creak open the small door, then entered. Maree could have told him his caution was not necessary, but she let him check the small cabin out and pronounce it safe. The two girls stepped into the cottage with him, and Kallem closed the door behind them. Maree couldn't help but feel the niggle of guilt as he did. She'd brought him here. A man. A former solider who'd once been an enemy. Yes, she trusted him more and more. But did she trust him completely? Chances were that no man had ever crossed that threshold before. Maybe none should.

The room was sparsely furnished. Two small beds, barren of blankets but with comfortable-looking mattresses. Zophia threw the quilt down on the nearest one. There was a small pot-bellied stove with a kettle on the top. Firewood was stacked neatly beside it. A table with two small chairs completed the one-room dwelling. And upon that table, sustenance. Similar to what the soldiers would carry—items of high protein, canteens (empty, which didn't surprise Maree; it must mean the water from the stream they could hear gurgling nearby was drinkable), strips of dried fish in a wooden box.

"My God!" Zophia breathed, echoing Maree's thoughts. "A feast!"

A feast for the rest of the journey. To take them through to the end of it. To carry them.

It was the smell of the room that struck Maree. Not musty. Not stale, but fresh. As if someone had aired it out, readied it for their arrival. Prepared it just for them. Valentina? She wondered. Had that living signpost on the road sent word ahead that seekers were coming? But if so, how? There were rumors that the highest-ranking officials of the compounds had communication devices. Radios that had miraculously survived the EMP pulses from the Electronic Wars and were somehow hardened to the constant interference from the sun. She'd seen one in the Prophet's desk, but had just assumed the silent device was a relic. Could the hags have such radios? Could Valentina somehow have communicated forward to the other hags to ready this stop for them?

Zophia touched Maree's arm. "Out here," she said. "We're free to…be."

That was all she said, but Maree caught the meaning. Psychic communication. Women's intuition; their great-grandmother used to call it. Telepathy. Surely Zophia wasn't the only one with that skill. That gift. Hadn't Valentina hinted at the same? And hadn't she hinted—no, flat out *said*—that Maree had a gift herself?

What?

As she pondered that question, Zophia moved away to veer across the room. A moment later, her sister cried excitedly, "Here!" Zophia pointed to the floorboards at her feet. She'd toed a small, worn carpet aside and found a trap door in the floor. Zophia went down on her knees and grabbed the handle.

"Wait!" Kallem said. "It might be a tr—"

She wasn't listening; neither was Maree, who'd shot over to her sister's side. Together they pulled on the heavy handle, and the trap door creaked open.

"Oh, wow!" Zophia gasped. Maree said nothing, but she felt that same sentiment with every fibre of her being as she reached for the earth-colored cloaks. Two of them, just like the one Valentina had worn. Their gender-shifted attire had given them a measure of protection, but these cloaks would completely camouflage them in the woods. They would be safer still.

Tail wagging, Roscoe came over to investigate, his wet nose touching Maree's hand as he sniffed the cloaks she held. Zophia slipped hers on. It fell to her ankles. She turned with delight and pulled the hood over her head. They both laughed out loud.

"Remarkable," Kallem said, moving closer to inspect Zophia's robe. "You'll melt right into the forest in that."

Maree turned to him. "We'll rest here," she said. "We need a good rest. All of us." She half expected him to balk at her command, but she wouldn't back down. Despite Zophia's buoyancy at the moment, she desperately needed rest. She was continuously pale now. Had been unusually irritable the last little while—angry. And though she tried to hide it, Maree knew she'd been ill this morning before they'd broken camp.

To her surprise, Kallem quickly agreed. "Yes. We're hidden. This cabin's well placed, high up. We'll be able to see any intruders before they see us. I'll rig some alarms. But first," he looked pointedly at Maree, "I agreed to teach you to shoot. We'll start today. You first, Maree."

Maree felt the thrill race its way through her. Knowing how to use the gun would keep her safer. Make her stronger. *She wanted this!*

"We're never going back, are we?"

At Zophia's plaintive words, Maree turned to see her sister's face wreathed in...what?...sadness? How could she miss anything about that horrible compound? "Never," she said. "You know we can't. Don't worry, Zophia—"

"I wasn't worried." Tears welled in her eyes.

"Then what is it?" Maree said, half exasperated.

"I'll go get us some water for tea." Zophia grabbed the kettle from the stove. She turned, and with Roscoe protectively on her heels again, she left the cabin. Maree opened the shuttered window and watched as Zophia headed in the direction of the stream.

"I should go after her."

"No," Kallem said. "You shouldn't. She needs to be alone right now."

"But the dangers—"

"The dog's with her. They've developed a real bond. He won't let anything happen to her," he said. "But something is clearly troubling the girl." Kallem paused, as if waiting for Maree to fill in the blank, volunteer the answer. Yet she couldn't have if she'd wanted to. She had no idea what was bothering her sister, beyond exhaustion.

"Okay, then." Kallem crossed the cabin to stand beside her, gazing out the narrow window. Instantly, Maree felt her pulse quicken as he stood there, so close she could smell the male musk of his skin. "About that shooting lesson…"

The idea of learning to shoot allowed her to focus on something other than the awareness humming beneath her skin. But was it really safe to be shooting in this, of all places? "What about the noise?" she asked. "What if the gunshots draw Reprobates?" *Or soldiers.*

Kallem shook his head. "Not a problem. I found a box of practice ammo in Aykroyd's rucksack."

She lifted an eyebrow. "Practice ammo?"

"Minimally explosive projectiles. Compared to a live round, it sounds more like a cap gun and won't carry very far. But accuracy and range are pretty much the same."

She chewed the inside of her lip. That sounded like an acceptable risk. Especially for the knowledge and skill she would gain. "When can we do it?"

"How about now?"

Grinning, she followed him outside.

"Zophia!" Kallem called after the young girl's retreating back. She turned to them. "I'm going to give your sister a shooting lesson, so don't be alarmed when you hear the shots. And stay between the cabin and the brook. Don't circle around."

Zophia lifted a hand in acknowledgement, then continued on.

In the yard, Kallem crouched down and opened his rucksack; both handguns—his and Aykroyd's—were stored in there, he brought the latter one forward. The gun lay flat in Kallem's palm for several seconds as he stared down at the weapon. He hefted it in his hands as if gauging the weight before he stood and turned to Maree again.

Eagerly, Maree reached for the gun.

"Not yet," Kallem said, pulling it from her reach.

"I thought—"

"What are you shooting at?"

She was perplexed. "Nothing. I mean, not yet. I'm just learning." As soon as she said it, Maree realized how dumb that sounded. "I need a target."

He smiled. "Aim, shoot, hit," Kallem said. "In that order. You need to set up a target before anything else."

"Or have a target come to you." She was thinking of the Reprobates, and the other soldiers.

Without a word, Kallem trotted off to where two large birches stood nearby. Between them on the ground, was a 'sheet' of the white bark, rolled and hard with age. Someone, sometime long ago, had peeled it from the tree and dropped it to the ground. Kallem leaned it off to the side of the first tree, but not before he looked quickly at both sides of the rolled bark.

In her childhood history classes before the Holy New Order came in, Maree had learned that people had in times past used birch bark for paper. That was often how they'd left messages for one another in the woods. But she knew immediately and with certainty that there was no message there. The hags were wise. They had their own ways of passing word along to their sisters without it coming to the inadvertent attention of others.

Kallem strode back to her. "There's your target."

"Ah, nice and still," Maree said. The dangers she would have to face out here weren't going to be so conveniently immobile, Maree knew. *Not unless I sicken them first with the vial from Valentina.*

Kallem chucked. "Well, unfortunately, we don't have any charging Reprobates for you to gun down at the moment."

"Or soldiers." She thrust out her chin.

Kallem's hard eyes met hers, and his smile was gone. "Or soldiers."

In a move so swift and practiced Maree could hardly follow the motions, he loaded the magazine into the gun and chambered a round. "You're right-handed?"

"Yes."

"Then you'll hold the gun in that hand. Your dominant hand." He placed the gun in her right hand, and the steel felt cold and heavy in her palm. She stood perfectly still. Powerful, yes. Dangerous, absolutely.

"Point the gun downrange," Kallem said, guiding her hand.

"In the direction I want to shoot, you mean?"

"Yeah."

Maree did, holding her right arm out and aiming the gun at the sheet of birch near the ground.

"For now, keep your finger outside the trigger guard."

"Trigger guard?" She'd crooked her finger inside the loop. It had just seemed natural.

"I'll show you." Kallem moved to stand behind her. Very close behind her; Maree could feel his warm breath on her neck, bristling the small hairs there as he stepped closer still. How she wished for her long hair now, to mask this effect he had on her! He covered her hand with his own. "The trigger guard is here."

Speechless, she nodded. He left his hand around hers.

"You've got to let the weapon be part of you," he said. "Let it be an extension of your arm, of your hand. You become the weapon. You don't just *hold* the power, the deadly force, you *are* it."

Maree drew a deep breath. "Okay," she said.

Kallem urged her fingers into position. "These three fingers and your thumb hold the gun firmly in place, and your trigger finger–when ready–pulls the trigger. But you have to be ready. Focused. Let nothing distract you."

And with that Kallem's other arm swung around her. He brushed his hand lightly against her breasts, down her ribs as he reached for her left hand. "A two-handed grip will give you better control," he said, his voice low in her ear. "Use your weak hand to cup under your dominant hand, support it. Now steady the weapon. Use all your concentration, Maree, and steady the weapon."

She did.

"You have to have the proper stance. Left foot slightly in front, feet shoulder-width apart."

She complied. "Like this?"

"More like this." With his powerful hands, he prompted her thighs until her stance was the way he wanted it. This time, Maree could not suppress a shudder of awareness.

"Steady," he said.

Gritting her teeth, she steadied her hands again.

"Which eye's the weakest?"

"Huh?"

"Which eye do you see better from?"

She closed one eye, then the other, then repeated the process. "The right one is weaker."

"Perfect. Now close that right eye." One hand settled on her hip. "Use your left eye–the dominant one–to align the front sight with the back sight."

"Got it."

Kallem's hands tightened on her hips and his breath tickled her ear as he whispered into it. "Now, fire!"

Maree fired. True to his word, it made an almost innocent-sounding pop. And missed the target by a good yard. "No fair!" Keeping the gun turned down, she twisted toward Kallem. She could feel the heat rising in her cheeks as she looked at the self-satisfied grin on his face. "You distracted me."

"My point," he said, "is that you have to always concentrate. Let nothing distract you. No one."

She lifted her chin. "Nothing will."

"Nothing? Is that so?" He cupped her face with one hand, then slid the other one down to cover hers on the gun. Gun secured, he proceeded to kiss her. Just as he'd done the other night, his kisses were designed to arouse, to seduce, and oh, God, she was ready to be seduced! Her free hand went to his chest, then roamed his back before finally dropping to squeeze that tight butt she'd been watching all day. He growled his approval into her mouth and his own free hand slid down to her buttocks, pulling her against him. If he hadn't been supporting her gun hand, it would have fallen to her side. Not to mention the way her knees wanted to buckle, taking them to the ground where—

Woof!

At Roscoe's bark, they pulled apart. Zophia and the dog were making their way back toward the cabin.

Kallem stared at Maree, his gaze hot as it skimmed her face. "Not much of a lesson, I guess," he said, sounding not at all disappointed.

"Oh, I don't know. I think we covered the basics, didn't we?" Maree turned to the two birches, steadied her stance, and cupped her left hand under the gun-holding right. Aligning the front sight with the rear, she squeezed the trigger gently, and blew the hell out of that rolled sheet of birch. Smiling victoriously, she turned to Kallem, but his gaze was not on her or the target she'd decimated. He was watching Zophia's approach with sober eyes.

Maree whirled to watch her robe-wrapped sister draw closer. When she was just a pace away, Zophia stopped and lowered her hood, and Maree saw her eyes. She'd been crying. No, not just crying; she looked completely cried out! As if there were no more tears to fall.

Maree handed the gun to Kallem and grasped her sister by the shoulders. "What is it, Zophia? What's wrong?"

Zophia looked up at her. She bit her lower lip. "I...I have something to tell you."

CHAPTER 20

THROUGH THE fog in his brain, the Prophet looked down at the woman, Liz. She slept now. But her sleep must be nightmarish, for she cried out even now.

Liz lay on his bed; beaten again. Nearly spent of life. But still not defeated. She'd pulled the thin coverlet over herself after he'd used her last night. He'd forced his will upon her and yet, he felt no victory with this one either! *For he'd not broken her soul.* She'd not begged for her life, begged for his mercy, nor whispered "Thou shalt not disbelieve" with *any* flicker of truth or fear in her eyes.

Liz is like Maree. The Prophet's pulse quickened as his mind stormed. *Strong, like Maree. Defiant, and dangerous in her defiance. She'll run too, given the chance.* And as Liz lay there in her injuries, he hated her all the more. Hated them both all the more. His hand moved toward the resting woman, ready to wrap his fingers around her throat and end this one once and for all. But he hesitated; even in his narcotic stupor, he paused. If he killed Liz before he broke her, then his victory was shallow. Taking a life was one thing; taking a soul was another. He wanted both. Didn't he deserve both? Hadn't Swagg always told him so?

Then too, there was the restlessness growing throughout the compound...

A knock sounded on his chamber's door. He turned, adjusting the belt on his robe to conceal himself. "Come in."

The soldier strode in, glancing at Liz a little too long for the Prophet's liking. Or had he? Through the glaze of his waning high, he just could not be sure. It was Minto. Again, one of his original One Hundred and One. He was a huge man. Powerful and deadly. Loyal. *As loyal as his soldier, Kallem? Or more so?*

The Prophet licked his dry lips.

"Shall I return the woman to the infirmary?" Minto asked, with a nod to Liz. Liz shifted on the bed behind the Prophet. *So she hadn't been sleeping.* At once he had a vision of her snapping to bite his hand if he had advanced on her further a moment ago. Premonition? Fear? Paranoia? He ran a frustrated hand through his hair. A hard hand—he had to, to feel it against his drug-tingling, numbed skull.

"Sir," Minto repeated. "Shall I take the woman?"

"In a moment, soldier."

The Prophet had an idea. Neither fear not paranoia, but *survival*.

He knew human nature. Every moment that Minto stood waiting, his curiosity would grow. And his worry along with it. Slowly, the Prophet went to his cabinet and opened the lock. He cringed as, unthinkingly, he raised his injured arm to extract the vials from the uppermost shelf. Three of them, syringes already attached. Slowly, he walked over to his desk, sat behind it, and placed the needles on the flat wood surface. "At ease, Soldier."

Minto assumed the more relaxed posture—hands linked behind his back, feet shoulder-width apart. But it was his eyes that betrayed him. The Prophet always watched the eyes. Minto's gaze went to the deadly vials on the table. Lingered there. Would he inject himself upon command?

How many days ago had Kallem stood here before him? Six? Seven? More? The Prophet had been so sure that he would do his blind bidding. But how sure was he, really, that that one soldier was the one who could follow her...where? Oh, yes, to that damnable Society Three. What if he'd made a mistake choosing that one? And Robinson too. His own general! What if Minto was disloyal too? No! He couldn't let his mind go there. He could not begin to disbelieve in himself...

"Thou shalt not disbelieve..." the Prophet mumbled.

Minto shifted.

A needle rolled to the stone floor, came to rest at the Prophet's bare feet. For a long, hard moment he stared at it as if just realizing it was there. His attention was broken by Minto.

"Can I...can I help you, Prophet?"

"No." He looked up, forcing his eyes to focus. "I mean...yes. I need to ask you something."

"Of course, sir."

"I've heard...stories." And he had. Luvanne. The old woman he'd pardoned when he'd knocked over his breakfast tray the other morning. She whispered the rumors, almost gleefully, he could swear, into the Prophet's ear every morning now. The females were watching the gates every day, secretly hoping and praying for no return of Maree and Zophia. Praying! Without his sanction! And the soldiers—the young ones—how loyal could they really be? Luvanne had asked that question more than once. And worst of all to his aching heart, she'd told him that some of these whispers had carried his former name. *Marcus Will Montag—he was just a man, you know.*

Minto pitched into the pause. "Stories, sir? What kinds of stories?" The soldier was apparently worried they were about him, judging by his uncomfortable tone.

"You've...you've worked with some of the new recruits, have you not?" The Prophet asked.

"Yes, sir."

"What age are these boys? Fifteen? Sixteen?"

Minto looked confused. "Yes, sir. As...as you've ordered. Fit males of that age go into soldiering."

"Are they...are they loyal?"

"Yes, sir! Finest bunch of recruits we—"

"The truth, Minto." He steadied his gaze. And waited.

The soldier swallowed before he spoke. "There are some who question the things we do. Some who are soft to the plights of the whores, the servants. Some wonder how Maree could have gotten away with injuring you. Just a common whore running so far, so well, and with that valuable bleeder." Minto glanced at the bandaged shoulder—the proverbial chink in the armour.

"And they question me?"

"Not openly, sir," the soldier said. "Not to me. All I've heard is—"

"Rumors."

"Yes, sir. But it's just talk, sir. Nothing concrete. They'll see. When the men return with the whore and the bleeder, they'll see all is right. All is as it should be."

He said no more. With a motioning hand, he bade Minto to take Liz from his chamber. And he could swear—almost swear—there was the slightest smile in her eyes as the soldier bore her away.

CHAPTER 21

THEY WERE sitting by the brook—Zophia gazing out over the clean, running water, Maree staring intently at her silent sister, waiting for her to speak. The tree branches swayed overhead with the slight breeze. Zophia was still wrapped up in the camouflage robe, and though the hood was down, she looked almost swallowed up by it.

Kallem was back at the hovel, searching it no doubt to see what could be useful for when they pulled out. Even Roscoe seemed to know to leave them alone. With a soft whine and a soulful, droopy-eyed glance at Maree and Zophia, he'd moved off to settle on a thick bed of brown pine needles a few yards off.

Maree's hand tingled. Not from any sting or fatigue from shooting the firearm, but rather with a residual excitement. She'd liked the feeling of holding a gun; the feeling of being able to defend herself. To shoot. To kill, if she had to. But she pushed that excitement aside now as she sat with her sister, waiting for Zophia to build up her courage to say what she needed to say.

Poor Zophia! She would draw a breath as if to speak, but bite back the words on the exhale.

And Maree was growing impatient. "Zophia, what is it?" she probed gently.

"It's complicated, that's what it is," Zophia answered. "As complicated as it gets." Then, with another indrawn breath, she placed her hands on her belly, smoothing the autumn-patterned fabric against her to reveal a definite bulge. "I wasn't sure before. How could I be? But now, I can feel it in there, Maree. And too, my intuition tells me now. It's really there. This is really happening. I am...oh God, there's a baby in me!"

Maree was stunned. She hadn't noticed Zophia's changing shape before. Between the baggy clothes, her preoccupied mind, and the inconceivability of it, she hadn't noticed what her sister now pointed out. But how would she be expected to? Breeders were kept separated in the compound. Though she had all her memories intact from before the instigation of the Holy New Order, pregnancy was such a rarity even back then.

Pregnancy.

Zophia was pregnant.

It was almost impossible to grasp the thought.

"You're pregnant?"

Zophia nodded. "I've missed my last two periods. And the two before that were...splotchy. Almost nothing at all."

Maree shook her head, trying to dispel the confusion. It didn't work. But that soon turned to anger as she thought of the ramifications. "But how could you be pregnant? The Prophet hadn't sent you to be bred yet. And no soldier would dare take you without—"

"No one *took* me," Zophia said. "No one took me at all."

"Then how...."

"It wasn't like that. Isn't like that between...this boy and me. No one 'takes.' He's not violent. He's good, and gentle."

"I don't understand."

Zophia looked suddenly sad, heartsick sad. "I know you don't. And how I wish you could." She turned her head, shifted closer to the brook. Maree watched as she picked up a thin branch and played the edge of it into the cool water. The water parted and flowed past the branch, making a little eddy in the current. "His name is John-Ryder."

"I don't know that name. Is he a soldier?"

"No," Zophia said, a smile in her voice. "John-Ryder was never a soldier. He lost an arm when he was young. One night, a few of the soldiers dared him to go close to a part of the fence where a Reprobate was lurking. You know how it is, the soldiers goad the young boys, and the boys try to be brave. It was John-Ryder's turn to be goaded that night. Usually, the Reprobates would just put a good scare into the boys. You know, roaring forward and making the kid jump back. Then the soldiers would laugh; throw a piece of bread or hunk of meat to the Reprobate. But this time...this one..."

"The Reprobate had a knife." Maree remembered now. She'd heard the story long ago; but never the name. It had been about seven years ago when a little boy had gotten too close to the fence and a demented Reprobate had grabbed the little fingers that had dared to touch the fence. He'd pulled the boy's hand through, and sliced it wrist to palm, then through two fingers. This must have been John-Ryder.

"Yes," Zophia said. "Infection set in. The medic couldn't save the hand. It had to be amputated from the elbow down."

"So no soldiering for John-Ryder," Maree said. And she was certain of it. There'd been a very few—boys born with birth defects or who'd became lame as the result of illness or accident. The hardiest of males were at the top of the pecking order; the physically challenged, at the bottom. They were practically outcasts. Treated as little better than women—and this too was supported by the doctrine in the Prophet's Ending Testament.

"John-Ryder's strong across his back. He bears the water for the rationer every morning as he makes his way around the houses. You've seen him, Maree."

She had. Maree remembered this young man. He was tall, strongly set, with a shock of curly brown hair that never seemed to look neat. Or as if it ever could. His eyes were a deep brown.

"I slipped him a note." Zophia raised her hands in a staving-off gesture. "I know, I know, I'd have been in deep trouble had I been caught. But I wasn't caught. And John-Ryder came over that evening and I went out to meet him. Then I went out another night...and then..."

"And then he took you and—"

"No, Maree," Zophia said. "And *then I fell in love with him.* And John-Ryder fell in love with me too. There was no *taking*. I told you! It wasn't like that at all."

Maree felt the ache in her throat. Her emotions were mixed. This complicated things; definitely complicated them.

If they were caught, Zophia, as a bleeder, certainly wouldn't be killed, but she'd definitely feel the wrath of the Prophet for having lain with someone outside his command. And if Zophia named John-Ryder as the one, Maree had no doubt he'd be put to death.

But in truth, she was happy that Zophia had found a love that was so unheard of, it wasn't even a thing of legend anymore. She hadn't been forced; she hadn't been raped. She'd—

"I chose," Zophia said, again as if reading Maree's thoughts. "I chose what to do with my body. With whom to share what I wanted. John-Ryder never harmed me. Never pressured me. I chose to be with him." Zophia let the branch go and it floated down along with the brook's gentle current. "Oh but, Maree, how I miss him now."

CHAPTER 22

PREGNANT. <u>ZOPHIA</u> was pregnant.

Kallem's hands moved automatically as he arranged his bedroll on the hard, cold ground. Roscoe plunked himself down beside it with a whine.

"I know, boy. You'd rather be in there with them. I don't blame you."

Kallem would rather be in there too. With Maree's hands on him as she'd done two nights ago... Well, not with the child there, of course.

Child. Not so much, it seemed. Old enough to have taken a man into her bed. Old enough to have gotten with child herself. And by a male not of the Prophet's choosing.

Oh, fuck! What if the Prophet blamed the breeder's pregnancy on *him*?

Not if you don't take her back. The Prophet won't even know about the pregnancy if you don't take her back.

Kallem squelched the traitorous thought viciously. Yet, he'd been having such thoughts for days, and they were literally eating away at him. It seemed no matter how many hares he snared or roots and tubers he dug up or apples they gathered, his stomach felt like an aching pit.

That was to say nothing of the lust, the sheer longing that plagued him every hour of every day. He'd thought perhaps tonight he and Maree would have a chance to lay hands on each other, but Zophia's news had completely thrown Maree. Always protective of the younger girl, she'd gone into mothering mode. He'd wanted to talk to her about so many things—this cabin, for instance, and how they happened to stumble upon it. And why it was seemingly provisioned for them. He wanted to talk about the existence of the map to Society Three, the one Zophia had let slip. He wanted to talk about those amazing camouflage robes that allowed the wearer to all but disappear.

About the weapons contained in the folds of the robes.

He'd found them when the two women were talking down by the water.

Maree had shut him out, focusing all her energy and attention on her younger sister. So Kallem had spent the waning hours of daylight scouting the area and setting up trip wires on the most likely approaches. If he didn't hear the tinkle of bells, Roscoe would, and he was trained to alert when he heard them.

They'd shared a supper—Kallem had come across a pheasant as he'd patrolled the area, and he'd dispatched the slow-witted bird with a well-aimed stone. That lucky circumstance allowed them to save the dried fish for their travels. It had been nice to supplement the succulent fowl with crusty bread and a bit of the cheese that had been left for them in the cabin.

But afterward, he'd eyed the two single cots with their thin mattresses and announced that he would sleep outside with Roscoe. Maree had sent him a grateful look which had warmed his heart at the time. Now, however, nothing felt warm. Now that full darkness had fallen, he'd let the cookfire die down. The girls would be plenty warm inside on their mattresses, so he didn't need to risk a fire this night.

He climbed into his bedroll and Roscoe got up and padded over. Kallem lifted the blanket automatically and let the dog settle beside him. The hound smelled…well, like a hound, but Kallem would need that extra body heat as the night grew colder. A soldier couldn't afford to be fussy. And a soldier who had a dog counted himself lucky.

Roscoe let out a half sigh/half groan. Kallem smiled. Belle used to groan like that when he and Errol camped out, reminding them that it was past her bedtime and they were keeping her up with all their laughing and roughhousing. She probably would have been happier on her little cushion at the foot of his parents' bed, but Errol always said it wasn't really camping unless—

Kallem caught himself.

Dear God, he could see him now! Errol. Dark hair, thin face, the slightly gangly body of a boy just beginning to be stretched by puberty. He'd been much younger than Kallem, younger even than Maree, by a few months...

Oh, shit! Maree, Errol...they had been close friends. In fact, Kallem had let the two of them hang with him much of the time. Their neighbourhood hadn't been the safest. Not that any of them had been especially safe, not with increasingly desperate people competing for shrinking resources.

He pressed his memory, searching for an image of a younger Maree, but it refused to come. Yet it was there in his head somewhere. It had to be. It was just as she'd said— their two families had spent a lot of time together. They'd had each other's backs in a time when such relationships were critical. They'd—

The door to the cabin creaked open and both Kallem and Roscoe lifted their heads. Maree stood framed in the doorway.

"Roscoe!" she called. "Come here boy. Come on in."

The dog stirred, and Kallem lifted his arm so it could get up and trot to Maree.

Great. Roscoe got the luxury of an indoor sleep. With a huff, he pulled the covers closer, reconciling himself to a fitful sleep as his source of heat disappeared inside the hovel with Maree.

He was still fidgeting with the blankets when he heard the door open again. What now? Maybe she'd ask for his bedroll too. Leave him out here with nothing but the clothes on his back. He lifted his head to see Maree making her way toward him across the grass, her progress marked by the moonlight.

He sat up. "What is it? Is Zophia okay?"

She stepped around the firepit, nearly cold now, to stand before him. Now that she was this close, he saw she wore one of the camouflage cloaks pulled tightly about her.

"She's fine. Sleeping, actually."

"But you're not." His words hung there, vibrating between them.

"No, I'm not."

Her voice was husky, and the desire he'd been trying to keep tamped down roared up.

"Are you choosing?" he asked, barely recognizing his own strangled voice.

Her answer was to open the cloak. Her nakedness gleamed pale in the night.

"My God, Maree." He pushed the words through a throat gone tight. "You are so beautiful."

"You make me feel that way, when you look at me." She dipped her head. "You make me feel all sorts of things."

He saw her shudder, and he knew it wasn't just desire. It was damned cold out.

"Here." He crawled out of the bedroll. "Crawl in there while I undress."

She wasted no time switching places with him.

He stripped quickly, efficiently, and when he was done, she held back the blanket for him. He crawled in, and the shock of naked skin against naked skin with no preliminaries just about blew his mind. She gasped, too, but it was probably the rude kind of shock for her. But her next words corrected that assumption.

"I've been wanting to feel you against me again so badly," she moaned.

Her arms came around him and he crushed her to him. "Me too," he confessed. "Last night when your sister needed you...I just about died from wanting you."

"I'm here now."

Yes, she was. And now she was pressing her lips to his, opening for him at the first brush of his tongue.

For long minutes they kissed, hands touching faces, fingers sliding through hair. When Kallem pulled back, they were both breathless.

"You said you'd teach me," he said.

She kissed his throat and her hand stroked his flank. "Teach you what?"

He shuddered at the heat of her mouth, then the chill it left behind. "Teach me to make you feel as good as you made me feel the other night."

She pulled back so she could look at him. "Are you serious? Do you really want to?"

Oddly, he did. It defied everything he knew about the relationship between men and women. Everything the Ending Testament taught. Yet there was no denying what he felt. He desperately wanted to transport her as she had done him.

He cleared his throat. "Yes. Tell me what to do."

There was a pause. "Well...um...mainly, females just need a little more warming up."

Warming up? "How do I do that?"

He felt her body shaking and realized she was laughing.

"What's so funny?"

"What's funny is I don't even know for sure what I like."

His smile faded. He didn't think that was funny at all. All she'd ever known was the Prophet's cruelty. He stroked a hand over her short hair. "Let's find out together, then. If you don't like it, I'll stop."

He felt her hand tighten on his side. "Okay. Um...I'm pretty sure I'll like it if you just stroked my body a bit with your hands."

Kallem's erection jerked against her, and from the way she contracted her stomach muscles, she was very much away aware of his response. He began to stroke her back lightly, then her side, feeling the gooseflesh rising under his hand as it glided around to her front.

"Cold?" he asked.

"No." Her voice was high, which made him smile.

"Do you like it?" He skimmed his hand across her midriff, knuckles brushing the underside of her breasts.

"Yes!" She arched against him and he opened his palm over her breast. "Oh, yes! That feels good."

Her nipple pebbled under his hands, and he adjusted his angle so he could drag his thumb across it. She gasped and surged against him. Inspired by that reaction, he drew his thumb and forefinger together to gently roll the hardened peak between them.

"Your mouth," she gasped. "Put your mouth on it. Please, Kallem."

His mouth. The idea shot another bolt to his groin, and he bent, shaping and lifting her breast until he closed his lips over her distended nipple, bathing it with his tongue. Her hands gripped his head and held him there.

"Harder." Her breath panted in and out. "Suckle me."

He did, and she made a harsh, sobbing sound that made his cock grow all the harder.

Suddenly, he knew exactly what else he could do with his mouth. Whether it was instinct or memory, he couldn't have said, but he knew what she needed. Judging by the way his member throbbed at the thought alone, he knew he was going to enjoy it, too.

She protested when he released her nipple, then tensed when she felt his mouth on her midriff, her stomach, gliding lower...

"Kallem!"

"What?" He breathed the word against the thatch of curls of he'd found with his questing hand.

"What are you doing?"

He smiled. "Warming you up, I hope. Is it working?"

She trembled. "God, yes."

He cupped her mound with his hand, then used his fingers to spread her slick folds. The scent that rose from her immediately hazed his mind with lust. It was all he could do not to cover her and drive his cock home. But the broken little noises she was making pulled him back from the edge. Instead, in the darkness beneath the blanket, he learned her anatomy with the tips of his fingers. When he found what was clearly a sensitive spot, she closed her hand over his and showed him the gentle but insistent motion. He smiled.

As he rubbed the little nub, her breathing grew faster, harsher. *Now,* he thought.

He bent and put his mouth on her, gliding his tongue over her aroused flesh, then drawing her in and suckling gently.

She cried out, her hips surging upward. His control broke and he all but buried his face in her. Then his fingers found her wet opening and he did bury two of them in her, thrusting deep into that wet warmth where his cock needed to be. She cried out again, bucking and surging against him. Then she stiffened and he felt her hands in his hair.

"Wait, Kallem! Stop!"

Stop? *Now?* Please, God, no! She couldn't mean it.

"I'm so close," she said. "I need you inside me now."

Kallem breathed again. *Thank God!*

He slid back up her body, but when she tried to pull him on top of her, he resisted. "I want to be inside you so bad, but I don't want to pin you down in case it triggers...bad memories. But I think we can do it on our sides like this, if you put your leg up and sort of hook it—"

"Kallem?"

"What?"

She'd stilled completely. "What if I was on top?"

He had an instant vision of her astride him. "Yes." He rolled to his back and pulled her with him. She drew her knees up to straddle him, her upper body bent over his chest beneath the covers. Between the two of them, they guided his cock to her opening and she sank down on him.

Jesus! He squeezed his eyes shut and gritted his teeth. In contrast to his relative coolness, her sheath was scalding hot, and so tight! But he needed to be completely buried in her.

"More," he croaked. "Take me deeper."

She sat up, and the blanket slipped from her back to pool on his legs. With a hand on his chest to steady herself, she rose and sank on him again, taking him deeper this time. He groaned and held himself still, letting her control the degree of penetration. She did it again, then yet again, until her slick channel had accepted all of him.

"You fit!" she marveled. "And it doesn't hurt. It doesn't hurt at all! It feels good."

"Good," he gritted, his hands tightening on her hips as he thrust upward.

She took his hands and lifted them to her breasts. He took the hint and began massaging them, and she began to ride him. When he pinched her nipples lightly she moaned and leaned closer, changed the angle of their connection, adding an insistent, gyrating grind.

She was trying to rub that little nub that brought her such pleasure. He knew it instantly. Slipping his hands between them, he spread her folds wider. Seconds later, she gasped and he felt her sheath tighten down on him in a pulsating grip. She was coming.

He gripped her hips, pumping wildly into her until his own orgasm seized him.

She collapsed on top of him, panting as hard as he was, and he pulled the blanket back over their rapidly cooling bodies. Before long, she rolled off him only to curl herself against his side. With one arm crooked around her and her head resting on his shoulder, he decided this was bliss.

He also decided he wasn't going back.

None of them were going back, ever. The Prophet would never lay another hand on Maree. Zophia would not be bred to death.

He wanted to blurt it all out. Wanted to declare that he would keep them safe, even against Robinson. That he would let no one take them back.

Except as far as Maree knew, General Robinson was dead and Kallem was already committed to helping them.

So he whispered to her instead about how beautiful she was and she whispered her ragged gratitude for the gift of pleasure he'd given her. Eventually her breathing evened out and she slept, her body relaxed and warm in his arms.

It would all sort itself out, he told himself as he followed her into slumber. He would deliver them to Society Three and then backtrack to deal with Robinson. His mind shied away from what "dealing" with Robinson would surely entail.

It would work out somehow. It had to.

He had chosen.

CHAPTER 23

THEY HEADED down to the brook early in the morning for a quick bath in the knee-deep water before moving on. Despite the fact that Maree and Zophia were in a sun-warmed spot, the water was shiver cold. Kallem was bathing, too, a little ways down the brook, out of sight but within earshot. Though the hovel's reprieve had been welcome, they had to move out this morning. Safety wouldn't allow them another day's rest.

They were so close to Society Three. They had come so far. But they weren't out of danger yet from the Reprobates; although Maree knew that cloaked as they were in the hags' garb, she and Zophia were a great deal safer than they had been. Nor were they out of danger from the damnable soldiers. Soldiers, in fact, were by far the worst threat. They would not be as deterred by a hag's garb as the Reprobates would.

Kallem had once been one of those damnable soldiers.

But now he was more. Hadn't he drawn a knife across the tattoo on his shoulder? Hadn't he proved it by that act? And by acts beyond that. He had killed for Maree and

Zophia, to keep them safe. Killed Reprobates and soldiers alike. And he had made love to her so thoroughly, intent on pleasuring her.

Maree found herself again thinking of last night, as if she'd ever stopped. Heat flashed through her as she thought of the things he'd done to her, had shown her. Oh God, the way he'd made her feel as he awakened her body. She splashed more frigid water on her skin, but it did little to dampen what Kallem Marsh had aroused in her.

"Lost in thought, are we, sister?" Zophia teased. She was on the bank, having rushed through her ablutions in record time.

Maree loved hearing that word 'sister.' The two had had to hide their connection so well, so carefully back at the compound. Not anymore. "Never you mind where my mind has gone."

Zophia laughed and dressed quickly. As she slid the robe over her clothes, Maree found herself staring at that little bulge of belly. As if it would bloom all at once, rounded with the baby. As if she'd see a movement, a sign. Oh hell, as if there was some kind of alien creature inside her little sister.

Maree could only remember ever seeing perhaps a dozen pregnant women in her lifetime in Falmouth. And breeders of course were segregated in the Holy New Order. Kept under the watchful control of the leaders in the respective colonies. Male leaders of course. Attended to by male medics as they gave birth. Even that—the process of birthing—had been taken from women. And it was the male 'leadership' who tore those babies from their mothers so the women could be bred all over again and the babies brought up to serve the Prophet, obey the Ending Testament and believe in the Holy New Order.

Sickening.

That would not be Zophia's fate. Nor the fate of her baby.

With a shiver, Maree raced to the shore, dried off using the threadbare towels they'd found neatly tucked behind the wood box, and began to dress.

"I'm glad I told you," Zophia said. "Glad you get to have this experience with me. Watch me grow. Watch her grow."

Zophia's eyed widened. She seemed to realize it just as Maree did. *Her*. She'd spoken the truth. She was having a girl. There was no doubt in Zophia's now-sparkling eyes nor in Maree's mind.

"A girl," Maree said. "A daughter for you!"

"A niece for you," Zophia answered. Then her voice became low.

It was almost a whisper. She stared straight ahead without blinking and spoke as if narrating, as if watching things unfold in the distance. "She'll grow up to be a warrior, like you, Maree."

The chill Maree felt now was bone deep. "Do you know this?"

"I see this. She'll be…my daughter…one with a scar on her beautiful face. She won't know a life free of pain. But she'll be free, this daughter of mine. Not right away…but somehow…I see my child being free. But there's danger." Her voice took on a whimpering tone, though no tears fell from her staring eyes. "And I see…you there with her, but there's terror on your face." Her face crumpled then, as though she herself were in pain. Grieving.

Maree grabbed Zophia's cold hands in her own. The contact startled Zophia. She blinked several times, then focused on Maree. "Don't tell Kallem," she whispered.

Maree frowned. "Don't tell him what? He already knows you're pregnant."

"Don't tell him the rest of it. The rest of what I see."

"Why?" Maree's heart felt as if it were beating stone.

Zophia shook her head. "I'm…I'm not sure. I just don't…"

Woof!

Roscoe bounded in between them, licked a few times at Zophia's hand before she bent to pat him. In fact, Zophia did more than pat him. She hugged the damp dog to herself and with both hands began stroking his fur as she talked to him. "Who's a good dog? Youz a good, good doggie, aren't you, Roscoe. Who's a happy puppy?"

The delighted animal rolled onto his belly. Zophia laughed as she scratched him.

"You're taking the soldier right out of that dog," Kallem said, shaking his head. "You know that, don't you?

Maree hadn't heard him approaching. She turned to greet his smiling eyes. She'd question Zophia more later, but for now, she found herself smiling back.

"Well, then that's a good thing," Zophia said. Roscoe rolled onto his belly again and jumped to his feet. He barked happily at Kallem, but still didn't leave Zophia's side.

"Turning him into a softie," Kallem said.

"Oh please!" This time it was Maree's turn to tease. "The way you used to carry on with Belle! I remember this one time when we thought Belle was lost. You—"

"Stayed out all night looking for her." Kallem swallowed. Twice.

Maree gasped. "You remember?"

"Only now, when you mentioned it," he said, his stone steadier. "We were kids. I was worried sick over Belle. There were people—angry people—who would have killed her if she wandered onto their neighborhoods. You stayed out all night looking for her with me, Maree."

Yes, she had.

"Oh, God," Zophia said. "That must have gone over well with the parents. Not to mention how dangerous it would have been."

Her eyes never leaving Kallem, Maree slowly started to smile. "We both got into so much trouble. But we did find Belle. And we—"

A sharp, reverberating boom came from the south, echoing in the morning.

Gunfire!

The fur on Roscoe's back bristled as he stood beside Zophia protectively. Ready for combat. His lips curled back in a snarl as he growled.

"Soldiers!" Zophia breathed.

Kallem ran a hand over his head. "One, at least," he muttered.

"What do you mean?" Maree asked.

"I mean, we're moving out. Now!"

It was an undisputed command. Within ten minutes they'd broken camp, erasing as best they could all evidence of their recent occupation. And as they set off at a brisk pace, Maree carried Aykroyd's gun well-hidden within her cloak.

CHAPTER 24

THE PROPHET was in his chamber, lying on his own bed. This much he knew. His head was flat on the mattress. Where…where were his pillows? The sheets? It was nighttime, judging by the darkness. By the fact that no sliver of light slipped through the heavy curtains. But the day? The hour? How long had he been like this? He ran a nearly numb hand over his bristled head.

Then the voices started again.

Marcus… We've been watching you, Marcus. Oh so very closely for oh so very long. You shouldn't have let the girl go; shouldn't have let that whore run. She injured you, so shamefully. That was the beginning of your end. Everyone saw it! Yes, everyone knows. Chink, chink, chink goes the armor, Marcus Will Montag. Soon—so very soon—the Prophet will be no more…

The Prophet pulled his mind into focus. *Where were those words coming from?* But the vision that swirled before him was just of Liz. Silent Liz. But he'd known it hadn't been her voice that taunted. That voice—dear God, those *voices*—were coming from within his own mind.

He needed…something. A needle for the pain. A needle to help with his breathing. Another one to keep him safe from the bats and rats—damnable monsters!—that were crawling back in even now. And another needle for the voices, those that nudged him into doubt.

Marcus, Marcus, we've been watching youuuu….

He focused on Liz, her bruised and battered face. Where was the hopelessness on that face? Where was the fear of damnation? And why did the smallest smile now play upon her split, swollen lips? Maree had looked like that, after she'd stabbed him. Now this one…Liz…looked so much like the other whore! He focused and focused until both women's faces swirled in his mind, and then swirled into one. He needed a needle!

"Ring the bell, Maree," he croaked.

She stood slowly. But it wasn't with a groan or pain or grimace. She backed away slowly, her eyes never leaving the Prophet in his torment. He closed his eyes against the assault of the flame that flickered from the candle she held.

"Prophet?" she said, her voice low.

He did not answer. There was effort in speaking he didn't want to expend. She asked again.

Silence.

"I'm not Maree," she whispered. "I'm not the one who stabbed you, not the one who caused you this pain. But, oh, you black-hearted devil, how I wish I had been! How I wish I could be yet!"

Did she think he couldn't hear? Her voice! This voice…this voice that swirled amongst the others. Didn't he…hadn't he heard her whisper something about the devil?

Chink, chink, chink goes the armor. Down goes the devil into hell. Soon, oh, so very soon, the Prophet will be no more—the Prophet that never was! We can see you, Marcus Will Montag—oh yes!—for what you really are…

"I'm not Maree! I'm not Maree! I am just your devil!"

161

He barely heard the ringing bell above these taunting voices. They danced around, sang around inside his drug-filled mind.

CHAPTER 25

"COME ON, ladies, pick it up." Kallem cursed silently as he urged the women faster.

Maree was right; gunshots meant soldiers. And the only reason Robinson would have discharged his weapon was if he were overwhelmed by Reprobates. Which meant there must have been a lot of them. A damned lot. Only a sizeable pack would dare threaten an armed soldier.

Damn that Robinson! What was he doing so close on their heels anyway? He was supposed to have hung back a day behind them. The old soldier must have started off after them almost immediately.

Or perhaps he *had* hung back, but new orders had come through and he'd double-timed it to catch up to them...

No, that didn't make sense. If new orders had come, Robinson wouldn't be alone. A soldier would have delivered them. And the old general almost certainly was alone to have resorted to using his firearm.

Maree stopped and looked back at him, her face pale with fear. Yet she gripped Aykroyd's pistol like she meant it.

"Which way?" She pushed the words out between panting breaths.

Kallem edged past Zophia and the dog, whom he and Maree had placed between them for protection, to see that they'd come to an escarpment. The rock face was too steep to descend to the wooded valley floor below.

He looked both ways. "West," he said, gesturing to his left. "We can work our way back when we've lost our tail."

No sooner had he spoken than a hound sounded. It was more of an agitated barking than the characteristic baying of a dog on a scent.

"My God." Maree's eyes went wide. "A dog. We'll never shake them."

Perhaps they wouldn't have to. The thought whispered in Kallem's head.

Perhaps the Reprobates would take care of Robinson for him. And then, Kallem wouldn't have to look his mentor— the man who'd taught him so much—in the eye and strike him dead. His heart quickened with hope. Could it be that easy?

When was his life ever that easy?

"They've been following us for days," Zophia announced.

Both Maree and Kallem turned to look at her.

"Zophia!" Maree cried. "Why didn't you say something?"

Zophia shrugged helplessly. "It's felt this way since that day you slew the soldiers who followed us and took Roscoe," she said. "I thought it was just an echo, a residual feeling."

The young girl dipped her head, looking impossibly fragile, and Maree put a hand on her shoulder.

"It's okay, Zophia," she murmured softly. "You couldn't have known." Then she turned to Kallem, her eyes fierce and determined. "Okay, soldier, how do we elude the bloodhound? You must know a way."

He shook his head. "Our party is too big."

"But there must be something! What if we went through water, maybe tramped down the middle of a stream..."

"It's not just our footprints the hound tracks. There are three of us, and Roscoe too. We're each of us shedding skin rafts at a rate of tens of thousands per minute. In the scent world where a bloodhound lives, we might as well be leaving a billowing trail of smoke in our wake."

"Trees, then," she said. "We could climb trees, get up off the ground..."

"And then we'd be treed when they caught up to us," Kallem said.

"What would you do, then?" she demanded. "If you were alone, what would you do to elude the soldiers?"

He nodded toward the precipice. "I'd go down that cliff face. Make up a few hours on them. And yes, I'd probably tramp a few miles along the first stream I came to in the hopes that by the time they caught up, my scent would have dissipated enough."

Maree peered over the cliff's edge and paled. "We could still do that."

He shook his head vehemently. "Not without rock-climbing gear. It would be suicide for the two of you without a safety harness. Besides, I'd have to kill Roscoe."

Both girls gasped and Zophia's hand went protectively to the dog's smooth coat.

"He'd just race along the escarpment until he could get down to the valley floor, then double back and catch up to us," he explained. "He'd lead them right to us."

Maree blew her breath out in exasperation. "There must be something we can do!"

"Yeah, keep moving."

Her eyes shot daggers at him. "How is that going to help? You just got done explaining we can't elude the hound."

"I'm thinking the Reprobates may take care of our problem for us."

Her eyebrows soared. "Reprobates killing soldiers?"

"Possibly," he said. "There had to have been a lot of them for a soldier to discharge his gun on a trail this hot. From the dog's demeanor, he'd have to have known they were closing in on us. No way would a soldier give himself away like that unless he was under attack."

"He's right," Zophia said, her eyes seeming to stare unfocused into the distance. "There are many back there, but they're not all soldiers."

Maree brightened. "Finally! Something Reprobates are good for."

"Maybe," Kallem muttered. "But remember, if they overpower the soldiers, they'll be Reprobates with guns. Or at least one gun."

"And a dog," Zophia added, shivering.

If they managed to overpower the General, they were apt to kill Beau for eating, Kallem figured, but Zophia didn't need to know that. Unless, of course, it actually happened, in which case he had no doubt she'd know about it with that weird vision of hers.

"Come on," he said gruffly. "Rest time is over. Let's get going."

CHAPTER 26

IT WAS Roscoe who tipped them off.

Suddenly, he growled and the fur on his back bristled. Maree felt the hair rise on the back of her own neck, particularly when she saw that the dog wasn't staring off in one specific direction. Rather, it did a full turn, scanning the surrounding thick woods in all directions, as though the danger were all around them.

Maree moved closer to her sister.

Though Kallem and Maree had kept Zophia between them as they'd traveled, he was now some distance from the two women. They'd needed a break to relieve themselves, so he'd run up ahead to do the same while scouting forward somewhat. Roscoe, as always now, had remained at Zophia's side.

"What is it, boy?" Zophia whispered. Maree could tell Zophia felt it too, whatever the dog was sensing. She put her hand on Roscoe's strong back. "What is...oh my God!"

Even as she whirled to see what had made Zophia scream, Maree was reaching deep into her robe for her gun.

Reprobates. Four of them. Coming from what felt like all directions, they charged. Two of them bore short knives, the other two thick, sharpened sticks. Their eyes were wild, not with fear, but excitement. And the fact that those eyes were the only parts of their faces showing above the layers of cloth that covered their faces only made the sight all the more terrifying.

"Kallem!" Maree shouted. "Kal—"

From behind, a powerful hand snaked around her, while another clamped over her mouth and nose. The Reprobate laughed as she gagged. His free hand raked her body roughly now, trying to tear away her clothes. The man with him laughed, his hand going to his crotch. Gang rape. That's what the bastards had in mind.

Reflexively, Maree reached to claw at her attacker's hand. She couldn't breathe, and panic welled in her. Welled, but didn't consume. And even as her left hand clawed her attacker, Maree's right hand wrapped around the hilt of the gun. With a practiced slide, she released the safety and withdrew the weapon. Twisting her lower body out of way, she shot the Reprobate in his right thigh at point blank range.

Screaming, he went down to the ground, clutching at a thigh that fountained blood. Maree could smell the burned flesh. She aimed and squeezed the trigger, ending the Reprobate's screams with a bullet to the head. She looked at the other. The laughing one laughed no more as she aimed at his crotch.

"No!" He covered himself with his hands, but to no avail. Her bullet shattered his right hand but still found its mark. He screamed as he went down, but quickly passed out.

"Maree!"

Zophia! Maree whirled to find the other two had her. Or were trying to. Roscoe kept attacking them as they tried to drag her away into the woods. One of them looked up and saw Maree focused on them. Cursing, he pulled Zophia in front of them, using her for a shield while they fought off the dog. One of them stabbed at Roscoe with his stick, while the other held a knife to Zophia's throat even as he kicked the poor dog.

"Stand back, whore!" The man who held Zophia called out. "Or I'll slit this one's throat!"

He held the knife closer to Zophia's fair skin, and Maree froze as a trickle of blood ran down.

"Drop your gun!" the Reprobate yelled. "And your knife!"

Her fingers trembled in this split-second moment of indecision. If she dropped the weapons, she was fucked. But if she didn't—how far would the one that held her sister go with that knife? She knew she was a good shot, even as new as she was to guns. But she couldn't shoot them both without risking Zophia's life.

Zophia cried out as the blood trickling down her throat widened into a one inch strip.

"Drop the fuckin' weapons! Drop them, or we'll kill her on the spot!"

Beyond the Reprobates, something caught Maree's attention in the trees. She knew then what she had to do.

She chucked the knife down a few feet away. The gun she hurled just as far as she could into the woods off to the right. As she'd hoped, the Reprobates' eyes followed the arc of the gun, no doubt planning to retrieve it later. That's when Kallem ghosted out of the woods behind them. He struck in a blur of motion. The one who held Zophia dropped to the ground, his neck obviously broken. Kallem pulled out his own gun now, but not fast enough. With Zophia still as a shield, the other pulled back.

"Call your dog off!" he yelled. "Call your dog off or I'll kill the girl now."

Kallem was silent.

"Roscoe, down." Zophia said through her tears. "Stop, boy. That's a good dog."

Roscoe, growling and bristling, stood down.

Out of nowhere, or so it seemed, another Reprobate seized Maree from behind. She fought, struggled, but he wrenched her arm behind her back till she thought it would break, forcing her to her knees. He crouched behind her, making her into a human shield like her sister.

Kallem's gaze darted from Maree to Zophia. He looked stricken. Stricken and furious beyond anything Maree had ever seen before.

The one behind Maree called out to Kallem. "We'll kill them both, soldier! Slit them from cunt to throat and back again if you come any nearer. And this one—" the pain was excruciating as he ratcheted Maree's arm higher. "This one's gonna pay for killing my brother, Jude!"

Jude. So that was the name of the one she'd killed. Good. She liked knowing the bastard's name.

"No!" Zophia cried.

Again Roscoe attacked, this time launching himself at Zophia's attacker's knife-holding hand. When Zophia saw the knife fly out of his hand, she made her move. Maree watched her go limp, using her dead weight to try to sink to the ground. The Reprobate couldn't hang on to her and fend off the dog too, so he let her fall. As she rolled away, the Reprobate screamed. Maree took her eyes off her sister long enough to see Roscoe tearing at the man's throat. The dog yelped a few times as the brute rained vicious blows on his head and ribs, but he hung on like a limpet, grinding his hold deeper. It was over quickly and Roscoe, muzzle bloodied from tearing the Reprobate's throat out, went straight to Zophia.

Kallem turned to the one holding Maree. He steadied his gun. Aimed. "Run," he said. "This is the only chance I'm giving you or you'll be as dead as the rest of these scum." The groin-injured man on the ground had regained consciousness and was moaning. With barely a glance, Kallem lowered his pistol, shot him in the head, then leveled his gun at the last Reprobate again. "Let go of the woman and run, you son of a bitch, or so help me, I'll—"

"You'll what?" the man snarled.

Maree trembled. He had no fear in him, this one. Or else he was just too enraged over the death of his brother to care.

"I'll shoot you right between your beady eyes, that's what."

"And risk the whore? She must have value, for your most legendary soldier to stalk you."

"Not that big a risk." Kallem's arm didn't waver. Nor did his voice. "I'm a damn good shot. This is a damn good gun."

"You soldiers, you're nothing without your guns," he spat. "Even the great General Robinson was no match against us until he drew his gun."

Robinson? Maree stiffened.

"We set upon him a day ago. He shot two of us dead, the cocksucker! But even with his gun, he couldn't stop us from taking his dog."

Maree saw the flicker of something in Kallem's face, and the Reprobate must have seen it, too.

"Yeah, that's right. We took his hound. We knew he had to be on the trail of something important—why else would the General be sent out by your precious Prophet? So we captured his dog, and didn't it lead us straight to you?" The Reprobate closed his hand on Maree's breast and squeezed cruelly. "These women must be something special for the great Robins—"

Maree saw Kallem's gun buck, heard the deafening report, felt the warm splash of blood on the side of her face. She tore herself away as the Reprobate fell to the ground, dead. For several seconds, she stared down at him and he stared back sightlessly, a bullet hole in the center of his forehead.

"Maree!"

Zophia's call broke her paralysis. She ran to her sister, crushing her in a tight embrace. It was short-lived, however, as Zophia pulled herself away to tend to the wounded Roscoe.

A yelp and a curse reached them from the forest, and Kallem crouched, gun ready. Branches snapped as someone—or multiple people—ran away.

"Go after them!" Maree said. "Kill every last one of them!"

"No," Kallem said, after a pause. "It could be a trap. They may want me to follow, leave you two alone so others can attack."

"Yes, soldier, it might very well be. And you'd know all about traps." With an angry hand, Maree wiped the blood from her face. She glared at Kallem.

"Maree—"

"Robinson is alive!" she shouted. "Yet you told us you'd killed him! Killed him and the hound too. That's what you said. But you goddamn well lied to us. You didn't kill either one of them. They've been tracking us."

"If you'd just—"

"You tricked us!" Her voice shook so hard, she barely recognized it as her own. "And you *fucked* me, you bastard! You fucked me like no one ever could. I let you *in*, damn you!"

She'd trusted him; made love with him. Brought him this close to Society Three. But he'd been using her, lying to her, all along.

Fucking her over.

Anger flared so high, Maree trembled with it. Trembled harder than she had even in the Reprobate's grip.

Kallem took a step toward her. The expression on his face looked...tortured.

How dare he! How dare he wear an expression like that after what he'd done? Maree's hand went to the pocket of her robe, searching for the weight of the gun that was no longer there. If it were there, she would use it. She'd end him right now.

He stopped in his tracks.

CHAPTER 27

MAREE SWALLOWED. A second time, a third. But the raw ache in her throat just would not go away. He'd used her. Lied to her. Kallem had betrayed her like no one ever had before. And she'd been fool enough to let him. Though the Prophet had used her wretchedly over the years, she'd never given herself to him. Never emotionally surrendered. That was the one thing the Prophet had always wanted—that release, that shuddering surrender. And she'd never given it to him. But she'd done so with Kallem Marsh, when she'd embraced him, opened herself completely to him, allowed herself to climax with him. And now she knew the truth. It had been a plot. A ploy. It had all been a lie.

"Zophia," she said. "I need to talk to Kallem, alone. Take Roscoe, go on ahead."

"But the dog's—"

"Go!" Maree's eyes never left Kallem's as she barked out the order. Zophia stood, walked away slowly with the limping dog beside her. Maree could feel her looking back at the two of them, but her sister said nothing. She heard her go off, tramping ahead into the woods. Zophia wouldn't go far, and Roscoe would alert her of any danger. This couldn't wait.

And this wouldn't take long.

"Maree..."

"Robinson lives!" Maree only realized how tightly clenched her fists were as her nails cut into her palms.

"The Reprobate—"

"Had no reason to lie! You did though, didn't you, Kallem of the First Guard? You had plenty of reason to lie. It was all a lie, wasn't it? Every goddamn word!"

He shook his head. "You're right that the Prophet sent me," he said. "Sent me to find you and Zophia, to bring you back. But not until..."

"Not until what?" Maree's eyes widened with the realization. "Oh God! Oh no! Not until we led you to Society Three. Jesus, is that it?" She felt sick.

"Yes," he said solemnly. "That was my mission."

Anger blurred her vision now. "How...how many ways did you use us? *Use me!* You're a monster. No better than Marcus Will Montag, the so-called Prophet. No, you're *worse*. I never believed in him. You made me believe in you."

Kallem grabbed her by the arms and held her tightly. "Maree, listen to me! It started out like that. I started out a soldier on a mission—single-minded and purpose-driven. Ready to do anything I was ordered to do. But that changed. I swear to you! Maree, *I* changed."

"Right," she said sarcastically, "as you remembered poor Belle? As you thought of your little lost dog? Your stone-cold soldier heart just melted with the mention of that dog?"

His jaw tightened. "Yes, dammit, as I remembered. But not just about Belle. I remembered you and me. My little brother. Our families.... Hazy as it still is—I remember some of it. Some of who I was before the inoculation. But those memories weren't what changed me. I changed because of you, Maree. Not because of who you were, but

175

who you *are*. You and Zophia. As we traveled and walked and talked. And yes, as you and I made love."

His grip had loosened just enough, but her heart hadn't. Maree raised her right hand and struck him hard across the face.

Anger flashed in Kallem's eyes, but he tamped it down immediately and released her. He raised his left hand, dabbed the droplets of blood forming on his bottom lip. "I deserve that."

And so much more!

"Enough, *soldier*," she said, her voice thick with disdain. "I don't believe a word you say. Not anymore. You may have made me into a fool with your knife through your precious tattoo, and teaching us these…tricks of self-defense." Just thinking about it fed her fury. How much had he left out of his instruction? Suddenly, she was convinced the knowledge he'd given her was no more than a pittance. Enough to keep her satisfied. Quiet. Enough to win her trust. "As of this moment, we are enemies. As of this moment, I know who you are and you know who I am. Now I'll give you a chance. Get the fuck out of here now, or I'll kill you on the spot."

He looked more heartbroken than angry as he stared back at her, which infuriated her all the more. Did he think her a complete fool? She wouldn't be taken in again, not by those soulful looks and not by the lies that tripped so easily off his tongue.

"Kill me, Maree?" he said softly. "You think you're such an apt student that you're ready to kill—"

He was about to say 'the master," but he knew better, and stopped short.

She narrowed her eyes. "I'll drop you where you stand."

"Maree, just listen to—"

"I won't listen to your lies!"

"Fine. Hate me if you must. Kill me if you can. Until then, I'll take you there."

"Where?"

"Closer to your Society Three. I know you won't trust me to take you all the way, or even very near. But I'll get you further along in your quest. Make the journey safer. That'll be the last you see of me."

"And what makes you think I'll let you come with us?"

He turned, his glare hardening. "Because you love Zophia. No matter what you may think of me, Maree, I care about you and Zophia. An obligation. I didn't put you into this mess, but I took advantage of it. Yes, I used you. But not...not how you think. I changed. I am changing still. Not just remembering, but feeling, dammit!"

She returned his hard look with one of her own. "Are you finished?"

"You have to listen. Reprobates have never been tracked this far north. What brings them here, I can only guess. But there's danger. From them, and yes, from Robinson. He does live. He's been on our trail, and that's why I've been pushing you to go so hard. So fast. You have to trust me, Maree. Trust me to at least get you out of danger. North as far as you need to go. Then I'll depart. You'll never see me again."

"Did you not hear me before? I'm going to kill you, Kallem."

The look in his eyes betrayed him; he didn't believe she could do it. "Look, I know what I did was wrong. Unforgivable. But you can't—"

He silenced when he saw it—the vial she pulled from the robe. Maree took a step back, holding it high over her head. If he made a lunge for the vial, or her, she'd drop it on the spot.

"What's that?" Kallem said.

"I have my own secrets, Soldier. I have my own weapons. My own ways to fuck *you*!"

He took a step back. "You're making a mistake, Maree. You have to trust me. I'll help you. Save you from the

Reprobates. And from Robinson. Oh, God, Maree, he's ruthless. Relentless. But I can help. I can lead him—"

Maree hurled the vial to the ground and it shattered.

Her heart thudded crazily in her chest as the smell reached up to her nostrils. The pungent odor turned her stomach and made her eyes water. But it was having a much more dramatic effect on Kallem.

He fell to the ground, amongst the vial's broken shards. His cheek bled just below the eye where a large sliver of glass had cut him. Immediately, he turned on his side and vomited. Then his body convulsed and he vomited again. Sweat sheened his face and dampened his hair, even soaking through parts of his clothing. When he opened his eyes, they were red and streaming tears.

Run.

Every fiber in her being told her to run after Zophia and get the hell away from this villain before he recovered himself.

Get away or kill him.

Those were the choices she'd discussed with Valentina. The potion worked on males for a reason. The hags had designed it so for a reason, to give the women the options of running from an enemy so he would tell the others the dangers of crossing the hags, or never having to run from him again.

Maree knelt down beside Kallem as he groaned in agony. She removed the sliver of glass that still protruded from his cheek, turned it in her hands. "I could kill you, Kallem." She dropped the glass and pulled her knife from her robe.

Though he was helpless to move against her, his eyes focused on the blade as she held it two-handed above him. She moved slowly, so that he could follow her motions.

"The throat," she said. "Though I can't believe much of what you told me, Soldier, I do believe what you told me about the throat being a vulnerable spot." He swallowed. "I stab my knife into your windpipe, slit open the jugular...just that easy."

Wasn't it? Shouldn't it be?

Kallem closed his eyes. "Do what you have to do, Maree. " He couldn't move, she could see that. He looked so sick, so weak. "Do what you must, but know this—how I started out is not how I ended up. I never meant to betray you. Not...not once I knew who you really were. Not once I saw everything. If I'm going to die, then...just know that."

His eyelids flickered. Then his eyes rolled up, irises disappearing as he passed out.

Maree blinked then stood up. Damn him! Damn Kallem Marsh and this damnable day. Damn the Reprobates and every fucking soldier there was. But most of all, Maree cursed herself as she resheathed the knife. Quickly, she rummaged through Kallem's clothing, found his compass and a couple other things she could use. Then she ran to her find sister.

CHAPTER 28

KALLEM CAME to with a hideous taste in his mouth, a heavy boot nudging his ribs, and the certainty that his life was in danger. Operating on sheer reflex, he rolled, caught the booted foot and upended his assailant. The next instant, he was on his feet, hand going for his gun.

"Christ, kid! Take it easy. It's me, Robinson."

Robinson. Only Robinson. Thank God. He'd thought it was Reprobates come back to scavenge what they could from the dead.

As relieved as he was, his heart still hammered—for the holster at his hip was empty.

How could that be? His brain was so foggy and his head throbbed like he'd been pounding whiskey shots for days. Even his vision felt shaky. Had someone kicked him in the head?

Robinson got to his feet again, dusting himself off. "Jesus, what a battle they gave you, kid." He glanced around the wooded area, and whistled. "Four Reprobates. Thought they'd killed you when I saw you lying there."

Kallem spat, trying to rid himself of that horrible taste in his mouth. What the hell was that foulness?

"Guess they got the whore and the bleeder," Robinson observed.

Maree and Zophia! Had they gone into hiding at Robinson's approach? Were they watching from the cover of the bushes even now? Or—oh, shit!—had they taken him for dead and moved on without him, with no one to defend them against another Reprobate attack?

"No shame in that, though," the general continued. "Bastards were organized. They got Beau offa me a day back, though he seems to have got loose again." Robinson nodded off to the left. "Got a piece of one of 'em in the process, I'd say, judging from the blood on his muzzle."

Kallem followed the direction he indicated to see Beau lying on the ground, panting. He immediately dismissed the idea that Maree and Zophia were hiding nearby. The hound wouldn't be resting if they were anywhere handy. They'd moved on, then.

Or—oh, fuck!—been *forced* to move on! Taken by Reprobates...

"No, there's no shame in bein' overpowered," Robinson repeated, no doubt because the same Reprobates had prised his dog away from him. "But I don't relish explaining that to the Prophet. So as soon as you collect yourself, how about we go fetch them back?"

Kallem blinked. Why didn't any of this make sense?

Robinson cocked his head. "You okay, Kallem? What'd they do to you, anyway? Don't see much blood on you besides that little scratch on your face."

Then Kallem glanced down at the ground at his feet and memory poured back.

"Maree!" he gasped her name without thinking. He bent and picked up the broken glass vial. Though he held it at arm's length, his stomach roiled sickly from the smell that still lingered. "This is what knocked me out! When she smashed the vial, it gave off a noxious gas."

"Maree?" Robinson barked. "The *whore* did this to you?" Robinson looked around wildly as though she might be lurking. "Jesus Christ, they weren't captured by the Reprobates, were they? She suckered you and ran!"

Robinson's voice was like a gnat buzzing in Kallem's ears. His mind was racing. Remembering…piecing together what had happened.

She'd been so angry! Livid. He'd shrugged off her wildly improbable threats and tried to explain. But then he'd found himself lying helpless on the ground, writhing in agony, puking his guts out, and then the paralysis… God, he'd really thought she was going to kill him. She could so easily have done it, too. He'd been completely defenseless. She could have dispatched him with that knife she'd learned to use so well. Had used before on the Prophet. Hell, a simple neck compression would have done it, her small foot pressed to his throat…

Or—*shit*—his gun! That's what had happened to it! She'd taken it off him. She could have used his own weapon to put a bullet in his brain and he couldn't have stopped her.

"Oh, for chrissakes! She got your weapon, too, didn't she?" Robinson's face was florid with fury. "That's it. I'm going to kill the bitch. I swear to God I will! The Prophet will understand. Swagg will back me up. When I tell him what she did to you…"

"No!"

Robinson cocked an eyebrow. "No?"

Dammit! He shouldn't have mentioned the vial and Maree's role in knocking him out. He'd better pull himself together and do a better job of managing Robinson. There was no way he was letting this or any other soldier get his hands on either of the women, but with Reprobates so thick in the woods it would be much safer for them to travel together. For now, he needed Robinson.

And later...well, later he'd deal with him.

A queasy sensation arose in his stomach again, but this time it was caused not by the chemical hangover, but by the thought of executing his old mentor.

"What the hell do you mean, *no*?"

"She didn't take my gun," Kallem lied. "She did remove it, but I saw her throw it as far as she could into the woods." He turned, tried to remember the precise direction in which Maree had thrown Aykroyd's gun, the exact arc and velocity... "It should be somewhere over there." He pointed in the general direction. "Give me ten minutes to see if I can find it."

The General sighed. "I'll help. Maybe Beau can help too, but don't hold your breath. If it doesn't breathe and run, he's not much interested."

They trudged into the woods and started searching. As predicted, Beau was not helpful.

"So," Robinson called, as he used a stick to move the undergrowth this way and that, "why did the whore turn on you, anyway? I thought you said you'd secured their trust."

Another punch to the gut. "I did," Kallem replied. "Until one of the Reprobates boasted of besting the great Robinson not a day ago and seizing his dog."

"Boasted, did he?" Robinson hawked and spat. "Did he also tell you I killed six of them as they ran like jackrabbits?"

Six? It was two, as Kallem recalled. "My point is that I'd told the women earlier, after Aykroyd was killed by the Reprobates, that I'd slain the both of you to keep them safe. And when I did, I used your names. I didn't think it would do any harm, since I thought you would be hanging well back. It was a convincing detail that helped me win their trust, as did my bringing them Roscoe. Unfortunately, the Reprobate blew my story before I could put a bullet between his eyes."

"So you saved their asses, and the bitches thanked you by *poisoning* you and leaving you for the Reprobates to come back and find?"

"If I'd deceived you like that, you wouldn't have left me breathing," Kallem pointed out.

Robinson merely grunted, and they resumed the search.

Fifteen minutes later, it was obvious to Kallem the gun was gone. "We're not going to find it," he conceded.

"The whore probably changed her mind and fetched it back again."

Kallem shook his head. "She wouldn't know how to chamber a round. My guess is that a Reprobate must have found it. We heard one running away after the attack. Well, at least one. Made such a thrashing, could have been more." He glanced around. "We'll have to look sharp as we travel."

"Great," Robinson muttered. "Armed Reprobates." He glared at Kallem. "This is still the whore's fault. If she'd left the gun on you, it wouldn't be in the hands of murderous criminals."

Kallem slanted Robinson a glance. "Again, can you blame her? She just discovered the man who was pretending to be her champion was actually using her to try to find Society Three, after which he planned to drag her back to the Prophet so he could take his time killing her."

The General studied him hard. And when he spoke his words were measured and slow. "You see, that's your problem, Kallem. You empathize too much. You're always putting yourself in someone else's shoes, trying to figure out how they feel. You always were too soft. Always."

And you, you old bastard, have always been too hard. You can't empathize with anyone because you don't give a damn and you're brainwashed. You didn't care about those female soldiers you persecuted. Didn't give a damn when they were sexually harassed by their colleagues, sometimes to the point of suicide. Hell, you practically gave it your blessing. And that was all before the New Order came in.

"Kallem?"

Memory was flooding in.

Kallem blinked Robinson back into focus, but instead of seeing his gruff but concerned mentor, he was seeing the masochistic fuck of a Commanding Officer from over a decade ago. The same CO he'd been planning to blow the whistle on. Except he'd ended up strapped to a gurney getting jabbed with needles instead.

Oh, fuck!

Kallem cleared his throat and forced a smile. "Yeah, yeah, I've heard this lecture before." He scrubbed a hand over his face, hoping to erase any expression that might be there. "Okay, hand over your backup piece, you old coot. Won't do you any good strapped to your ankle. We need to be able to cover each other."

Robinson grunted, but bent to unstrap the .22.

Kallem held out his hand for it.

Robinson slapped it into Kallem's palm. "Think you can hang on to this one?"

"I aim to try, sir. Think you can hang on to that dog this time?"

Robinson gave a great guffaw and clapped Kallem on the back. "Good one, son. Now let's go track us a whore."

CHAPTER 29

ZOPHIA COLLAPSED to the ground, and Maree went down beside her. She wrapped her arms around her sister. "Just a little bit further," she whispered.

They'd come to a huge fallen tree in their path—a thick-trunked maple. They'd have to climb over, or tramp through even thicker forest to skirt around it. It might as well have been a mountain in their way. And Zophia leaned up against it, as if it were just that formidable.

Maree folded Kallem's compass—*her* compass now—into the pocket of her robe. She'd taken his compass and his gun. All the rations she could quickly grab. Not just so they'd have the resources to guide and protect themselves, but so he'd have a harder time tracking them down.

Not for the first time since she'd left Kallem hours ago, Maree doubted her decision to let him live. She shook her head. It was too late now. Too late to second-guess that mercy. Whatever his motive, he had helped her and Zophia. Without his help with the lone Reprobate that first day—the one who'd tried to rape her—Zophia would have been raped too. Then he'd have butchered them both. And the gang of

Reprobates earlier this day had promised an even worse fate. Even her struggle with Aykroyd—she'd knifed him good, but he'd still been able to draw his gun. He'd have shot her had Kallem not finished him before he could pull the trigger. To say nothing of keeping the cruel General off them that day. Were it not for Kallem, she'd have had to fight both Aykroyd and Robinson. She couldn't possibly have won, but she'd have died trying.

A shiver shuddered through Zophia, pulling Maree from her thoughts.

"You okay?" Maree lowered Zophia's hood and pushed a strand of flaming red hair aside from her sister's sweat-damp forehead. The pins had fallen out of her hair now, as if her unruly locks had a mind of their own. Or maybe it was her unruly spirit. But looking like a man now to fool the Reprobates was the least of Maree's worries. With the robes, they did blend into the background, especially after night fell, but that was no guarantee.

Zophia gulped a breath before she answered. "I've got to rest, Maree."

"The baby?" *Oh no, she'd pushed her too hard!*

Zophia shook her head. "No, she's fine. I don't feel a danger there. But...*I'm* exhausted. Beyond exhausted. I just can't go on. I...I just can't." With a whine of sympathy, the battle-scarred Roscoe lay down beside her.

Maree closed her eyes a moment, as she fought against the flood of defeating thoughts that welled inside her. They'd come so far; fought so hard. And Maree had had her fool heart broken.

How could you, Maree? How could you have come to care?

Maree opened her eyes. She stiffened her spine. Whatever she'd allowed with her foolish heart, her spirit was unbroken. She unfolded her precious quilt and covered Zophia and Roscoe with it. The robes were heavy and warm;

but the quilt would be warmer. "We'll rest. Just for a bit, and then—"

"No," Zophia cried softly. "I'm sorry." With her finger she traced a piece of the intricate pattern on the quilt. It was a small crescent moon design—one of three crescent moons—as Maree had spotted so long ago carved into the trunk of the oaks. "I don't know if I can go on at all."

"Zophia, we have to."

Her younger sister looked so defeated. Cold and forlorn.

"Can you light a fire? Can you light one like Kallem did?"

She pulled a hard breath. She couldn't. For so many reasons, not the least of which was that Kallem could be very close behind them. Waiting for a slipup so he could attack. Capture. Again she cursed her decision to let the bastard live.

The compass had led them into a thick growth of forest— the thickest she'd seen yet along their trail. Trees grew tall and wide around them, their branches strong, full and somehow always reaching, fighting them. Clawing as they went. Tangles of bramble were all around. Alders grew thick where they could.

But that wasn't all Maree had seen, and she'd shown the signs to Zophia in an attempt to buoy her spirits as they'd traveled. She'd seen those same signs on the map. They'd almost reached it. As far North as they needed to be. The piles of white feathers. Dear God, hadn't they seen the cradle carved into the rocks? Hadn't she...hadn't she truly seen them? In her fatigue, she was second-guessing herself.

As she'd been lost in her thoughts, Zophia had been lost in her own. "I can't go on, Maree. Not now. I'm—"

"Oh Zophia, don't say it!"

"I'm not strong like you." The tears started to fall.

"You are! You—"

"No, I never was! I've been running for days. We've been running for days and avoiding the inevitable truth. That I'm just slowing you down now. And I'm...I'm the one the soldiers want. The bleeder the Prophet so desperately wants returned. Needs returned. They'll...they'll stop if they get me. I know this, know it like I know so much else.

"You go on, Maree. Climb this log and take this quilt and make it to Society Three. Make it for both of us. I'll stay here. Stay here and wait for the soldiers. If it's just Kallem and the other one, they'll both have to return with me to keep me unharmed from the Reprobates, which will give you even more time."

Maree's heart hammered against her ribs. Oh Jesus! "No!" Maree grated. "Zophia, think about what you're saying! A life as a bleeder, locked away and bred over and over by men chosen by the Prophet. Alone and locked up. And what will become of this daughter you're carrying?"

"He'll...he'll let her live."

"And for what? So she can grow up in a compound where her fate is breeder, whore or slave?"

Zophia cried all the harder. "I don't...I don't know. But I do know I can't do this to you anymore. You ran because of me. And now you're being hunted because—"

"Because there will always be enemies who hunt those who demand to be free! Those of us who rebel against the tyranny. *Against the dogma they use to keep us down!* That's why I'm hunted, Zophia. That's why *we're* hunted. Because we won't be broken—they may use our bodies and cast us out when they can't use us anymore. Make us villains in our own society because we refuse to be trampled by men—self-proclaimed holy men, or hellish men—who can tell the difference? So yes, they hunt us. They hurt us in the name of their God. But we fight on. We run on. Always."

"Then go," Zophia begged softly. "Go and fight on. Because you are stronger than I am, sister. Fight for your life."

There was a stirring in the thick woods beside her. Instantly, Roscoe was on his feet, his fur bristling on his back. Maree stood more slowly, quietly, but pulling her knife as she did so. She wouldn't fire blind in the dim light. But the knife, she could use if she had to.

"She may be right, Maree."

Maree heard the voice, low and soft and definitely female. She followed it and saw the hag standing there among the boughs and branches. The woman stepped forward.

"You can put your weapon away," she said easily, fearlessly. "You know I've not come to hurt you." Whining, Roscoe lowered himself to lie with his head upon his big front paws.

Sagging with relief, Maree put the knife away. "I'm Maree, and this is—"

"Zophia," the hag finished. "I know. We've been watching you. Oh, you've traveled so far. My name is Leola."

"Are you from Society Three?"

Leola smiled as she nodded. "Yes. We're from Society Three."

Society Three. The name rang like a chorus of Hallelujah in Maree's mind.

"We're...so tired," Zophia said.

"I know," Leola answered. "You've been running so long."

Maree dared to hope. Then, pausing, she dared to ask. "What do you mean, Zophia may be right?"

Leola came closer, her palms outstretched in a gesture of ease. "Maybe it is time for you to go on—keep going—without your sister, Maree. She's tired. She's grown weak and weary. She's slowing you down. She's become a liability."

Maree couldn't believe what she was hearing. And from whom she was hearing it. "A liability?"

"If you continue your quest with Zophia, will you make it? Will you reach us? Or will the soldiers get you both?"

"We travel together," Maree snapped, livid.

"But you'd have more of a chance if—"

"If what?" she spat. "If I abandoned my sister?"

"You could join us tonight! You're almost there. You've almost found sanctuary. But are you strong enough to leave the weak behind so you can grab it?"

Maree's eyes filled with tears. Truly hot with tears. "Strong enough? You'd consider it a strength to abandon my sister?" she whispered. "Never! I haven't found a sanctuary at all if I find it without Zophia. There could never be one if I left her behind. If I...if I left any woman behind to perish so I could be free."

"But she's weaker! She can barely walk any further."

"Then I'll carry her." Maree vowed. "I'll carry her and I'll fight for her. I'll carry her as far as I have to till we find freedom and a place of belonging. Where we can be safe! Free, dammit! And we'll keep going, together, one way or the other. That's the only way."

Maree fell again to the ground, embracing Zophia tightly, protectively.

"You have a decision to make," Leola said, crisply. "Society Three or your sister."

"That's no decision at all," Maree said. "I choose my sister. I will *always* choose my sister. And never a society where the weaker are cast out, or left behind for being in need. Never!"

"You'd *die* for her?"

"How could I live if I didn't?"

In the moonlight, Maree saw it: Leola smiled at the both of them. Her eyes sparkled. She turned to signal

More figures stepped out of the forest, from behind the fallen oak tree until a dozen robed figures stood there. They slowly lowered their hoods. Mostly women, a couple men, all opening their hands once their hoods were lowered, and smiling warmly as they moved to help Zophia, and Maree, to their feet.

"Welcome, sisters," Leola said.

"You're here. You're with your kindred. You've made it. This is Society Three."

CHAPTER 30

THE PROPHET hadn't heard the door opening. Hadn't heard any footsteps crossing the room to where he lay on the floor. But suddenly, there was a silhouette above him, dark against the blinding light aimed down at him. Oh God, was it a demon, finally come to take him fully down to hell?

But it was a man, not a demon who stood above him, cursing.

The Prophet covered his eyes with his hand. "Turn...turn the light off."

His order was ignored. Instead, the harsh beam of light swept over him—head to toe and back again.

There was a further sound of disgust. "God, Marcus! What the fuck are you doing? You're going to ruin everything. *Everything!* Sit up!"

Marcus? *Marcus?*

It took a panicked moment before he realized it was Swagg Keenan addressing him by this former name. Only Swagg would dare talk to him like that. Only Swagg could. Not quite his friend... No, not his friend. But he needed

Swagg. Swagg was his advisor. That thought swirled on the periphery of his way-down-deep mind.

"How many of these have you had?" Swagg swiped his hand across a table close to the Prophet's head. Syringes rattled down around him. Glass crunched against hard, stone tile as he stepped on the needles and ground them under foot. The sharp, grating sound was like chilling pins along the Prophet's spine.

"The needles...I need them for the pain." The Prophet's mouth was dry. He swallowed, then went on. "It's medicine. For the pain in my shoulder."

"The pain in your shoulder? You've got enough opkalaphine in you to knock a fucking horse out," Swagg sneered. "For Christ's sake, cover yourself!"

The Prophet realized his nakedness only then.

Swagg stomped across the room, pulled a cover from the unmade bed and threw it on him as he sat up, still on the floor. Swagg sat in a chair across from him. The Prophet's chair.

No, not his chair...*his throne.*

"Any word?" the Prophet asked. "Any word on the girl?"

"Which one? The whore or the bleeder?"

The Prophet licked his lips. "The bleeder, of course."

"Really? Because it's all over the fucking compound—hell, beyond this one fucking compound—that you're more concerned about finding that bitch, Maree, than you are that valuable breeder."

"She tried to kill—"

"Revenge?" Swagg roared. "You want her back to mete out revenge? Bullshit! Marcus, no one believes that. *No one!* You're falling apart."

"But—"

"Do you know what your followers are saying? They're saying that you were too close to the whore. You gave her privileges. Never once sent her to the soldiers to show her her place. That she was more than a whore to you. That you *fell* for her! That she rebuked you, over and over. Made a fool of you. Marcus, they're saying she broke your goddamned heart! People are laughing at you! You're more concerned with getting the whore back than the breeder, even though whores are as common as dirt. And breeders, you imbecile, are not!"

The Prophet's head swirled. "That's not true!" *Surely it wasn't! Couldn't be.* "I only want her back to punish her. To show the people that we won't stand for disobedience. For disbelief!"

"They're already starting to disbelieve, in *you!* And you know what that means! If they question the man, Marcus, they question the Testament! Then *The Order!* If that happens, we're done for."

"But how...how can they question *me*? I'm their Prophet; their chosen one. I wrote that testament by God's own..."

"You?" Swagg Keenan's laughter started out low, a chuckle the Prophet had to strain to hear. But it grew as he sat there. Grew to a roar. "*You* wrote the Ending Testament? *You* founded the Holy New Order? Holy hell, Marcus! *I* wrote those rules. Put them out in front of you and let you run with them."

The Prophet's throat ached. His mind whirled. He heard the words he feared. Recalled the whispers before they'd been crushed beneath his martial law. Before the inoculations. Swagg had told him...Swagg had shown him the words he should write, should know, but...

"You're a fool. You were a mouthpiece for my bidding, a salesman in shiny shoes. Not a prophet. Jesus, man, you sit up here on this throne and order your needles and bang your whores and know nothing of what's going on."

"No!" he protested, but his voice was weak. "I'm the Prophet."

"You're a puppet."

Swagg rose. Kicking the broken glass out of his way, he strode to the door and turned. "You've bungled this long enough. I'm handling it from here. When Marsh, Robinson and Aykroyd return, they'd better have both girls. I've left orders with the gate guard that they're to be brought straight to me."

"How did you know I sent...?"

"I know everything! I've bartered the bleeder out to another community. She can't return here. The whore will be killed, after the soldiers rape her, publically. Her head stuck on the highest post. We'll have order again. We'll put the fear of God into them. The people damn well will believe again. Or else!"

"No!"

"Yes, Marcus. And I suggest you clean yourself up. At least look presentable—that's why you're here, after all. Don't make me replace you. And Marcus, don't think I can't. A new puppet can always be found."

He slammed the door and again the Prophet's room was in darkness. But just for a moment, till a match struck and a candle was lit. *Liz!* He'd forgotten she was her, hidden in the corner where he'd left her. He looked at her in the candle's light, her mouth unsmiling, her lips unmoving. Her eyes full of knowledge.

CHAPTER 31

IT WAS Kallem who heard the Reprobates first, perhaps because his hearing was a little more acute than Robinson's.

They'd been traveling for about an hour and a half, moving at a much faster pace than Kallem had been able to when he'd had the girls in tow. He certainly hadn't had to slow down for Robinson. The old bastard might have decades on him, but he was tough as boot leather. At least his breath seemed to come a little harder than Kallem's. Perhaps that's why Robinson hadn't heard the Reprobates sooner.

Kallem had tapped Robinson's shoulder, then signalled for silence. They'd sunk down behind some nearby bushes, and Robinson had gripped Beau's muzzle to ensure he didn't give them away. The dog knew not to bark, but panting could just as easily betray them.

There were four of them, Kallem saw. Not enough to pose a significant threat to a pair of armed soldiers, even if one of the Reprobates might be packing Aykroyd's weapon now. But there was no way they could handle that many without discharging their weapons, and neither of them was eager to do that. Besides, the Reprobates were traveling on a course almost perpendicular to theirs and thus posed no immediate threat to Maree and Zophia.

They'd waited a good ten minutes to make sure there were no stragglers bringing up the rear. In the enforced inactivity and silence, Kallem finally had a chance to think. Not that his brain hadn't been fucking *exploding* with memories and images these past hours. The door that Maree had pried open a crack with the little bit she'd told him, had been flung wide. It was almost as though his lapse into unconsciousness had reset something in his brain.

But the need to stay mentally sharp and avoid blundering into hostiles—of which Maree now had to be considered one—had forced him to shelve the memories. Of course, he hadn't been able to clear his mind entirely. Bits and pieces kept breaking through. He'd found himself more than once with his hand on his blade, itching to use it on Robinson's throat.

He'd been going to leave the Army. Maree had still been there in Falmouth; he'd known that from his brother, Errol. She'd graduated high school and was attending university part-time, waiting tables at a restaurant. She would be turning eighteen within weeks, and he was going home to see if the crush she'd had on him at fourteen had survived four years of growing up.

Except he'd wound up in the program for the First Guard, which was supposed to be voluntary. Kallem knew damned well who had *volunteered* him. That cocksucker Robinson.

Kallem had told the fucker to his face that he planned to lodge a complaint about his horrifying ill-treatment of female officers. His mistake was in forewarning the bastard. The officers Robinson had victimized had paid Kallem a visit, begging him not to make a report, swearing they wouldn't corroborate any accusations he might make. Knowing they acted out of fear for their lives, he'd backed down. But apparently Robinson had seen an opportunity to kill two birds with one stone, removing a threat and taking revenge on Kallem.

Yes, revenge. What else could you call it? Robinson well knew how much Kallem despised his cruelty toward women, so he'd forcibly inducted him into the loathsome First Guard. Robinson must have been laughing up his sleeve all this while, presenting himself as a friend and mentor to a mind-wiped and reprogrammed Kallem. Steeping him in misogyny, harshly "correcting" his impulses to empathy. To mercy. Humanity.

Dammit, no wonder he'd felt like such a fraud inside, even as the Prophet recognized his loyal service as one of his *best* soldiers.

He'd been a good soldier once. He truly had, back when the world was different. But this...this was not soldiering. Bile rose as the thought of the things he'd done in service of the Prophet's army...

"Jesus, Kallem, you look like a man with murder on his mind."

Kallem blinked. Not murder. *Justice.*

He cleared his throat and stood. "Reprobates. It pains me to let them pass. They've been the bane of our travels."

"I'll bet." Robinson stood also. "I'm still looking to avenge Aykroyd. As far as the women are concerned, all these brutes ever see is dried-up old hags. And there you go, waltzing through with not one but *two* of the most fuckable females they're ever likely to see. I expect it pained them, too."

Kallem realized his hands had fisted and forced his fingers to relax. Yet he could not let the comment go unanswered. "The breeder is a child still."

Robinson snorted. "She appeared to have all the equipment to me. But you're right. She's too skinny and green. Now the whore...she's a different story." His gaze sharpened on Kallem. "Tell me you been hittin' that, son. If she believed you were helping her out, I can't think she'd mind spreading her legs for you. You'd be a fool not to take what you could get."

Kallem felt his face suffuse with rage. And yes, with shame. There was more than a little truth in Robinson's words, and Kallem hated him all the more for it. Jesus, hated himself. He *had* abused her trust.

But there was more to it than that, dammit. He'd loved Maree once, and some part of him had remembered that, right from the time he laid eyes on her as she'd entered the gates of the compound. And she'd remembered too. Had remembered all along. That's what had drawn them together, not some ugly transaction, not payment for bodyguard services rendered.

And now, he loved her again, but it was so much more real.

Robinson scowled. "Oh, Jesus, you're blushing like a twelve-year-old! She got to you, didn't she?" Robinson dragged a hand over his white buzz cut. "Jesus, Kallem, what have I always told you about being so goddamned soft?"

"Don't worry about me, old man," he shot back. "When the time comes, I can do what needs to be done." *Which is put a 9mm silver-tipped hollow-point bullet in your brain, you evil bastard.*

Robinson held Kallem's glare for a few measuring moments. "Okay," he said at last. "If you say so, kid. That's good enough for me."

But as they got underway again, with Beau leading the way once more, Kallem had the distinct impression he'd given Robinson reason for suspicion. He'd have to do what he could to allay that. He couldn't make a move on Robinson until he was confident he would no longer need a second gun, a second pair of eyes, a second lookout so they could spell each other off when they needed to sleep. Then, when the time came, he wouldn't hesitate. Robinson would never see it coming.

That time came much quicker than Kallem would have imagined. Within another hour, just as dusk was falling, they caught up with the Maree and Zophia.

"There!" Robinson said softly, going to the ground with Beau and holding his muzzle again.

Straight ahead, the women were stopped on the trail in a very dense part of the wood. A massive tree had fallen across the trail, and the two women were contemplating it as though it were an unscalable, uncircumnavigable obstacle. Kallem's heart squeezed to see the exhausted defeat in Zophia's posture and the anguish in Maree's.

Kallem drew his knife, careful to make sure it came out of its sheath silently. Robinson could not have made it easier, kneeling on one knee as he had. All Kallem needed to do was seize him in a headlock and draw his blade across the bastard's throat.

So why was his stomach churning? Why did his heart pound so, and sweat break out all over his body?

Because you thought of him as a father figure for all these years. Because he took such interest in you. Because you thought he was helping you become a better soldier in service of the Prophet.

But it was all a lie.

Kallem took a step forward just as Robinson raised his arm and pointed. "Look!" he hissed.

Kallem lifted his gaze to see a dozen or more figures come seemingly out of nowhere to surround the girls. They wore robes like the ones Zophia and Maree had taken from the hovel, and were all but invisible in the fading light. Society Three! They'd reached it.

Damn the timing. He'd planned to kill Robinson, then disarm Maree and Zophia and take them hostage long enough to show them Robinson's body and persuade them that he really was on their side, completely and unequivocally. But he couldn't do that now. Couldn't capture her and make her listen. If he showed himself now, wearing a soldier's uniform and without having had that conversation with Maree, he'd have a pitched battle on his hands. He didn't have a death wish, and he had even less desire to see any of these people hurt if it became necessary to defend himself.

No, he needed Maree to introduce him, to vouch for him. And no way in hell would she do that until he could make her listen.

But you could still kill Robinson.

His hand tightened on the knife.

Then pain exploded in his knee as Robinson struck it from the side. Another blow knocked the knife from his hand as he went down. Before he could cry out or hit the ground, Robinson grabbed him, controlling his descent. Instead of landing with a crash, he folded with a gasp.

"Be quiet!" Robinson hissed the words in Kallem's ear even as he pressed his own blade to Kallem's throat. "If you even *breathe* too loud, you're dead. Got it?"

Kallem had a feeling he was dead anyway, but he bit back on the shout of pain and rage that sought release. Jesus, he *had* to survive. Had to find a way to keep the promise he'd made to Maree to protect her and Zophia.

"Robinson..."

Robinson shoved his handkerchief into Kallem's mouth before he could get another word out, then produced a set of plastic zipcuffs. "I fucking knew that whore had you pussy-whipped," he murmured softly. "But you've always been a pussy, haven't you, Kallem?"

Clearly, he didn't want a response, because he grabbed Kallem and tried to roll him over. Instantly, new pain shrieked out over his nervous system. Christ, his ligaments must be torn to hell! Still, Kallem knew that if the old man got his arms together behind his back long enough to get the zipcuffs on him, he was finished. So he resisted. And when Robinson bent closer to leverage more power, Kallem lurched upward and headbutted him as hard as he could.

Robinson reeled backward, but the pain from Kallem's knee hazed his vision. Then Robinson was back, blood dripping from a cut over his eyebrow as he crouched over him with his blade.

Voices drifted to him now. Female laughter and buzzing voices, and they were starting to recede, as though the party were moving off. Shit. He should have shouted earlier. Except that would just have gotten a lot of people killed.

Dammit, he had to find a way out of this!

His heart jerking in his chest, breath puffing in and out through his nostrils, Kallem steeled himself to grapple with Robinson when he came at him. If he could get possession of the knife, or find his own knife on the ground, he could cut the old bastard down...

But Robinson didn't come at him with the knife. Instead, he stepped on the side of Kallem's injured knee and ground it viciously beneath his boot.

Kallem shouted, but the sound was muffled. Except in his mind. In his mind, his scream echoed around and around as blackness claimed him.

CHAPTER 32

ZOPHIA WAS sleeping peacefully—snoring, actually—the last time Maree had checked on her. Roscoe was bedded down at her side in the small room the hags had afforded them. Maree would join her later.

For now, she sat at the table in a small, dimly-lit kitchen. A small plate of food—delicious smelling, greasy dark meat and fall vegetables—was placed before her by a smiling young girl. The girl put the kettle on the stove and left her alone in the room. It was then that the weariness and the relief finally claimed her, right down to her bones. *They'd made it! They'd finally arrived.* She could hardly believe it.

Zophia had had to be carried. A beautiful young woman named April and an older man, Xavier, had carried her sister the rest of the way in a makeshift hammock.

Yes, a *man*! Maree had been shocked to see the men appear, then alarmed as one reached for Zophia. She'd almost pulled her knife from her boot before Leola placed a restraining hand on her arm. By Leola's manner, Maree knew the man meant no harm. And that he meant something to Leola.

Zophia, as tired as she was—who must have been profoundly exhausted not to have sensed the sisters and brothers of Society Three so close at hand—hadn't balked. She'd lain down in the hammock when Xavier bade her to. He and April had skillfully pulled her over the huge fallen tree. The rest of the camouflaged troupe had helped each other over the obstacle, and then the trek had begun. At the memory, Maree swallowed down emotion; the tears that would surely fall if she let them.

"Let them," Leola said gently.

Maree startled, partly because of Leola's soundless approach, but mostly because the other woman had clearly read her mind. "You're…you're…"

"An empath. Like your sister. We all have our gifts. Our talents within Society Three."

Society Three. Relief shuddered through her again.

They'd walked five miles or so past the fallen tree into forest so thick and foreboding, it seemed almost to belong to another world. Dark, but not sinister. And the hags traveled almost silently over the rough terrain and past the heavy branches; they traveled liked ghosts. As if they were one with the woods, moving within it rather than through it. Eventually, they reached open fields which they traversed more quickly. Then back into the forest, where they soon came to a small compound. A *very* small compound, compared to the one the girls had fled. From what she could see, there were just a handful of buildings, low to the ground and practically disappearing in the woods. And Maree knew it was another world indeed.

Though the hour was late, several villagers came out of the small buildings. Maree and Zophia were welcomed, embraced. Two children—a boy and a girl—both of whom appeared to be perhaps seven years old—greeted them shyly with fistfuls of fall flowers. Zophia, her strength restored somewhat, had risen from the hammock and marveled at the gift the young ones had provided. The kids moved on to greet Xavier with a hug, calling him 'Daddy'. Maree watched the gentle interaction, fascinated.

Suspicious.

"He's a good man," Leola had whispered to Maree. Leola had the scar. The tell-tale one from cheek to chin that meant she'd been evicted by her colony. Yet she looked so youthful, so alive. So free.

Maree nodded, reluctant to admit it aloud. Wary to admit it. *Once burned, twice shy?* Wasn't that the old expression her mother used to use? Though of course her mother had said it in a romantic context, which didn't apply here. But Maree had been so much more than once burned. She'd been torched to a goddamned crisp by every man that had ever crossed her path since the Holy New Order came in. Every single one of them. And by Kallem Marsh worst of all. She'd never trust a man—*any* man—again.

"Milk?"

Leola's query pulled her from her drifting thoughts. She cleared her throat. "Pardon?"

"For the tea, dear…would you like some milk for your tea?"

Did she? It had been ages since she'd had a warm drink. Tea? She hadn't liked it when she was younger back in Falmouth. At all. But there was comfort even in the promising aroma of it now as it steamed through the small kitchen. Again, Maree supposed it was a kitchen—it held a woodstove, two small tables and high cupboards. But there were also two small bunk beds in there. Leola caught her looking. Maree smiled. "Milk would be nice."

"We make use of every space," she said, as she poured the hot tea. The teacup was delicate, old and stained. Leola poured her own tea in an unmatched cup, one without a handle. "Every space and everything is appreciated. There is no waste here. We can't afford for there to be. And we don't want there to be...not after what happened with the old world—the world we once knew."

Maree suddenly felt uneasy, defensive. She shifted in her seat. "Zophia and I won't be a burden. We'll work. I…I can learn a skill. I'm strong. My sister will be strong again too. We can—"

With a gentle gesture, Leola quieted her. "No one is a burden here. We care for our infirm. We love our weak as we do our strong. And only those who feel as we do find their way here."

Maree took that first sip of her hot tea. She fought the urge to grimace as she did. It was definite; she still didn't like the bitter drink, but she couldn't deny the comfort in the warmth she felt sitting here with the hag, Leola. The cup was warm in her grasp, and that felt wonderful too. The second sip wasn't quite so bad. "But I was on course to find it. "

"Yes, you had the quilt's map. And you followed it well, persevering and staying together. You needed strength to get as far as you did—well beyond the physical. Always, just that little bit more to keep you going. And more still to keep you going with your sister." Leola sighed. "We all seem to have our challenges just as we reach the almost-there point. A last hurdle we have to get over. Who puts it there? Ourselves? The Goddess?"

Goddess. Maree blanched and her stomach clenched at the word. Such language was sacrilege punishable by a hideous death in the world that the Proph—the world that *Marcus Will Montag*—had manufactured. Those who disbelieved, or dared to believe in something else, something more comforting, were summarily executed. But not here. Not in Society Three.

Maree blinked, as something dawned on her. "It's not just a place I've been looking for, is it? All these years, I thought…"

"All these years you've *known*, Maree. In your heart, you must have known. It's so more than a place."

Maree supposed she had. And she'd found it. Fought for it. Fought for her sister. And as she sat there in the comfort of this world, she knew she'd fight for any one of her sisters here.

The brothers? Well, that might take some time.

As if beckoned by her thoughts, Xavier walked in. "Excuse my interruption," he said. "Just getting ready for first watch. Needed a few supplies."

"Of course. Come in, Xavier." To Maree, Leola explained, "We have constant enemies and thus we must have constant guards. Watchmen and watchwomen. Xavier heads that group."

"I can't believe you allow men here." The words were out of Maree's mouth before she could bite them back.

But Leola took no offense, in fact she only chuckled. "There are men who wish to be free too. Free of the oppressive worlds built by that puppet Montag, Swagg and the like. Some men ran and hid before the initial inoculation—Xavier was one of these men. He and his late wife, Goddess keep her soul. For some, like you, the inoculation didn't take effect. They balked at the horrible duties imposed by the Holy New Order and stole away from the compounds. And for a few, a rare few, the inoculation *did* work, but they nevertheless managed to change."

"No!" It was that last one that Maree couldn't swallow. Her body tightened. "They don't change—not the soldiers, not those in charge. Those who take us for their whores. For breeders."

Her words seemed to pain the beautiful hag, as they did Xavier who stood silently now.

"Haven't you ever cared for a man, Maree?" Leola asked gently. "If not after the inoculation—then before? Some of the young males were never poisoned with the needles. Yes, they lived in a society that was mind-warping, were brainwashed with the pounding broadcasts of the Cursed New Order's message, but there is goodness in some of them."

Cursed New Order. Maree smiled at Leola's words. No one here used the term 'Holy New Order'. They knew: there was nothing holy about it. There was power in renaming.

"Have you ever seen a soldier...?"

"Turn? Change?"

Maree nodded.

"No," Leola admitted. "It would take a strong man to resist that pull—not just the inoculation—and the first soldiers got many needles, not just one—but the ongoing indoctrination. They live and breathe in an environment where they are all-powerful. All-privileged."

"All damned!" Maree grated. *Kallem Marsh, Captain of the First Guard!* He'd used her. Lied to her. Made her care and believe. "Damn them all to hell."

At the thought of Kallem, a flood of worry swamped her as suddenly and thoroughly as if a cold ocean wave had knocked her flat on her ass. *Kallem Marsh was still out there. Potentially on their trail. If he found her and Zophia, he found this whole Society.*

"Leola!" she cried. "A soldier traveled with us! One of the Prophet's First Guard! If he followed us here—"

"We know." This time it was Xavier who answered. "Valentina sent word ahead."

"Telepathically?" Maree asked.

"Yes, many of the women here are telepathic to some degree. Some, like Zophia, outstandingly so." Leola's smiled was proud. "Nature is taking back. We are taking back—all of our skills. All of our gifts."

"Then you know I've put you in danger!" Maree felt sick. "Oh, God, if anything happens to you because I trusted him, because I let him live, I'll—"

"No," Leola said, her voice rising for the first time. "The Cursed New Order put us in danger. You brought no wolf to our doorstep that wasn't already lurking in the woods."

Maree watched as Leola stood. She moved aside a table and the braided mat that had lain beneath it to reveal a trapdoor in the floor, much like the one back at the small hovel wherein they'd found the robes days ago. Leola opened it; Xavier merely assisted her as she brought out the weapons: throwing knives and spears, and bottles small and large that could only contain poisonous potions.

Maree stood to join them. Accepting a long knife from Xavier's offering hand, she hefted it in her grip, testing its weight. The bulk felt easy. And the weapon felt like a part of her.

"And your soldier put himself in danger," Leola said. "If he comes to our home, we'll defend it. If he hurts one of ours, we'll hurt him."

"We'll kill him if we have to." Maree met Leola's glare as she made her declaration. "Defend the strong and weak. And our home. And each other."

Leola nodded.

Grim-faced Xavier did too. "You are a warrior, Maree," he said. "That is your gift."

She looked up to meet his gaze, then Leola's approving one. "This is so, Maree. Oh how I feel it in you."

Maree knew they were right.

CHAPTER 33

KALLEM CAME to with the memory of his own scream still reverberating in his mind.

No, not the memory of a scream. It was a brand new one.

The shock of waking with a gag in his taped-over mouth and his hands cuffed behind his back had sent him lurching to his knees. Or trying to. But the effort had caused fresh agony, white-hot and mind-shredding, to erupt in his knee. He'd subsided again, fighting the dimming of his vision, clinging to the tatters of consciousness.

Several minutes of deep breathing later—nose-breathing, thanks to the damned gag—he rolled over very gingerly and sat up. After working through another flare of pain, he dragged himself to the nearest sturdy tree. Bracing his back against it, he was able to grip its trunk with his hands and use his good leg to push himself to his feet. Or *foot*, rather. His left leg would bear no weight.

Leaning there against the tree, panting out fresh pain, he took stock of the situation.

It looked pretty grim, but at least he was alive.

Which raised a good question—why hadn't Robinson killed him? Not out of any kind of softness or sentiment, that was for damned sure. And he couldn't be planning to drag Kallem back to the Prophet as a prisoner along with the women. With his leg ruined this badly, it would slow them down too much. Besides, he would know Kallem would find a way to kill him before they got back to the compound, bound or not. Injured or not.

Maybe the General had intended for the Reprobates to find him trussed up and helpless. Now that sounded like the Robinson he'd come to know and hate. After the body count Kallem had racked up, the Reprobates would love to get their hands on him. If he fell into their clutches, the torture would go on for days...

His mind veered away from that line of thought.

At least Maree and Zophia had found what they'd sought. They were now in the bosom of Society Three. But Robinson was on their trail, with a bloodhound, no less.

They couldn't have been gone too long, though, thank God. Dusk had descended with a vengeance, but it was still too early for the moon and stars to offer much illumination.

Oh, God, he had to get moving! Had to catch up to them. Find them. Keep his promise to Maree!

Except he couldn't do anything, not in his present state. His ACL was definitely fucked. What Robinson hadn't done with his initial blow, he'd finished beneath the grinding tread of his boot. But the knee could be braced. He had ACE bandages in his pack, if Robinson hadn't taken it. But even if he had, he could still figure a way to splint the knee. Then, he could fashion some kind of crutch and get mobile. If nothing else, the military had taught him to improvise.

However, he couldn't do any of that until he had the use of his hands again. Right now, they were bound behind him in plasticuffs that weren't coming off unless they were sawn off with a knife.

What were the chances Robinson had left him any such tools? Nil, he supposed.

Unless...

Kallem started hopping his way toward where his rucksack lay on the ground. His knee screamed with every jarring hop, but there was nothing else for it. Reaching the rucksack, he turned his back on it and sat down. This time the jolt to his knee left him fighting nausea. It struck him then—he must not vomit! Not with the gag in his mouth.

His stomach lurched and his mouth watered, but he managed to fight it back down.

As soon as the nausea subsided, he groped behind him for the rucksack, wrestling with it until he'd shaken most of its contents out on the ground. Blindly searching the jumble, his left hand encountered what he was looking for—his sewing kit. The one he'd used to mend the bodice of Maree's dress after the Reprobate tore it open. And the one she'd use to fashion pants for herself and Zophia. God, it seemed like an eternity ago, though he knew it was only a matter of days.

He shook thoughts of Maree away and forced himself to concentrate on the job at hand. Awkwardly, he extracted one of several needles, then went to work on the cuffs. What he needed to do was jam the needle in between the roller lock and the strap so that the lock could no longer engage the teeth on the strap. Theoretically, that should work. It took an eternity and two more needles, since he kept dropping them, before he managed to get one wedged into the retaining block. Cautiously, he pulled on the strap and it gave a few millimetres. *Holy shit, it was working!* Applying more tension, he eased the cuff wider until he could pull his hand free.

Instantly, his shoulder sockets screamed with pain from having been rotated in that unnatural position so long, and his arms felt like they weighed a ton. Nevertheless, he lifted a hand to his mouth, tore the tape off and pulled the gag out. He then extracted the needle and shoved it into the retaining block for the other cuff, yanked the strap wide and threw the cuffs to the ground. "There, you fucking bastard!"

Ten minutes later, he'd fashioned a splint from two sticks and bound the whole works tightly with the ACE bandage Robinson had left behind.

Too bad he hadn't left a small axe, because the next order of business was improvising a crutch so he could ambulate without having to hop. If he had an axe, he could have cut a sizeable branch from any number of trees, one with a Y-notch to fit under his armpit. But lacking any kind of cutting tool, he had to make do with a shorter piece of deadwood he found on the ground. It was more of a cane than a crutch, but it was stout enough to support his weight.

He then sorted through his first aid kit to find the waterproof packet of extra-strength painkillers. He withdrew two pills and swallowed them with a swig of tepid water from his canteen. Shoving everything back into his rucksack, he headed off in the direction Maree and Zophia had gone. In the dark, with no visible trail to follow and no hound to guide him, he figured his best bet was just to stay on that northerly course, following the North Star. When the sun came up, he could reassess the situation.

Of course, he came to the obstacle of the huge fallen tree right away. With pain throbbing vividly in his knee, he considered circumventing it. Then he thought about all the roots and branches he could trip over if he did. Cursing, he leaned over the tree and dragged himself up and over. On the other side, he slumped to the ground, cursing and panting out the fresh red wave of pain.

Jesus, he wanted to rest already. No, not rest. He wanted to pass out again. Slide off into unconsciousness and away from the pain. But he couldn't. He fucking wouldn't. He had to reach Maree. Zophia too. He couldn't let anything happen to them.

He hauled himself up and started off again, moving as quickly as he could, which—dammit all to hell!—was considerably slower than he'd traveled with the women.

Anxiety clenched his stomach in an iron fist. What if he was too late? What if he couldn't find them?

Before his panic could spiral out of control, he clamped down on it, bringing logic to bear to rein it in. He still had time. The girls were now in the arms of Society Three. Robinson would not try to recover them in the dark. Well, at least not *this* night. He would merely track them to their village or encampment or compound, or wherever it was they were going. But seasoned soldier that he was, he wouldn't make a move on his targets until he'd learned everything he could about their security. He'd wait until he could breech it safely.

They would no doubt have watchmen. Or watch*women,* perhaps. And if they were smart—which they unquestionably were, having established this illicit Society and eluded detection for so long—they would have alarms, perhaps even booby traps, lurking at every approach. Robinson would need to study the encampment, watch their comings and goings, determine how many guards there were and when shifts changed. He would have to inspect the lay of the land in daylight, mentally mapping out the safe paths as used by the guards. And the old soldier would find out everything he could about Society Three to report back to the Prophet, Swagg, and the leaders of the other compounds. So they could try to destroy it.

Kallem knew this. He knew it because if he were in Robinson's shoes, that's exactly what he'd do himself. What he'd literally set out to do himself. Kallem had been trained by Robinson. And Kallem had been a *very* conscientious student.

Despite the jolting pain that every step cost him, he smiled fiercely.

He knew what he had to do.

"I'm coming for you, Robinson, you son of a bitch."

CHAPTER 34

IN A sleep born of exhaustion, Maree dreamed.

She was back home in Falmouth. It was the same Falmouth of yesterday—her house, the town. But she was not the same Maree Krystek she'd been all those years ago. Zophia was little again, the same inquisitive, beautiful, red-haired little girl who was always tagging along behind her. Their parents were the same as they had been before the Holy New Order. As ever, her mother was hurried and focused in everything she did, while her father pored over the email alerts that he'd never let Maree see when she was of tender years.

"That Maree's gone," her mother said abruptly, rushing up with a pile of quilts in her arms. She dropped them at Maree's feet before she turned and was gone. "And you know it as well as we do!"

"Oh look," her dream father said, turning to her now, for the first time acknowledging her presence. "The young Maree is gone now; Warrior Maree is here. That's the one we need." He pushed with his feet and the chair on which he sat slid back from the computer. Maree's eyes scanned the

screen down through dozens of subject lines, all displaying one word. RESIST, RESIST, RESIST.

She was startled by a sudden, loud pounding at the door.

"Zophia, no!" Maree cried, turning around immediately. But her sister either didn't hear her or chose to ignore the command. As if in slow-motion, Zophia punched in the code to unlock the door, she turned the handle, stepping aside just in time as the door flew open.

And Kallem Marsh came charging in.

Not the youth she'd known—he hadn't been locked in time in this dream of yesteryear. No, the Kallem who'd burst through the door was the man she'd known in a different way. The soldier with the X-shaped wound drawn across his tattooed arm. He crossed the room to her, his stride urgent, his eyes pleading.

In the periphery, and it barely registered, there was a low pitched background whining sound. Frustrating. Annoying.

Kallem stopped just short of Maree. And suddenly now in the dream, the other characters faded away, leaving just the two of them.

"Maree, you're in danger!" he said. "Let me help you! I can help you!"

He looked bedraggled. Tired. Sorry. All fucking wrong! She would not allow the smallest bit of sympathy.

"You're the one in danger, Kallem Marsh! You're the one we have to fear. And you'd better fear me!"

"Just listen!"

But Maree could listen no more. Because she could hear no more. The whining sound had grown steadily. Oh God, persistently! And it was all she could hear now. Kallem continued to talk, she could see his lips moving, knew the words were pouring out of him with urgency. But she couldn't hear a single word of the lies he spun.

Kallem grabbed her hand, and Maree looked down. She was about to use her other hand to slug him in the face, but she hesitated. There was something odd about the sensation of his grip. It felt strangely wet, warm, almost as if someone were—

Maree woke up to find Roscoe licking her fingers. She drew it back under the covers. "Roscoe, you mutt!" Though the room had started to lighten, it was still dim enough that Maree knew she had at least another hour of sleep coming to her.

He whined all the more loudly, adding a couple of urgent 'woofs' to the mix and nudging her in the side with his nose.

"Go crawl in beside Zoph—"

Maree sat up straight. *He would have gone to her first.* In the dim light of dawn seeping in through the room's window, Maree could see it. Zophia wasn't in her bed. Roscoe took two backwards steps out of her way as Maree threw back the blankets and shot across the small room. *Where was Zophia?*

Bathroom?

No. Roscoe would have gone with her to the outdoor latrine. Maree was sure of it.

She pulled back the quilt and her heart sank. The nightgown Leola had given Zophia to sleep in was rolled up by the pillow. Moving to the bedside dresser, she yanked open the bottom of the two drawers. Zophia's clothes—the cloak, the makeshift pants and tunic, all of it—were gone. Even before she glanced toward the door, Maree knew her shoes would not be there.

Zophia had left, and had taken pains to leave Roscoe behind.

That's what the whining was in her dream, she realized. Roscoe trying to waken her.

Cursing, Maree dressed hurriedly, pulling her hag cloak over the other garments. Worry gnawed at her as she imagined every possible scenario as to what could have happened, where her sister had gone. Oh, Jesus Christ! Of who could have taken her!

Had Maree pushed her too hard today? She wasn't physically as big or as strong. And she was pregnant. Was she lost? Disoriented out there somewhere? Oh, God, what if something was wrong with the baby girl she was carrying?

Maree's mind was racing as she reached for the door handle, but before she could turn the old-fashioned latch, the door opened.

Leola stood there, and Maree could see the worry in her face in the grey light.

"Zophia is missing!" Maree nearly shouted. "Roscoe woke me and—"

"I…I hoped that wouldn't be the case, but I thought—*I knew*—something had to be wrong here." Leola's tone was grim.

Of course she'd known. She was an intuitive, like Zophia. Maree stepped back to allow Leola to enter the cottage. "Tell me."

"I was on watch," the older woman said, "and I sensed something was wrong with one among us. I had to calm myself, settle, so I could ascertain the source. The moment I was sure it was Zophia who was in trouble, I came straight away."

Maree straightened. "She's in *trouble*?"

Leola wet her lips, then nodded.

"Where is she?"

"She's left the encampment."

Maree blinked. "Didn't the watchwomen see her?" she asked, her voice chipped with anger. "Didn't they try to stop her?"

"We come and go freely, here, Maree. This isn't a prison. If a sister or brother saw her moving among the houses or into the woods, they'd think nothing of it. Many women prefer the night, the moon's strength."

Maree bit back on her frustration. It wouldn't serve anyone to vent it. "I'm going after her," she said, heading toward the building's exit.

"As am I." Leola's stride matched Maree's.

Maree threw the door open and they stepped into the dawn, followed by a limping Roscoe. The eastern sky was lightening by the minute. "Can you feel where she is?"

Leola turned to face southeast. "This way…this way is pulling me."

"Wait," Maree gestured toward the dog. "See what Roscoe says."

Nose to the ground, Roscoe cast back and forth, searching for the scent of his beloved, adopted master. Then he took off, headed into the woods in the direction Leola had indicated.

Beside her, Leola gasped suddenly. "Oh, God, we have to hurry. We have to get to her before—" She stopped abruptly, put a hand to her chest as if it pained her.

"What?" Maree demanded. "Before what?"

"Before *he* does! There is a man somewhere…he'll harm her. And he's looking for her."

"*Her,* specifically?"

Catching the meaning, Leola nodded. "This isn't random. Not a Reprobate looking for any woman to victimize. This man wants Zophia. But Maree, he wants you too. Oh my Good Goddess! Maree, you're in danger too if you step into those woods."

Maree's heart thundered. *Kallem.* Not a Reprobate, it had to be a soldier. It had to be him. Again she cursed herself for not finishing him off.

Maree took off, following Roscoe's trail through the woods.

Leola's voice was low beside her. "We should go back for more warriors."

"Can't you alert them telepathically?"

"Most telepaths are still asleep—only a handful of us serve as watchwomen also. I can invade their dreams, but to awaken them is nearly impossible. We could go back quickly. Alert Xavier, and—"

"No," Maree said. "The man following me and Zophia may not know that we've reached you, Leola. That we've reached Society Three. If I find him, I'll kill him. Or he'll kill me. But either way, he won't find this place of sanctuary. Won't know that we have. I know this soldier. This pursuit won't stop until either of those things happen. One of us must die. But I protect my sisters. Every single one of them."

Even as she spoke the words, Maree knew even more strongly that she had indeed arrived. Society Three wasn't a physical place.

As Maree's logic sunk in, Leola nodded. "Okay. We'll—"

"We?"

"Yes, we," Leola said firmly. She adjusted the hood and the sleeves of her cloak. Somehow she adjusted her presence, and though Maree knew she was right there beside her, Leola blended in with the shapes and colors of the forest which were slowly emerging as the sun climbed further into the morning. And blended in all that much more as they continued, following Roscoe's progress through the thick forest.

Suddenly, Roscoe stopped at the edge of a clearing. Maree could feel more than see the bristling of the hair down the length of his back. But she knew the dog had spotted something. Spotted danger. His growl was low in his throat. Roscoe didn't lose one iota of focus as Maree caught up to him and placed a hand on his neck. She crouched down beside him, followed his gaze.

Zophia!

There she was, sitting on the ground beneath a tall birch on the other side of the small clearing. She had a piece of the tree's bark in her hand and a writing instrument of some sort. She looked pale in the grey light, troubled, and yes, sick. Maree was about to call out to her, about to run forward and wrap her arms around her. But at the last instant, just as she opened her mouth to call out, she saw the reason for the tension in Roscoe's vibrating body and the sudden menacing note in his growl.

CHAPTER 35

ROBINSON! AND he had her sister!

Oh God, the bastard had Zophia!

Maree felt the sudden shift beside her as Roscoe sprang forward.

Snarling, barking, the injured dog raced from the cover of the trees straight at Robinson. The soldier's eyes widened as he saw the charging dog. Maree prayed Roscoe'd get the fucker's throat. But just as Roscoe lifted off his hind legs to lunge for his target, Beau was on him. The two dogs were a tangled blur of fur and fury as they fought—but Maree's eyes were on them for only a second. Her glare shot to Robinson.

Distracted by the dogs, he still didn't know she and Leola were there. He was swearing, kicking at both animals. Though he still held the knife close to Zophia's throat, his focus was elsewhere.

Beau was besting the injured Roscoe, but with an agile twist, Roscoe was up and sinking his teeth into Robinson's left leg, just above the ankle.

"Fuck!" The General tore loose. In the dull morning light, the blood soaking his pant leg looked improbably vivid.

Then Beau was on top of Roscoe again. But Roscoe had won his mistress a chance. As Robinson bent to check his leg, Zophia dropped to the ground, rolling away from the blade. Seeing that, Maree made her move.

Every muscle in her body had been tensed like a piston ready to explode. As she broke from the cover of the trees and raced toward Robinson, she could feel it in her muscles, the buildup of power and desire so strong it was absolutely fucking primal. This man—this soldier—had her sister. Wanted to hurt her. Maree felt as if she could tear him to pieces with her bare hands. She wanted to—there *was* a warrior in her. And it was bursting forth. No, it was fucking *raging* forth.

She had her hand on her gun—Kallem's gun—in the robe's pocket when Zophia stood to face Robinson. Dammit! Her clear shot at the old soldier was gone. But she had her knife. Maree pulled it, held it firm as she sprang at Robinson. Clutching the power of it in her right hand, with a warrior's yell right up from her toes, she flew at him.

From the corner of her eye, she caught a glimpse of bloody muzzle and flashing white teeth as Beau sprang at her. Without taking her eyes off Robinson for a second, Maree swung the knife, raking Beau with it as she passed. The dog dropped away with a whimper and Maree launched herself at Robinson.

"Maree, no!" Zophia cried.

But Maree was already flying into Robinson, locking the bastard in battle. She flew into him with such force that she upended him onto the ground a few feet away from Zophia, who now crouched low, away from the fray, beside the bloodied Roscoe. Robinson's knife flew from his hand. His gun holstered, he couldn't reach it without releasing his grip on Maree.

Even in the midst of battle, Maree worried for her sister. Out of the corner of her eye, she could see Leola embracing both Zophia and Roscoe protectively, pulling them back from the battleground. Good. That was good.

Maree returned her full focus to Robinson and the need to bury her blade in his throat. Using her weight, she pushed it closer. But he had closed both hands over hers, and she couldn't bridge those last few inches. Sweat broke out on her body. With every ounce of her strength and rage, she battled to press the knife home.

But it was no use. He was stronger than she was. Her arms had begun to tremble. Slowly, Robinson took more and more control of that blade she held. Though she resisted, he managed to angle the blade upward. Millimetre by millimetre, the knife came closer to her face. She couldn't even rear her head back without losing still more control. Then, with an extra spurt of strength, Robinson forced the blade to her face and drew it down, slicing the skin from cheek to chin. Maree gasped with the shock of it, and he took the opportunity to reverse their positions, rolling her beneath him.

The mark of the hag, she realized.

Maree grinned fiercely even as her cheek flamed with pain. He probably thought he was breaking her by slashing that mark on her face. Hadn't they both been conditioned to believe this the greatest of a woman's insults? But if Robinson only knew, his action only made her stronger.

Robinson was sneering at her now, confident of victory, waiting for her to wilt, cry out in shame and pain.

He was a fool.

As he lowered the blade to her throat, she brought her knee up as hard as she could. Reading her intention, Robinson braced and shifted, but the blow struck him solidly enough to loosen his hand's control on the blade.

Maree yanked her hands from beneath his and rolled away. She had to release the knife in order to do so, but she still had the gun. She tasted blood—her own blood from the dripping wound on her face. But the blood she thirsted for was *his*.

His left hand shot out to grab her right arm before she could scuttle further away. "Not so fast, cunt."

"Your blood will spill yet, you motherfucker!" she said. She didn't have to possess second sight to know it—Maree just swore that it would be so.

"I don't like what's gotten into you." Robinson pressed his face close to hers. The man was powerfully strong. That left hand of his clamped around her arm like a punishing vice and she strained against him with every fibre of her pissed-off being. "Now I see what Marsh saw in you. Some men like their fucks to fight. His only problem was that while his dick got hard, his mind got soft. You'll find that's not a problem with me, whore. So will your sister."

Maree raged against him—with her body and with her spirit. "You'll be dead before you touch my sister," she hissed.

"Not likely." He released his grip on her left shoulder so he could two-hand the knife.

Maree knew she didn't have time to draw her gun, chamber a round and shoot the bastard. But she had something just as effective. Better maybe, because it would allow her to kill him more slowly after it took effect.

Maree slid her hand into the well-placed side pocket of her hag cloak and pulled out a small vial of dark clear liquid—one of several Leola had given her in the kitchen earlier in the evening. Splinters of glass jabbed into her thumb as she broke it in her hands. She slapped at Robinson's face, but he pulled his head back, just in the nick of time.

Robinson rolled away and jumped up. He backed away from Maree, raising the thick collar of rolled cloth at his neck as he did so. He covered his mouth and nose with his elbow. *My God*, Maree thought. *He's holding his breath!*

Robinson knew about the hag potion. Knew how to protect himself against it. He swayed on his feet, looking nauseous, at least momentarily. He was feeling it—but not nearly enough to be disabled. Barely weakened. Still, Maree jumped to her feet, her hand going for her gun. But experienced soldier that he was, Robinson had beaten her to it. His own pistol was aimed at her head.

"Don't try it," he said through the muffled cloth. The immediate effects of the potion had been lost in the morning's cool wind. Realizing this too, Robinson let the cloth fall. His grin struck impotent rage into Maree's heart.

Maree's eyes never left his as she gripped the gun in the folds of her robe.

"I'm going to need you to pull that gun out by the handle using just two fingers and toss it over to me," Robinson said. "You may have disarmed that pussy Kallem Marsh, but one wrong move and I'll shoot the gun right out of your hand. Then I'll let you watch as I shoot the breeder and this one—" he gestured to Zophia and Leola with his gun "—before I finish you off."

"I'll give you the gun!" Maree drew it out of her pocket as instructed and tossed it toward him. "Just don't hurt them. Take me. Leave Zophia; she's pregnant. And she's very weak. She wouldn't make it back to the compound anyway. But I'll go without a fight. Do what you want with me, Soldier. The Prophet wants me back. He—"

Robinson spat. "You're dispensable," he said. "The Prophet may want you back, but Swagg doesn't. He wants you dead. You're worthless now. He only wants the breeder. But I can offer him something more."

The gooseflesh rose on her arms at the implications of Robinson's words. "What do you mean?"

"I've found Society Three. I've seen a few kids—healthy young females. I can offer even more breeders. I kill all three of you here, make it look like the Reprobates did it—not one of those dimwitted hags will know the difference. Then I go back to the compound and tell Swagg I've found the whole Society. The soldiers I come back with will feast on the whores. The bleeders we'll take back to the compound. The rest we'll kill. So, suddenly you and your slut sister aren't so damn valuable anymore. Hardly worth the trouble."

"You bastard!" Maree cried. Her mind whirled as she tried to formulate a plan. She'd run at him, dive at him. Yes, he'd kill her, but Zophia and Leola could potentially get away. Have a chance at least to run, and warn the others.

Robinson chuckled. "Say your prayers, whore."

Maree's eyes were wild now, and she knew they were—she meant for them to be. Mad in the glow of the rising sun. Her breath came raggedly as she advanced—step by step—on Robinson and his gun. Closer. Closer still. Planning her moment—the very split second—to launch toward him. The potion was still on her hand from when she'd broken the vial. If she could just get close to his face.... "Prayers? To whom? Nothing could make me believe the Cursed New Order's self-serving propaganda! I'll die a disbeliever in your false prophet and the lot of you!"

"Glad to accommodate." Robinson steadied his gun, and took a bead on her head.

But as the shot rang through the clearing, something burst from the woods in a blur of speed and knocked Robinson on his ass again.

Kallem! He'd sprung out of nowhere and toppled Robinson, but Robinson wasn't out of the game by any means. The two men were locked in combat.

"Maree!" It was Leola's cry this time. But her cry seemed distant, somehow. Not in space, but in dimension. It was then that she looked down at herself, then that she realized—the warm wetness spreading across her stomach was her own blood.

CHAPTER 36

KALLEM'S VISION dimmed with agony, but he fought to hang on, fought to keep his grip on consciousness and on the neck of the furious Robinson wriggling beneath him. The bastard had almost blown Maree's head off! Unless Kallem could stop him, Robinson was going to find the gun that had gone skittering into the fallen leaves and finish the job.

Not a fuckin' option.

Kallem tried to tighten his headlock, but with his arm exhausted and trembling from having supported his weight for the whole pursuit, he couldn't muster enough strength to completely obstruct the flow of air or blood. Still, Robinson seemed to be weakening, and Kallem took heart. He'd pass out eventually. Or Maree would come and shoot him.

As soon as that thought formed, it struck him that Maree should be looming over them, waiting for her chance to knife or shoot or even kick the man who'd just tried to kill her. He risked a glance in her direction and his already pounding heart took a crashing leap.

Jesus, she was shot! Robinson had hit her. Another cloaked female—not Zophia but an older woman—attended her, but there was so much blood....

Robinson must have felt his distraction, because he chose that moment to drive his fist into Kallem's grossly swollen and severely abused knee. Just like that, Kallem was fighting the blackness again. Robinson started to slip free of his headlock. Kallem roared and tried to correct his grip, but it was too late.

Robinson was on his feet in seconds.

"You stupid bastard!" Robinson kicked him viciously in the ribs. "You dragged your crippled ass all this way just in time to see me kill the whore."

No! Kallem's heart thundered in panic. And the next time when Robinson's boot lashed out, instead of trying to protect himself, he grabbed that booted foot and wrenched. Robinson went down again, hitting the ground hard this time.

The gun. He had to find the gun. As Robinson wheezed out curses, Kallem crawled in the direction he figured the gun must have gone. Before he'd gone more than a few feet, Robinson was on him again, stepping on the injured knee once more.

Kallem gave a shout of pain and fought a surge of nausea. In an instant, his former mentor had him flat on his back, then sank down to sit astride him, pinning Kallem's arms to his sides.

"Goddammit, Soldier!" Robinson roared.

Kallem glanced in Maree's direction. She hadn't moved, he didn't think. Maybe she was already dead. No. He refused to believe that. She was passed out! That had to be it. He rolled his head to look at Robinson in the watery light of dawn and saw that his enemy had sized up the situation, too. He had to buy Maree time to come to, or for Zophia and that other woman to carry her off.

"Soldier?" Kallem ground out. "I'm no soldier. Not anymore."

"Huh! You were *never* a soldier!"

"No," Kallem agreed. "But that didn't stop you from trying to turn me into a killer, did it? Even after I quit the goddamned army!"

Robinson's body tensed a moment, then relaxed. "So you remembered that?"

"I could kill you for that alone." Kallem choked the words out. "The things I've done in the Prophet's service..."

Robinson pulled a knife from the sheath strapped to his thigh and snorted. "You couldn't kill an ant right now, Marsh." Robinson leaned forward, the blade grasped firmly in his hand. "I did you a fucking favor, you pansy-assed baby." The general was so close now, Kallem could feel the warm breath on his face. "If I hadn't invested my time in you, you wouldn't have survived in this world."

Kallem fisted his hands impotently. "I didn't want to survive in this fucked-up world. I wanted to *fight* for a better one."

Robinson shook his head. "What is wrong with you? You're literally throwing your life away. And for what? The life of a whore?"

Kallem scorched Robinson with his eyes. "She's not a whore! She's just a woman who got fucked over by the New Order. Like every woman did. And I could kill you for making me party to it!"

Robinson sneered. "Once a pussy, always a pussy, I guess. And now you're going to die over pussy."

Kallem swallowed convulsively. If Robinson would just move a little closer, maybe he could headbutt him before the old bastard slammed that knife into his heart. "I love her," he said simply, dropping his voice in the hope that Robinson would lean closer. "I love Maree, and I would do *anything* for her. Kill for her. Die for her. And I sure as hell would die before I went back to being what you made me into."

"I would die for my sister, too."

At the sound of the female voice, both Kallem and Robinson swiveled their heads to the right. There stood Zophia, clutching a 9mm pistol. It looked as big as a cannon in her tiny hands, but those hands were steady.

Robinson held out a hand toward her. "Now, missy, just put that gun down. Ain't no one gonna hurt you."

"I would die for my sister," Zophia repeated. "I'd kill for her, too."

Zophia pulled the trigger.

CHAPTER 37

"OH, GOD, Maree, you can't leave me!"

Zophia? Yes, those were her sister's words. Maree reached for them. Not to hold on to them, but to assess their meaning.

Zophia...had shot Robinson. Shot him! Her mind tried to grasp the nearly unthinkable. Where had her sister gotten a gun? Unless... Maree had thrown Aykroyd's gun into the woods when the Reprobates had attacked. Had Zophia found it? Taken it?

She was drifting away; she knew it. There was no longer any pain. And her sister—her safe, safe little sister—was calling to her. As if through a sound-muffling snowstorm. As if through a thick fog. As if on the other side of this wall between life and death.

"Maree! Maree, stay with me! Oh God, please stay with me!"

Maree heard the words, but it was so peaceful as she pulled away. Her mind, her soul.

But her body...strong arms were carrying her quickly through the woods. Xavier, she supposed. And Leola ran

alongside him. She was calling desperately to Maree too—
*Hang on, stay strong...we've almost reached the
healers...don't be afraid.*

No, she wasn't afraid.

Healers? Couldn't Leola see she was too far gone for
healers?

But...stay strong. Maree knew she was smiling. Felt the
turning of her lips, heard her own small chuckle amidst
Zophia's cries and the chaos. Stay strong.

She had been strong. Strong enough to escape the
clutches of the false prophet—the false world. Strong
enough to disbelieve in all that was wrong with the world.
Strong enough to secure the freedom of her sister, and the
baby girl she was carrying. Strong enough to fight. And she
had fought.

"Fight more," Zophia's words again, tear-choked as they
were. "Fight for your own life now. Fight for Maree."

"Fight for me." The male's voice broke in. "I just found
you, Maree. Just found myself. I can't lose you again."

Kallem Marsh.

There was an unexpected sadness there as she thought of
him—God, a hesitation. The soldier who'd betrayed
her...the man who'd saved her. Yes. Those memories were
there in the fog of her mind. Motionless, she weaved through
them.

Motionless? Had Xavier stopped running? Or had she run
out of time? And wasn't that...okay? Wasn't that justice
now that she should get this rest? Find this peace that called
to her on the other side of consciousness?

Maree felt Xavier laying her on what could only be a bed.
Then the others surrounding her. She felt their presence, felt
the press of hands holding hers. Someone placed a blanket
over her lower body. And someone whispered to her, "My
name is Ginger. I'm here to help. I want you to look at me,
Maree. Look at my eyes, dear child, as I..."

But she couldn't look into Ginger's eyes—her own eyes were drifting closed. And she could barely hear the voices now, the cries... Leola, Zophia, the beseeching words of Kallem Marsh—they were all fading.

There was a contentedness as she let them go. Then she reached, drifted, oh God—flew now!—toward the other side. Her battle was over. Her life spent.

Resist.

Maree saw the flash of the word in what threads of consciousness remained in her mind.

Resist. Resist. Resist.

"Do you understand, Maree, what it is I am telling you? What I've told you all along?"

Her heart clutched. "Dad?"

She was hearing her dad's voice now. Oh God, it had been so long, and if she took that final leap of faith, he'd be there.

"No, Maree! Resist." Her father's voice was commanding. "You've so much more to do. More to protect and fight for. Not just Zophia and her daughter. Not just Leola and the other women of this compound. It's bigger than this, sweetheart. Bigger than you and me and Zophia. Child of mine, it's bigger than any of us could have ever imagined. You must resist the pull of this peace for now. You must—"

"Fight on..." That whisper was her own. But was it too late? She felt Ginger's hands upon her, heard Zophia crying there. And Kallem Marsh begging her to hang on to this life.

Yet death pulled at Maree, warm and welcoming and utterly peaceful.

But so did life. More than ever now. Life pulled at the sister, the woman, the warrior.

This is Ginger. She's a healer.

And you're a fighter, Maree. A warrior. Now fight and war for yourself.

Death beckoned again, stronger still. It would be so easy to surrender to it. Resistance would be so damned hard. Too hard, maybe....

Oh, Maree, I can't lose you again.

Resist, resist, resist.

CHAPTER 38

THE SUN was slipping in through the high window on the other side of the room, brightening still further the whitewashed space. There was a moment of unfamiliarity, but just a moment. Maree knew this wasn't the first time she'd opened her eyes to those dazzling white walls—she'd seen too much of them in her fever dreams to have imagined them. How many dreams had there been? How long had she lain here?

Her head swirled with the memories, not just of battling Robinson, finding Society Three in her soul and in the world, but also flashes of the recovery. Ginger must have been at her side for most of that time, soothing her with those whispered words Maree couldn't comprehend. Laying her hands on her wound and over her heart, chanting, sending prayers around the room, to the sky. Maree frowned. There had been others, too. More healers—one just a small female child with eyes that looked as black as coal, among the group that chanted and prayed and anointed her forehead with a sweet-smelling oil. Zophia, Leola, even Xavier—these three had never been far away from her sick bed.

No, Maree thought. Her *recovery* bed.

And now, as the sun dropped lower, reaching down as if for the sole purpose of warming her, Maree realized she still was not alone. She raised her head and turned her gaze to the figure sitting on the chair at the side of her bed. Kallem Marsh, arms crossed over his chest, his heavily-wrapped leg propped up on a low stool beside him, dozed there in the chair.

Maree swallowed hard—torn between anger and something else she could not—*would* not—put words to. Tears filled her eyes and she blinked them back quickly. "Damn you, Kallem Marsh," she whispered. And she'd hold on to that thought.

She let her head fall back on her pillow.

But he was *here*. Which meant her sisters must believe he was not a danger to her. If they thought otherwise, she was certain he'd be far away—or dead—by now.

Kallem. He was the one who'd hunted her, yet he'd tried to kill his own mentor, his old commander, for her. He had been the one who'd endangered her life; the one who'd saved it. The one she swore she'd kill after all if she ever got the chance again. And now? How could she ever forgive him?

She put a hand to her pounding head.

"You're awake." Kallem's voice was gravelly.

Maree lowered her hand, met his gaze and nodded. She tried to sit up, but quickly abandoned the idea when she felt her injured abdomen protest. Kallem lurched awkwardly to his feet, or *foot*, rather. She could see he couldn't bear weight on his injured leg. Nevertheless, he made it to her side. Carefully, he put his arms around her and helped ease her up. But when he pulled back, she saw the pain etched on his face and the beads of perspiration that had sprang out on his brow.

"God, Kallem, sit down before you fall down."

He looked back toward the chair he'd been occupying a moment ago and the crutches propped up against the wall beside it. From the look of him, you'd think he was contemplating crossing a vast distance, not a few feet of polished floor.

"Here." She patted the bed. There was plenty of room on the edge of the mattress for him to perch.

He did just that, but to her surprise, he lifted his injured leg—God, it looked like dead weight—onto the bed, then swung his other leg up so he was sitting right beside her. Her shock over that development took a back seat to the fact that his weight on the edge of the mattress had sent her body leaning into him. He put his arm around her to catch her against his chest, then kept it there, cradling her like a piece of fragile china.

Oh, God, that felt so good. Good, but dangerous. She closed her eyes, tensing to gather her strength to move away.

"Don't," he said, his voice muffled above her head. "Just lie still a moment. Let my leg calm down."

She heard the pain in his voice, knew it wasn't all from his physical discomfort. She knew if she lifted her head to look into those dark brown eyes, she'd see something more. So she complied, focusing on letting the tension drain out of her body with her breathing. Except with every inhalation, she drew him into her, his musk, his breath... She stiffened again.

"Does it hurt?" he asked.

"No," she lied, but the word came out as barely more than a croak. God, her throat was parched. "Well, a little. But it's okay."

Kallem must have detected the hoarseness of her voice, for he swiveled his body to snag a glass of water from the bedside table. He handed it to her, pulling away slightly so she could drink it as he held it to her lips. When she signaled she was finished with it, he put it back on the table, then returned his attention to her.

Gravity required that she settle against him again, so she did. Maree could feel the tension in Kallem's embrace easing a bit. Adjusting. Probably just as he could feel it easing and adjusting out of her.

"I'm surprised they let you stay here with me," Maree said, suddenly. "Alone."

"A rare occurrence, I assure you." His voice rumbled beneath her ear. "Ginger is never far from your side. Hasn't been since they brought you here. But Zophia convinced them it was all right. That I could be trusted to take a turn watching over you. That I was..." His words trailed off. He cleared his throat. "I should go get Ginger," he whispered.

She felt him tense again, as though he were gathering the will to move away from her. Or maybe he just dreaded the pain his leg would give him when he got up.

"Wait, Kallem." She put a hand on his chest and felt the tension in him change.

"What?"

Maree licked her lips, knowing their sudden dryness wasn't due entirely to the fever she'd battled. "You...you risked your life to save me."

He didn't respond immediately. Maree found herself counting the heartbeats beneath her hand until he finally said, "Yes."

"Why?" Oh, Christ, she couldn't help it—the skepticism in her voice even now.

"You know why."

She realized her fingers had spread open on his chest and drew them together into a fist.

"You still don't trust me." His voice sounded so bleak, she wanted to deny it. But she couldn't.

"I just can't, Kallem. I can't trust any man. Despite everything—oh hell, *because* of everything—I just don't know who you are."

The silence in the white-walled room throbbed with pain. His, hers.

Then he pulled back far enough to look into her eyes. They burned dark, just as she knew they would. Worse, they searched her eyes and she knew he saw the tortured conflict there.

"Maree, I—"

"Don't." Maree's throat ached with tears she damned well was not going to shed. "I'm not in any shape for this."

"Of course." His body had grown tense again, and the light in his eyes had gone flat. "You're right. How *could* you know who I am? Hell, I don't know anymore."

"Well, would you look at the two of you!"

Maree startled at Zophia's voice, then gasped at the pain in her belly. She hadn't heard the door swing open, but she certainly heard her sister Zophia's exclamation at the sight of her lying there on the bed in Kallem's arms. And the giggle that followed.

Zophia glided to a stop beside the bed. "Did I come at a bad time, Maree?"

"Not at all. I'd say your timing was impeccable." Kallem disengaged his arm and swiveled, using his hands to ease the bad leg off the bed. He cleared his throat. "Could you pass me those crutches, Zophia?"

"Sure."

As Zophia circled the bed to fetch the crutches, Maree eyed Kallem's broad back. It spoke volumes. It was all she could do not to lay a comforting hand on it.

Maree's gaze never left Kallem as he carried himself swiftly across the room and out the door with the aid of the crutches he'd obviously become proficient with.

"His leg—"

"Robinson ruined it," Zophia said. She'd watched the former soldier's exit too, but now turned her attention back to her sister. "And Kallem refused treatment, other than allowing Ginger to rewrap it. He insisted that all the healers—all their energies—be focused on you. Ginger says

242

he's got a lot of healing and rehab ahead of him, and it still will never be right."

She felt a stab of guilt. Then shoved it away. Her need had been greater. For a decade she'd seen women go without, go behind, go after. It didn't work that way anymore. Not in this society.

"The dogs are better though."

Maree raised a questioning eyebrow at Zophia's impromptu announcement.

"There are animal healers here, also," she explained. "Most of them are animal husbandry experts."

"Roscoe made it?"

"Yes," Zophia said. "Beau, too. He's our dog now. Well, my dog. Seems this one's adopted me too."

Maree shivered at the memory of the way the two hounds had gone at each other, each in defense of their masters. "They must be very skilled healers."

"Maree, this Society...everyone has their gifts. My intuitive abilities have grown so much! But even so, I can't compare to Leola. She's amazing! Of course, she's been here much longer. And you know Ginger, the girl who did most of the healing?"

Maree nodded, smiling at Zophia's enthusiasm.

"She didn't even know how powerful of a healer she was until she escaped her own compound and came here. There are sisters who can take the plainest food and staples and make the most amazing meals to feed the whole lot of us. Only a few of the woman—gifted seamstresses—can sew our cloaks so powerfully well. Everyone who lives here, who belongs, has their gifts; it's just as Leola said. And you, Maree, are a warrior." Her smile faltered. "The warrior I almost lost. The sister..."

Sister. The word always made Maree smile. And she smiled even wider when Zophia lifted the blanket and crawled in beside her to claim the place Kallem had just abandoned. It was only then that Maree saw the tears that spilled from Zophia's eyes.

"Zophia?"

She wiped them from her cheek, then put her arms around Maree. "I'm okay," she whispered. "Does it hurt? Your wound?"

Maree hesitated. "Not like before. I'm healing."

"If you'd died, I'd never have forgiven myself!"

"Forgiven yourself?" Maree frowned. "It was Robinson who did this to me."

Zophia sniffled. "But it was me you were looking for. You would have been safe in bed if I'd not gone to the woods..."

"Why did you?" It wasn't a reprimand, but Maree had to know.

"I...I wanted to get a note to John-Ryder. I remembered what you'd said about writings on birch bark, and I just wanted to write him a letter—an explanation."

"Zophia, how did you think you were going to get it to him?"

She shook her head. "I...one of the girls I met the night we arrived, she told me that sometimes when the hags enter the compounds to barter, they take messages to the others there. I thought...I thought if I could get word to John-Ryder, he might try to come find me. He might escape, too. Or at least he'd be able to understand why I left like I did, without saying goodbye." Zophia was full-on crying now, and Maree stroked her head as she lay in her arms. "But my action almost killed you!"

"No," Maree said firmly. "That fucker Robinson almost killed me. That's it. And besides, I'm tougher than that. Silver bullet through the heart...that's the only way I'm checking out of here."

Zophia snorted a watery laugh, then wiped her tears away with the back of her hand. "God, Maree, they had to *operate* on you. Your wounds were almost fatal, more than Ginger and the healers could deal with. But there's a surgeon here. She was a medical student before the Cursed New Order. She's like you—the inoculation didn't take. But still, we nearly lost you. Ginger said you actually died while she was operating! It's a miracle that they brought you back. And it's all my fault—*forever!*"

"Nonsense," Maree said firmly. "You saved my life, Zophia. If you hadn't shot Robinson, he would have killed Kallem and finished me. Probably you and Leola, too."

She could feel her sister shudder, but Maree didn't know which thought prompted it: the memory of taking a man's life, or of nearly losing Maree. She didn't have to wait long for the answer. "I'd kill for my sister still," Zophia said in a low tone. "There's blood on my hands, I know, but there's no stain there. I did what I had to do. And I know I'd do it again, if I had to."

"I'm glad." Maree squeezed Zophia's hand. "But the gun...where did you get the gun? Was it the one I threw?"

"That's right." Zophia pulled back so Maree could see her grin. "When you told me to run ahead while you dealt with Kallem—"

"You sort of ran sideways," Maree said.

"Aren't you glad I did?"

Maree hugged her closely. "Very glad you did."

The quietness hung welcome in the room. They both knew these precious moments would be interrupted soon. Ginger would be in to check on her. One of the nurses would be in to change the bedding, the dressing on her wound. Take care of her. Leola would no doubt stop by. Xavier, maybe. But for now, Maree held her sister, and her sister held her back. This was what she'd fought for. What she had to fight for, still.

Suddenly, Zophia asked, "Did you feel that?"

Maree blinked. "I think...was that *the baby*?"

"Yes, that was her!" Zophia smiled, then laughed out loud. "That's our free little girl."

CHAPTER 39

KALLEM HARDLY had time to get back to his room, park his crutches and stretch out on the straw-stuffed mattress before someone knocked on his bedroom door.

Company. Great. Fucking wonderful. All he wanted was to be alone with this terrible weight crushing down on his chest. Maree didn't trust him. Wouldn't even hear him out. Not that he could much blame her...

The knock sounded again, harder this time.

Well, if they thought he was going to get up and greet them, they could think again. "It's unlocked," he growled. "Come in if you're going to."

The door swung open and a slender woman carrying a basket let herself into the room. Ginger, he realized. The healer.

He pulled himself up on his elbows. "I think you've got the wrong quarters. Of course, all the time you spent by Maree's side, I guess you should be able to find her room."

Ginger smiled, and the glint in her eye was unnerving. "It's not Maree I've come for."

He eyed the basket which he'd seen her carry to and from the infirmary. She meant to stay and work on his knee.

"We had a deal, Healer. Maree is still in pain and—"

"Maree is out of danger, well on her way to healing. While you, tough guy, are almost as bad off as the day you came to us."

He sighed. She was right about that. "Come back tomorrow. You can get started then."

"Tonight," she said, in a tone that brooked no argument. "You're going to have to stay on that pallet for a couple of days, Kallem. You might as well get your first treatment in so you can sleep away eight hours of your confinement."

What the hell? "Confinement?"

She laughed aloud, and the high, musical sound reminded him that she was a woman. "Don't worry. We won't actually tie you down. But I'm telling you, if you want functionality of that knee restored to anything approaching what it used to be, you'll comply."

Dammit. She was right. He *would* comply. He needed his leg back. Not that he imagined it would ever be the same. Hell, even if he had access to a skilled orthopedic surgeon like the military used to have back in the day, it probably still would never be a hundred percent. But he had to get back what he could. He couldn't—*wouldn't*—be a burden on this Society. If he were to stay here, he needed to be a strong contributor.

Maybe if Maree saw that, saw how much he could help...

He quashed that line of thought before it could go any further. Yes, he was going to have to demonstrate his worth, his trustworthiness. He would need to prove where his loyalty now lay. But it wasn't going to happen overnight. Winning Maree's trust was going to be a long road, and one he needed to be whole to walk.

"Okay, what do I do?"

"Let's expose that knee so I can work on it."

That was easily enough done. Ginger herself had slit Kallem's trousers to the upper thigh that first day, to access the knee and re-wrap it. He'd used a couple of safety pins to close the pant leg again, knowing it was premature to mend the seam.

When she'd removed his bandages, she stood back and looked at him assessingly. "Okay, take off your shirt now."

His hands went to the buttons of his shirt before it struck him that her order was a little odd. He frowned. "Ummm…why do I need to remove my shirt for you to treat my knee?"

"You don't." She grinned. "I just wanted a look at that upper body. Can't blame a girl for trying, can you?"

Kallem's eyes shot wide. "You're not…I mean…" He blushed furiously. "I thought you were a healer."

"I am." She lifted an eyebrow and tilted her head. "What else did you think I was?"

"Nothing. You can treat my knee now."

Her eyes narrowed. "Look, I know you were a soldier. I know what that means. Where most of us got one inoculation, you got hit with a bunch of them. You got brainwashed. But hear this, Kallem Marsh. I'm a healer, but I'm also a woman. I'm neither a breeder nor a whore, but I am a sexual being and I flirt. So does most everyone else here, eventually. Once they feel safe enough. Once they know that some jerk isn't going to presume that it means they're a whore volunteering to be used."

He swallowed. "Got it."

"Good."

She bent to her basket and retrieved a small brown glass bottle and shook it well. From it, she measured a quantity of liquid in a large spoon. "Open up."

He obliged, and she deposited the liquid into his mouth.

He swallowed and grimaced. "What the hell was that?"

She smiled. "Fish oil, ground ginger and turmeric."

He shuddered, tasting the hideous fishy aftertaste. "Why?"

Her smile broadened. "Natural anti-inflammatories. So is this." She bent to retrieve a Thermos—a precious commodity out here—unscrewed the cap and poured him a cup of gently steaming liquid.

"Willow bark tea." He recognized it, having been forced to drink at least two cups of it each day since he'd arrived.

"It helps with the pain. I'm sure you've noticed."

He had. "Thank you."

She adjusted his pillows so his head was up far enough to drink, and handed him the mug. He took a sip right away, grateful that she'd added honey to cut the bitter taste. Grateful, too, that it took the fishy taste away.

"Drink it up quickly," she advised. "You'll want to get it working for you."

"Yes, ma'am." He took another sip to show he was following medical orders.

She sat down on the edge of his bed and began treating his knee as he'd seen her treat Maree's abdomen. Her hands hovered close, never touching the skin. If he hadn't seen with his own eyes what Ginger and the others had done for Maree, pulling her back from the brink of death from acute sepsis with nothing more than their hovering hands and some herbal concoctions, he'd have dismissed it as quackery. But he couldn't now.

Besides, he could feel the heat of her hands. They couldn't have felt any hotter if she'd warmed them by a blazing fire and laid them right on his skin. He closed his eyes as she worked, and before long, he thought he felt an improvement.

"It feels better already," he said, surprising himself.

"Good," Ginger said, "because it's about to feel worse."

Just then, another knock came at the door, but the newcomer didn't wait for permission to enter. The door opened and a grinning young man stepped into the tiny room. Dragon. Kallem knew him; he aided the healers in their tasks. And right now, he was carrying a bucket.

"You can put that in the corner, Dragon," Ginger directed. "Then take the rags from my kit and toss them in."

Kallem lifted his head. "What's in it?"

"Frigid spring water," Dragon replied cheerfully. "Cold as I could get it."

Kallem returned his attention to the Healer. "Is that what's going to make my knee feel worse?"

"No," she answered. "Dragon is."

Grinning still, the young man cracked his knuckles, as if warming up for the task.

"Physical therapy," Ginger supplied. "While we need to keep you off your feet for a few days, you desperately need some range of motion work. Dragon is going to supply the manpower to manipulate your leg."

"Sorry," Dragon said.

"Okay by me. Whatever it takes." Kallem knew it was going to hurt like hell. He downed the rest of the medicinal tea and handed the empty mug back to Ginger, who placed it in her basket.

"Don't worry," she said. "I'll work the knee for a bit longer to give the anti-inflammatories a chance to kick in."

True to her word, Ginger continued doing her thing. Whether it was her ministrations or the stuff she'd given him, his knee was feeling distinctly better. But all too soon, she stood. To Kallem's surprise, she laid a hand on the biceps of Dragon's right arm. "Okay, big guy, time to put those lovely muscles to work."

Dragon didn't start or stutter or do any of the things Kallem would have done in his place. What he did do was waggle his eyebrows and flex for her, making her laugh. Then he sat down on the chair she'd just vacated as if nothing had happened.

Kallem blinked. Why would Ginger touch him? And why would Dragon respond so casually?

Ah, yes—flirting. Freely having sport with men. Fearlessly.

Maree used to do that....

The memory hit him like a ton of bricks. Suddenly, he was back there. Back in Falmouth, and he was seventeen and Maree just turning thirteen, and she was practicing her fledgling flirting skills on him. He'd pretended long-suffering tolerance, but the truth was, even then, he hadn't wanted her honing those skills on anyone else. And speaking of truth, her innocent efforts were far more effective than she could have dreamed. He'd lived in a state of guilty semi-arousal that whole year.

An excruciating stab of pain jolted him out of his reverie. For the next few minutes, Kallem had no room for anything else but the pain as Ginger showed Dragon several manipulations to improve knee flexion, knee extension and patellar movement. None of them felt good. A fine sweat had broken out all over his body before Dragon mastered them all.

"Perfect," Ginger announced. "Now, we'll need ten reps of each to start with. Think you can handle it?"

Dragon shrugged. "Sure."

Ginger laughed. "I meant him."

Kallem gritted his teeth. "No problem."

"Good. I'll leave the both of you to it. And afterward, Dragon, if you could wrap his knee in the cold bandages, I'd be obliged. Just make sure to put the plastic and the towel under it to keep the mattress dry. I'll be back in an hour or so to switch them out for a dry wrap."

With that, she left Kallem to Dragon's not-so-tender mercies.

"Sorry, man, I know this has gotta hurt," Dragon said, as he helped Kallem draw his leg up until it was flexed well beyond the comfort range. "Feel free to scream or cuss or whatever you need to do."

Kallem blew the pain out in a series of short puffs. "Thanks, I'm okay." And he would be. He just needed something else to focus on.... "Hey, can you talk while you're torturing me, or does it require your undivided attention?"

Dragon snorted. "I can talk."

"Then tell me about what security measures you have in place to protect the Society. I may be able to help you improve them."

Dragon lowered Kallem's leg, let it rest a merciful few seconds, then started flexing it again. "I don't think so." His voice was cold.

"Oh, but I can help. I'm sure of it. That was my bailiwick, as Captain of the Guard. You really have to think about your multiple layers of security like they're made of Swiss cheese. Every layer has a few holes in it, because that's the nature of things when you're working with humans. We're all fallible. But the thing is, even with multiple layers of security in place, if things line up just right—or *wrong*, I should say—then those holes in the various layers all align in such a way that harm can slip through. My job was to configure security so those holes never lined up."

"I'm sure you're very good at your job, Kallem. But that's not what I meant. What I meant is there's no way I'm going to disclose top secret security information to a—"

"Soldier?" Kallem locked his gaze with Dragon's. "How many times do I have to tell you people, I'm an *ex*-soldier! Even if I wanted to go back—which I sure as hell don't—I'd be a dead man."

"I was going to say newcomer." Dragon flexed Kallem's knee again, this time moving it a millimetre past the point of severe pain into searing agony. "We don't just hand that kind of information over the minute you join our ranks. But you're right. The fact that you were a soldier in the First Guard...that's going to take some time to live down."

Kallem dropped his gaze, forcing his indignation down. "It was a stupid thought. I'm just...I need to...." He shrugged helplessly. "I just need to contribute, somehow. I need to find a way to prove you can trust me."

"You will," Dragon said, his voice reassuring. "But I'd suggest you focus on rehabbing this knee first. You're not much use to anyone like this."

Kallem dragged in a deep breath. He was wanting things to happen overnight, but life didn't work like that. And he had a lot to atone for. He would do it, though. He would gain their trust. Maree's trust. "You're right. I need to learn to be more patient."

"Agreed." Dragon bent and retrieved something from the floor by his chair. "Given our conversation, this might be a good time to mention this little gadget."

Kallem looked at the metallic-looking circlet the other man held up. "What's that?"

"A leash, in a manner of speaking." Dragon did something and the circlet—oh, Christ, the *cuff*—opened up to make its nature known.

"Jesus, is that an *ankle bracelet*? Where did you get batteries for it? And radios to monitor it?"

"It doesn't require batteries, and the 'radios' are basically the empaths." Dragon leaned forward and clicked the thing closed around the ankle of Kallem's injured leg. "Any one of them will be able to fix on you, track you, know your intent. You understand?"

Kallem nodded tightly, reminding himself that until recently, he *was* the monster they worried he might still be. They had every right to monitor his movements. He'd do the same if their positions were reversed. He didn't have to like it, though. "Fine," he clipped.

"Don't even bother trying to get it off," the young man advised. "Only Leola or one of the other strongest empaths can open it now. I couldn't even pull it off if I had to."

Jesus, he felt like a goddamned dog. Leashed. Reprimanded. Okay, a pissed-off dog. Monitoring his *intent*? Christ, had Ginger known this was coming even as she'd flirted with him? He dragged a hand through his rough hair. There wasn't a fucking thing he could do about it. Comply. Wait it out till they trusted him.

Dragon nodded. "Okay, tough guy, ready for some extensions?"

Kallem sucked in a deep breath and blew it out. "Ready as I'll ever be."

CHAPTER 40

KALLEM STOOD—yes, actually stood—to resume stripping the bark from the piece of ash he'd been working with all afternoon.

It had been almost three weeks since his first session with Ginger, and his knee was much improved. He continued to do the exercises, and Ginger had added a few to help strengthen the ligaments. He was having much less of that back-and-forth drawer-slide movement that had punished his cartilage so heavily. He could even do some gentle pivot/rotation work, and the ligaments were holding up. He had to be pleased with that.

He was less pleased with his progress in other areas.

His gaze went automatically to Maree, who was taking advantage of the unseasonably warm October day to do her physical therapy exercises outdoors, assisted by Zophia. Kallem hadn't spoken to Maree directly since that day in the infirmary when she'd finally come around, but Ginger had given him periodic updates.

He'd actually come to like Ginger a lot. And he'd also observed something about her. She flirted the hardest with men who were already attached, no doubt because it was safe. Kallem could see why. The few men in the village were either too young, too old, or otherwise not a good match, and she was far too kind-hearted to give any of them false hope. Besides, Kallem was beginning to think she might prefer women. Homosexual relationships were banned as sinful in the Cursed New Order, but here, it wasn't even frowned upon.

What he'd learned from Ginger was that Maree was healing quickly, but the injury and the weeks she spent fighting the massive infection had taken a toll on her muscles. She was working now to improve the strength of the whole abdominal/back/pelvic area.

Realizing he was staring again, Kallem returned his attention to the staff he was working on. A quarterstaff, to be specific.

He'd cast about for something to do while he was healing, and found precious little. But when he'd found a supply of nicely cured ash saplings, he'd asked for and been granted a handful of them to turn into quarterstaffs. Now that his knee was so much better, he was going to start pestering Leola to let him start some martial arts instruction with this most ancient of weapons.

He'd just gotten back into a rhythm again when a commotion arose at the gates. Clearly, someone must be approaching, for a handful of villagers had rushed out to greet them.

Or help them.

The thought had him leaning the partially stripped staff against the porch rail and taking up his walking stick. Before he'd even gotten down the steps, a female began wailing and a man's voice shouted for a healer. Kallem put a press on and covered the yard quickly, reaching the gates just in time to see two somber scouts bearing a bloodied female on a litter. He recognized the scouts as Daniel Elias and Twila

Nelson. The woman on the makeshift stretcher he didn't recognize.

Ginger came hurrying up to them, placing a hand on the girl's bloodied head. Dragon was right behind her. The stretcher bearers paused so she could have a quick look. "What happened?" Ginger asked, even as her fingers searched out the evidence on the girl's skull.

"Reprobate attack," Twila said. "We didn't see it. Didn't hear anything, either. But when Kendra didn't make the last rendezvous, we went looking for her."

Maree and Zophia came jogging up.

"Has she been unconscious long?" Ginger asked.

"She's been in and out," Twila said, obviously taking on the spokesperson role for the team. "Looks like he hit her on the head with something, then sexually assaulted her."

Kallem's eyes met Maree's, saw the horror there. His fists tightened.

Just then, Leola and Xavier came racing through the gates, both of them shiny with sweat and breathing hard. Leola must have sensed the trouble and they'd double-timed it home. "What is it?" she called as she crossed the last few yards. "It's Kendra, isn't it?"

Ginger turned. "Yes. She has a head injury. We're about to take her to the infirmary."

Leola looked down at the still form on the improvised gurney and sagged. But in the next instant, she'd stiffened her spine, straightening to her full height. "Go," she said gently to Ginger. "Take care of the poor girl."

A crowd had gathered, but they parted quickly to allow the stretcher bearers to pass. Ginger started off after them, and several other healers fell into step beside her.

Kallem met Maree's gaze again, and this time her eyes were full of black rage. He imagined she saw much the same in his.

"Shall I assemble a hunting party?" Xavier asked.

Leola nodded. "Yes. And do it quickly. We leave in fifteen minutes."

As she turned, Kallem touched her arm. "I'd like to go with you. I'm a very good shot and an excellent tracker. And I've worked with both hounds."

She dropped her gaze to where his hand rested on her arm. He removed it immediately.

"Sorry, soldier, we're not quite there with you yet, and Xavier can handle the hounds well enough. Besides, your knee is not stable enough." She looked pointedly at his walking stick. "One awkward step on that uneven terrain and you'll twist that knee, undo all the work my healers and your efforts have done."

"But—"

"You'll stay here," she said sharply. Then, more gently, "If you want to help, you can do so by ensuring our settlement is safe in our absence."

Kallem bit back any further protest. "Very well." He glanced at Maree, half expecting to see a gloating expression on her face. But she was focused completely on Leola. He understood why when she spoke.

"I'm coming with you," she announced.

Leola looked like she was suppressing an exasperated sigh. "Sorry, Maree. I admire your courage, but—"

"You *have* to let me go with you. I know what that girl Kendra went through. I was almost raped by one of those bastards, too. He'd have killed me, if Kallem hadn't come upon us and killed him. Dammit, I *deserve* a spot on your hunting party."

Kallem was stunned, both that she'd tell these people what had happened and that she would credit him with saving her.

Leola's eyes darkened. "I'm sorry, Maree. Sorry that that happened to you, and sorrier still that I can't accede to your request. It's too soon. You're still regaining your strength and form."

Maree looked like she would argue the point, but Zophia put a hand on her arm. "She's right, Maree. You're a hell of a warrior, but you're not up to it yet. Just as Kallem's leg would slow the party down, your lack of stamina right now could do the same. Or worse, put someone at risk."

"Dammit!" Maree threw up her hands and stormed away.

Zophia grimaced. "She'll be okay," she told Leola. "She knows we're right. Or will know, when she calms down enough to think about it rationally."

Leola rounded on Kallem. "How about you, soldier? Would you like to swear at me too?"

"No, ma'am. But I'd like to ready the dogs for your party, if that's okay with you."

She looked surprised by the offer. Surprised and grateful. "Thank you, Kallem. That would be helpful."

Fifteen minutes later, a group of ten able-bodied women and men stood in the yard. Some of them Kallem knew to be seasoned warriors. At least two were empaths—Leola and one other. One was the male guard who'd helped carry Kendra home. Several others were also regular patrol. A few of the latter seemed pretty young to Kallem to be heading out on such an assignment, but he had to trust that Leola and Xavier knew their people.

Kallem handed the leash for Beau, the bigger of the bloodhounds, to Xavier. "You'll need a second person to handle the other hound, if you want to take both of them along. One straining bloodhound is more than enough to contend with when it's hot on a scent. No way could you hold two back."

"I'll do it." Dragon stepped forward to take Roscoe's leash.

Kallem handed each man an extra canteen and a collapsible water dish. "They'll run until they drop on a track, so it's up to you to make sure they pause long enough to drink once in a while. No point trying to interest them in food. And for God's sake, don't let them off the lead.

They'll leave you behind quicker than you can get the first cuss word out. Plus, it's your job to make sure they don't run off any cliffs."

Someone chuckled.

Kallem gave them a black look. "I'm serious. Once a bloodhound gets a scent, they'll follow it anywhere. I've seen cases where a fugitive walks right up to a cliff, then doubles back in their own tracks for a bit, then jumps sideways and scuttles off. When the dog comes along, it follows the heavier scent—the double-laid trail—right on over the cliff, if the handler isn't paying attention."

"Thanks, man," Dragon said.

"Yes, thank you, Kallem." Leola inclined her camouflage-hooded head graciously. "Maree, since you and Kallem both want to be of service, I'm going to ask you to act as sentries. There are rifles in the lookout and ammunition enough to hold off an army of unarmed Reprobates. I really don't expect an attack, but you never know. This might have been a ploy to get us to send a party out, depleting our numbers back here."

"Let them come," Maree said with obvious bloodthirstiness .

Leola almost laughed. "Perhaps it would be a good thing at that." Sobering, she turned to her group. "Are we ready?"

Ten cries of "Ready!" rang out.

Within another minute, the group had said their goodbyes to the villagers. The moment they stepped outside of the compound, the gates closed behind them.

Kallem looked at Maree. "Shall we?"

Her answer was to stride off in the direction of the guard tower, or what served as a guard tower. It was basically little more than a hunting blind in the tallest tree on the compound. Kallem picked up the other full canteen of water and sack of biscuits he'd thrown together and followed.

Maree climbed the rope ladder with more ease than he did, he noticed. His knee still didn't bend all that easily. But when she reached the platform, he noticed her hand go to her left side. Then she dropped it, clearly loathe to let him see that it still bothered her.

He levered himself up on the platform, then pulled up the ladder, stashing it in a wooden box obviously intended for that purpose. When he turned to check the station out, he saw the pair of rifles Leola had promised would be waiting for them. They were lying on the narrow bench that circled the tree and he covered the few feet of platform to examine them. One was a semi-automatic and the second was a bolt action rifle. Good combo. The semi was faster, but semis were prone to jamming. Good to have a more basic backup. The bolt action would be slower, since the bolt had to be operated between shots, but the biggest drawback would be manually reloading the magazine.

"Ever fire a rifle?" he asked.

Maree, who'd come to stand beside him, shook her head.

"It's a piece of cake." He gave her an orientation, showing her how to hold the rifle, how to sight, and explaining the semi-automatic action. "You'll have to cycle it manually for the first shot, but after that, you just have to release the trigger, then squeeze again. Until your clip runs out, that is. If that happens, just remove the magazine like this and shove another clip in." He demonstrated the action for her. "Again, with the new magazine, you have to cycle the first round, then you're good to go. Should be ten rounds to a clip."

She accepted the rifle from him, and then nodded at the other weapon. "Yours looks different." She looked closer. "It doesn't have a clip." She looked up at him. "Does that mean it's single shot?" She frowned.

"No. It's got an internal magazine that holds...I don't know...probably five shells. But you're right—it's not semi-automatic like that one. I'll have to operate the bolt action between each shot. That won't slow me down much. Reloading, on the other hand, takes longer."

"Five rounds, you say?" She reached behind her and produced a handful of chargers, each bristling with five lethal-looking shells. "These must be for you, then."

"Stripper clips! Sweet!" He took them from her, leaning around to see there were several more loaded and ready. "This is what we call a speedloader," he explained. "I can just shove that clip into the magazine, hold the rounds down, then pull the loader itself right out. The rounds are 'stripped' off the loader and stay behind in the magazine. It's a helluva lot faster than trying to reload the magazine manually. And easier on the thumbs."

She regarded him oddly for a moment. "You gave me the best gun, didn't you?"

Truth, Marsh, he reminded himself. *That's the only way forward now.* "Yes and no."

She lifted an eyebrow.

"It's faster, holds more rounds, and is easier to use, so yeah, you could say it's better. But the more automatic action a firearm has going on, the more likely it is to jam. That won't happen with the bolt action, so in that respect, you might say I've got the better gun."

She blinked. "What do I do if it jams?"

"We'll switch. I'll clear the jam for you, reload and then we can switch back."

"I need to know how to do it myself."

He nodded. "And I'll be happy to teach you. But can we do it another time, when the village isn't potentially under attack?"

She rolled her eyes. "God, Kallem, I'm not that tyrannical. I wouldn't make you stop to teach me something when we're under fire."

He held her gaze. "You're a *little* tyrannical."

Her lips quirked in a half smile, before she quashed it. "Okay, then, tyrant that I am, I demand to know everything I need to know about firing a rifle from a tower. I mean, it's gotta be different, right? Shooting downhill?"

He suppressed a grin of his own. "Good deduction. It *is* different. Basically, if you take a bead on your target the same way you would if shooting horizontally, you'd miss high. So aim a little lower."

"How much lower? Knees?"

"That's probably too low. I'd say aim for the crotch. That should get him dead center in the chest."

A slow smile spread across her face.

"What?" he asked.

"I was just thinking, if I aimed for their knees…"

Kallem laughed. "Yeah, that'd likely hit him where it hurts."

Her face sobered. "Anything else I need to know?"

Besides how much I love you? Jesus, how much I miss you? He cleared his throat. "No. But I should be on the other side of you, so we can both reach our respective ammo more easily."

They sidled around each other on the narrow platform. He could tell Maree had sucked in her breath to minimize the space her chest occupied, as had he, but her breasts nevertheless brushed his abdomen as she squeezed past.

The desire to lay hands on her—God, to crush her against him and kiss her senseless!—blindsided him, especially when she made that little gasp. But, dammit, now was not the time. Making a move on her when they were supposed to be protecting the Society was *not* the way to her heart. And the villagers—these people who'd harbored him despite his having once been a soldier committed to bringing them down—deserved better.

Kallem pivoted away from her, levered the bolt on his rifle to chamber a round, then leaned the weapon, cocked and ready, against the platform railing, and took a seat on the narrow bench. His knee protested, but he refused to stretch his leg out to relieve it. It needed a good flexing. His eyes scanned the land below.

Maree took a seat a few feet away, propping her rifle up on the railing as he'd done.

After a silence that seemed to grow more awkward by the minute, she spoke. "Your knee seems much better."

"Thanks. So does your abdomen."

She laughed, a sharp bark of amusement. "You obviously haven't seen it lately."

Awkward silence fell again at the reminder of that body he'd once known so intimately, but no longer had the privilege of seeing. Or touching.

It wouldn't be so beautiful now, he suspected. The damage done by Robinson's bullet, then the surgeon's knife, followed by infection the likes of which he'd never seen anyone recover from before. The scarring would be awful. And Kallem longed to trace every one of those scars with his fingertips, his lips...

More awkward silence.

A sound from below had both of them on their feet, guns in hand, looking down.

"Zophia," Maree said, putting her rifle down again.

"Toss the ladder down," Zophia called. "I need to get up there."

"What are you doing out here?" Maree asked. "You should be in the common room, with the others." All but the healers and the surgeon—who would be in the infirmary— were gathered there.

"You need an empath up here," she announced. "I volunteered."

Kallem examined Zophia's face carefully, unsure whether she spoke the truth or whether she'd just sensed Maree's discomfort with being alone with him. Whatever the case, her presence was welcome to buffer this awkwardness. He tossed down the ladder and she climbed it carefully. Then, he slid over to make room for her between him and Maree.

"So…can you sense stuff that's happening out there?" Kallem asked.

"That's the idea."

She folded her hands and closed her eyes. Kallem took the hint and shut up.

They sat silently for a while. Kallem, well accustomed to guard duty, let his gaze run over the intervening space between the compound fences and the forest even as he allowed his mind to wander. From experience, he knew the slightest flicker of movement out of the norm would yank him back. Of course, his mind went straight to Maree. He allowed himself to relive the soft brush of her breast against his chest, but this time he imagined acting on the impulse to seize her and—

"For heaven's sake!" Zophia huffed out a sigh. "Would you two keep a lid on it, please? How am I supposed to sense anything out there with you guys mooning over each other?"

Kallem blinked. *You guys, plural?* Had Maree been fantasizing about him, too?

Zophia gave him a hard look and he yanked his mind away from Maree and onto other things. Boring things. Practical things. Surprisingly, it wasn't as hard as he would have thought. Zophia's energy there between them seemed to calm things. It certainly diffused the awkwardness. Now the silence felt much more comfortable. Whatever the reason, the next hour and a half passed quite peacefully.

Then Zophia stiffened suddenly. Kallem turned toward her to see that her eyes had rounded in horror. "Something's wrong. Someone's been hurt. Oh, no, killed! One of ours. The Reprobate, too, or maybe several of them. But oh, one of ours!"

Maree and Kallem leapt up, scanning the horizon.

Zophia stood. "No, not here. A few miles off, in that direction." She pointed to the southwest.

Maree took Zophia's hand. "Who is it, Zophia? Who's been killed? Can you tell?" Kallem saw her hand squeeze Zophia's tighter. "Please, not Leola..."

"No...Brittney, I think."

Oh, Jesus, *Brittney*? She was one of the youngest of a handful of guards who did routine patrol duty. Had she ever been out on a special assignment like this? Zophia was speaking again, breaking in on his thoughts.

"There are other injuries," she said. "They're coming back now. I have to go down and warn the healers, tell them to make ready for incoming wounded."

Maree's eyes flew to Kallem's.

"Go with your sister, Maree. Do what you can to prepare. I'll stand guard until the others get back."

"Are you sure?"

"I'm sure. Sounds like the hunting party probably eliminated any Reprobates in the area anyway."

With a worried look, she disappeared down the ladder after Zophia.

As soon as he was alone, the recriminations started. He should have been with them. He might have been able to save that young girl.

Hell, he should have been training that young girl this past week. Yes, Reprobates were a fact of life for Society Three, all Societies, but there was a damned lot he could teach them. Firearms, hand-to-hand combat, knife work, martial arts, dirty tricks. Maybe it would have made the difference out there today if he'd spent a few days with the young patrolwoman.

He would do it, goddammit. And this time, he wouldn't take no for an answer.

CHAPTER 41

MAREE STOPPED only because Ginger insisted she'd had enough for the day.

It was a clear and cool fall morning, perfect for the grunting-hard work of physical combat training. Maree'd been working on her knife-fighting skills—a particular favorite of hers. And she hadn't been pleased when the healer had called her over from the training rings.

Maree wiped the sweat from her forehead now with the small towel Ginger handed to her. She'd been out since six o'clock this morning, working on maneuvers and learning techniques for the last three hours.

"You did good out there," Ginger said.

"Thanks. It felt good." Maree rubbed the back of her neck with the towel. Her hair was too short still to tie up, but it was plenty long enough to get soaked with sweat. "I'll be ready to go again this afternoon."

Though she'd been out of her recovery bed for weeks now, she still tired easily. But she wasn't about to let a little fatigue stop her.

Apparently Ginger was, however. "Not a chance, Maree. You'll be ready for more training when I say you are. And right now, I say you're done for the day."

"But you need warriors ready *now*."

"We need them strong. Healthy. Alive."

The statement silenced both women. As Maree's eyes shifted from Ginger's gaze, she knew they were both thinking the same thing. Or rather of the same one.

Brittney. The sister so recently lost in battle just a few short weeks ago.

Her cruel death was still felt throughout the Society. Maree had only just met her, but Ginger had known her for a couple of years. Had eased her, physically and emotionally, through a miscarriage just a few months ago. Leola had taken Brittney's death even harder. Xavier blamed himself. Maree couldn't imagine their pain. But even as newcomers, Maree and Zophia felt a loss of their own. And at the funeral, the two had felt the loss of the collective. Brittney's death was so wrong, another injustice served to them all.

Maree knew in her heart that if she'd been out there, she wouldn't have perished in the battle that claimed young Brittney's life. And she truly wanted nothing more right now than to rush back into one of those training rings and ready herself for the next time. But, begrudgingly, she also knew Ginger was right. It wasn't just about her; it was about them all. And each of them had to be as strong as they possibly could be. Maree picked up her hag robe, slid it back on, and nodded her acceptance to the healer.

"You can help Kallem instruct," Ginger offered. "But hands off. Nothing physical."

Maree eyed Ginger's coy smile. "No, thanks. I'll watch from the sidelines."

"Ah, of course. The better to study his...um...techniques." Grinning, Ginger walked away.

Maree walked over to one of the low benches off to the sides of the three training rings. Only then, when she sat down, did she realize how tired she really was from her workout. She lifted the glass water bottle she'd left out earlier, tilted her head back and drank. The water had grown a little tepid, but it tasted wonderful going down her parched throat. And when she set it down again on the bench and looked up, her gaze fell on Kallem.

He was working with a group comprised mostly of watchwomen and men, those who guarded the posts day and night. Most in this particular group lacked the sixth sense some of the sisters were graced with. Xavier was part of the group too, which surprised her a little. He was already highly skilled in his own right. Kallem was teaching them hand-to-hand combat. Guns and ammunition being so rare and precious, all watchers had to be prepared to defend their Society by whatever means they could. Maree knew the moves Kallem was working with now, flipping an attacker, then delivering a hard blow to the top of the head, preferably with an elbow. A good strike to the cranial cavity. The move could be deadly, if delivered with enough force.

One of the younger women cringed as he flipped her to the ground. Victoria. She was new to Society Three, too. Her hag scar—like Maree's—hadn't faded yet. Though she was a harvester, a crop worker, by gift, she was needed as a watchwoman also. More watchers were being assigned since the attack on Kendra. They all knew it; they all felt it. Reprobates weren't the only danger.

And defense was not the only sentiment within Society Three. There was a feeling of resistance growing. There was talk of it. In the evenings around the warm stoves in the various kitchens, Maree had sat with her sisters, and the few brothers. She could feel it in their words. Knew the anger was growing. And yes, she had no compunction about stoking it.

Every single one of those impromptu meetings had ended when Kallem had come in. People shifted from their seats and drifted away, one by one, until it was only Maree there with the ex-soldier. And then she had shifted away too. He'd hidden the hurt.

She saw a different kind of hurt etched on his face now as he flipped Xavier in another demonstration. Maree couldn't help but notice how much harder Kallem threw Xavier than he did Victoria and the other young women he trained. At least at first... Maree knew he would dial the degree of force up as training continued. It would serve no good for any of them to go easier on the women. An enemy wouldn't.

Maree felt a surge of resentment that Ginger hadn't ordered Kallem to stand down. On the other hand, his injury hadn't been life threatening. *He* hadn't lain in bed for weeks. He hadn't lost muscle mass or strength or stamina, apart from that one limb. If anything, she thought he'd developed more upper body strength. She found herself staring at his chest, his biceps, mentally measuring them against her memories.

Catching herself, she forced her attention to his legs, trying to gauge how they were holding up. Pretty damned good, she decided. Of course, the knee would be braced and wrapped under his combat pants. In fact, she wouldn't be surprised if it would always have to be braced and wrapped except when he slept. She'd overheard him yesterday telling Ginger he feared the knee was as good as it was going to get, and she hadn't contradicted him. Which meant the limp would never completely leave, nor would the pain.

He winced against it now. Kallem was working as hard as any of the instructors. More so, even. As if he was proving himself. Which was exactly what he was doing. Proving himself to Leola and the rest of the Society. To Xavier and the ones he trained. He'd been a soldier, and he'd rejected that life. And she couldn't help but think it too; maybe he was trying to prove something to Maree.

And God help her, it was starting to work. Not just the way he threw himself into it and worked harder than anyone else. But in *what* he was teaching them. She'd suspected that the skills he'd taught her and Zophia on their journey were minimal, and she'd been right. There was so much more! Yesterday, he'd wowed everyone with the martial arts moves he'd shown them with the sticks he'd made. Okay, *quarterstaffs*, as he insisted on calling them.

Maree watched as another young watchwoman took her turn charging at Kallem. He bent, using her own momentum to flip her onto her backside. As he pivoted, Maree caught a flash of the ankle cuff beneath his combat pants. It gave her an uneasy feeling, this device. But the Society would protect itself no matter the cost. It would only be removed when Kallem was completely trusted. That decision would be Leola's. And the leader had made it clear that it was a decision she wouldn't be quick to make.

Kallem Marsh had saved Maree; he'd endangered her. He'd made love with her like no man ever could. Ever would. He'd made her feel things so foreign, yet she longed to feel them again. Her eyes traveled upward, to see Kallem staring back, his gaze hot with yearning. She swallowed hard, stood, and walked away from the training grounds.

Trusting Kallem Marsh was a decision she wouldn't be making soon either. But she couldn't deny how much she wanted him.

CHAPTER 42

MAREE MADE her way through the forest. Stars studded the sky, but their lonely, distant brilliance was dimmed by the soothing wash of moonlight. She pulled her hag cloak closer, though she wasn't terribly cold. The layers of clothing she wore beneath her cloak, not to mention the pace she set, warmed her.

Near the river, about two miles from Society Three—the furthest she'd ventured since arriving with Zophia those many weeks ago—she stopped.

No, not stopped. *Paused.* She was ready, body, heart and soul, for what lay before her. She knew she might not survive this mission, but she was ready to die trying. She knew what she had to do. What desperate wrong she had to right.

She'd left a note for Zophia as she'd stolen out of the small room she shared with her sister and Zophia's precious, tiny daughter, Torree. The baby had arrived early—a good six weeks premature, according to Zophia's calculations—but she'd been a scrapper from the start. Maree had been alarmed by how small and delicate her new niece was, her skin nearly translucent, but Ginger had pronounced her strong and healthy. Nevertheless, the healer had made a sling for Zophia and shown her how to carry the premature infant next to her bare skin beneath her shirt. Nature's perfect incubator, she'd called it.

In retrospect, it had been a blessing, really, that Torree had come so early. Now Maree was free to do what she must, a task that grew more urgent with each passing day. Had Zophia still been pregnant, Maree could not have left her young sister to face the terrors of childbirth alone. Not just the fear of pain, nor even fear of death in childbirth, but rather fear for the child's health. So few live births happened these days, and of those who were born alive, few escaped the gene-warping effects of environmental degradation. Somehow—miraculously—Torree was one of the lucky ones.

Yes, Zophia would be frantic to find Maree gone, but both she and the babe were safe. Ginger would see to it. As would Leola.

Suffice to say Leola would not be pleased to learn where Maree had gone. Nor would Xavier, whom Maree was coming to accept. Maybe even befriend.

And Kallem...

Kallem Marsh would try to stop her, if he knew where she was going.

It was early December. The ground was frozen and hard, but no dusting of snow covered it yet. That would work to her advantage, Maree knew. No visible tracks. She could only pray that conditions would remain the same for the return journey.

If there was one.

She shook the thought away.

The cover of night was also in her favor. When she'd first arrived, Leola had told her that some women preferred the moonlight. And Maree could see that now. Hell, she could *feel* it. It was spiritual. So although she wanted to put as many miles as possible behind her this night before she took cover to sleep in the daytime beneath her hag cloak to avoid the sun's rays as well as detection, Maree allowed herself a few minutes' rest, just to stop and stare up at that moon as she stood by the river.

She'd follow the river southward for the next few miles. Amazingly, this river—this watershed—was beginning to recover too. Not completely; not yet. Mankind had exacted a terrible toll on every aspect of the environment. But nature was taking back. The ecosystem was cleaning itself, purifying the river's waters. The evidence could be seen in the occasional jump of a fish or glimpse of a river otter. When they'd first arrived weeks ago, Maree had even heard frogs, though they were silent now, hibernating beneath the mud. And she hadn't heard frogs in years and years.

The sisters of Society Three were helping, of course. Somehow, Maree had not been surprised to learn that just as there were healers of women and men, there were healers of other aspects of nature too. These women were extremely rare. One of the children back in the village—a shy, almost silent child—was such a healer.

A bird stirred overhead. An owl, she realized, seeing its shadow silhouetted in the moon's gleam upon the water as it flew over. Maree smiled at the majestic sight. At the majestic night!

She'd longed for this freedom for the last ten years. Now that she'd attained it, she would give herself these few moments within it. Dropping the heavily-packed rucksack, Maree sat on the ground and pulled her hag cloak around her. But it wasn't just a physical tucking of fabric. Maree tucked herself into it mentally, spiritually. She could do it as well as the more seasoned hags now, make this slight shift that rendered her all but invisible in the natural environment.

All was quiet. All was calm and still. And Maree was thankful.

Minutes later, she heard it—the snapping through the woods behind her. Unlike her own stealthy passage, whoever was coming wasn't trying to conceal their presence. It couldn't be one of the sisters of the encampment—they would walk quietly. Especially after what had happened to young Kendra. It had to be someone who didn't care if they were heard or not.

A Reprobate? Maybe the one who killed Brittney...

She'd kill the fucker.

Her body tensed, nerves leaping with adrenaline as she felt the person directly behind her. And felt him stop. The rucksack! Crap, she might be well-hidden in her cloak, but her pack was not. Stupid mistake.

As the man reached for the bag beside her, she made her move. And here, there was no mistake. She'd trained long and hard for this. With a sudden twist of her body and a thrust of both feet, she lunged and the man was down. Seconds later, Maree was on top of him, her blade at his throat.

Oh God, at *Kallem's* throat. He stared up at her wide-eyed for all of one second before he flipped her off of him.

They both bounced to their feet, staring at each other.

"Dammit, Maree. If I hadn't recognized you, I'd have thrown harder," Kallem grated.

"And if I hadn't recognized you, you wouldn't have had the chance to. You'd be dead." She put the knife away. "What are you doing out here, Kallem?"

He looked pointedly at the rucksack. *His* rucksack, once upon a time. "I could ask you the same thing."

She ignored his question. "I thought that cuff on your leg was to keep you—"

"My leash isn't that short!" He ran a frustrated hand through his hair. He was wearing it longer now, not soldier-short as it had been. Maree's own hair was growing back in. "Sorry," Kallem said gruffly. "This fucking cuff...I'm sick of it."

Of course he was sick of it. Maree felt herself soften. Then she fought that instinct immediately. "It's just till they're sure, Leola and the others."

"I'm like a damned pariah in this colony. And Leola—"

"You can't blame her, Kallem. She's the leader. She has to be sure she can trust you. Completely sure. Leola just isn't there yet."

He marked her with a cold stare. "And what about you, Maree. Are you there? Do *you* trust me?"

She fought the hesitation as she delivered him the truth. "I don't know, Kallem. I don't know that I ever can. You were once—"

He raised a hand to forestall her. "Yeah, yeah, I get it. I was once a soldier of the First Guard. The enemy."

"You were once that boy in Falmouth who left me!" The words were out before Maree knew she was going to utter them. And not just out. She practically hurled the words at him.

He looked shocked. Stunned, even. Well, that made two of them. But now that it was out there, she had no choice but to forge on.

"You were the one who left me and our families behind when all hell was breaking loose! And you never came back, Kallem Marsh. Even before the inoculation, you never came back for me!"

She saw him swallow hard. "I tried, Maree."

"Yeah, right. You—"

"Just listen, dammit! I've fought so goddamned hard to regain these memories! The least you could do is hear me out!"

His vehemence shook her. Her heart started hammering harder than it had when she thought he was a Reprobate approaching. "Go ahead, then," she said, with only the slightest tremor in her voice. "Say your piece."

He drew a breath. "I've never told anyone this. I was going to come back. In fact, I was going to come back the very night that Robinson delivered the first of the needles that turned me into his monster. His and the Prophet's."

Maree's held perfectly still, except for her pounding heart. "I'm listening."

"I'd found out the truth about Marcus Will Montag, the politician. And Swagg Keenan, the real manipulator. It was out there, of course—his misogynistic ideals, the way he perverted religion for his own murderous means. He had more than hinted at the extent to which he'd take the armies to protect his 'Holy' New Order. But what was I? Just a private. A grunt. A tiny cog in the military machine. But when the politician turned prophet as the world was crumbling around us, I realized how dangerous the man—the system—had become. And I wanted no part of it. I put in for release—I was waiting for it.

"Then I caught wind of the needles. From Robinson himself, no less. Swagg's biggest supporter. A month earlier, I'd confronted him for ill treatment of a couple of the female soldiers. And by ill treatment, I mean the bastard raped them. But the female officers refused to corroborate, out of fear for their lives. That's when Robinson arranged to get me assigned to him personally."

"My God, Kallem," Maree breathed, but Kallem didn't seem to hear her. His eyes looked inward now.

"I stood guard within their meetings often enough—though they were so powerful there wasn't much 'guarding' to be done. But I stood there as the obedient and blank-faced soldier, melting into the walls, oh God, into the madness of the corrupt plotting I listened to. The needles. The false epidemic that was being cooked up. Already a 'virus' was being introduced into some of the denser populations. Except it wasn't a virus; it was deliberate poisoning! Many people were getting violently ill, and those with compromised immune systems were dying. And Montag's media machine kicked into action, driving fear into the nation. The plan, of course, was for Marcus Will Montag to 'save' them. He delivered that 'divine' Ending Testament. Then he would deliver the medicine within that spoonful of sugar—the inoculations. That was to be the first wave, and the one that would catch many. And those who didn't take that first round of needles voluntarily would be forced to take the next."

"All for the sake of the New Order, the greater good," Maree whispered. That had been the Prophet's claim.

"But there never was a real pandemic. The drug's only purpose was to scrub minds, erase memories. And all that would be left were blank slates to be indoctrinated into Montag's New Order. Live his way, believe what he told them."

"You knew...even before."

"Robinson made sure I knew—I realize that now. He wanted me to know what was in store. He wanted me to resist just so he'd have more to break. I was determined to have no part of it, enlisted man or not. Waiting for discharge? Fuck that! I was through waiting for something that was never going to come. Instead, I planned to go AWOL. To get my ass the hell out of there and join the resistance. It was small, the resistance, but growing. Your parents were part of it, Maree."

Maree simply nodded. Since the night she'd nearly died after Robinson shot her, the night her father's spirit had spoken to her, she'd known. Of course, she should have realized it sooner. If she hadn't been so young, so self-absorbed back then, she could have seen it for herself. All those talks on the back stoop when she crept out to sit with him while he smoked the one cigarette a day he allowed himself. And the way her parents would put their heads together and whisper. She'd thought it was just the usual worries they always tried to protect their children from—money, food, medicine. God, she'd been so blind.

"I was on my way back to Falmouth."

Kallem's words ripped her out of her reverie. "Sorry...what?"

"I was going back to Falmouth. Going home."

God, could it be true? Had he really been coming back? "I…I didn't know."

"You couldn't have. And until the last few weeks, I'd completely forgotten about it myself. Once Robinson got a hold of me, the needles…I forgot everything. But these past weeks—it's all been flooding back in." He took her hand in his. "Maree, I wasn't coming back just to join your mother and father and the others in the resistance. I was coming back for you."

She didn't want to hear those words; yet, oh God, she did! Desperately. Maree studied Kallem under the moonlight. Studied the unmistakable depth in those eyes. The truth in them.

"By then, you were almost eighteen. Before…you were so young. Too young for what I felt for you. I left because I was too damned tempted to take what you so innocently offered. I couldn't trust myself. But I never should have left, Maree. I should have found another way. Waited, dammit. If I could go back in time, I'd do a lot of things differently. But I swear, I was coming back to you, and I was ready to desert my post to do it. I needed to know if there was still something between us, or the possibility of something. For all I knew, it might have been just a teenage crush that you'd grown out of, but I needed to know. And I never stopped thinking about you, Maree. Never stopped loving you."

She drew a shaky breath. "Kallem, I…"

He held a finger to her lips. "Robinson caught me the night I planned to desert. Hell, he waited at the base gates. And he laughed as he told me what was in store—as his minions strapped me to the table, gave me that first shot. The very first one delivered. Wiping my mind, destroying my soul. Turning me into the monster I was."

Tears stung at the backs of her eyes. Maree laid a hand on his arm. Immediately Kallem tensed.

"Kallem, I am so sor—"

"Don't say you're sorry!" Kallem gripped both her arms. "Just say I haven't gotten back too late. That there's still something between us. Even if only a chance of it."

Oh, Kallem. So much had been stolen from him. From her. From them. The wall around her heart dissolved like a sand castle in the face of a tidal wave. It was a terrifying feeling, but exhilarating, too. Quaking, she went up on her tiptoes, splayed her hands against his chest for balance, and pressed her mouth to his.

He crushed her to him almost violently then, kissing her with an urgency that blasted everything else from her mind. And, oh, God, his hands! They were running all over her body, sending shocks of desire rippling through her. Her own hands had been trapped against his chest when he'd caught her up, and she made use of them now, gliding them across his pecs then down his flanks. Some part of her mind registered that she'd been right; his upper body *was* even more magnificent than before.

He broke the kiss and surprised her by hoisting her high against him, arms wrapped around her bottom. "Say it, Maree." The hoarse words were half command, half plea, as he looked up at her. "Say we still have a chance."

She braced her arms on his shoulders, looking down into that fierce face. It was the face of the Kallem she'd known so long ago, yet, at the same time, the new Kallem. A man tempered by loss and suffering in an unspeakably cruel world. She wanted to burst into tears. Instead, she resorted to levity. "This can't be good for your knee. I've gained a few pounds since coming north."

"Stop torturing me, Maree. Say it!"

Her face was as serious as his now as she gazed down at him. He'd been coming back to her. He really had. She believed that utterly. She swallowed the lump of emotion in her throat. "Welcome back, Kallem."

His arms crushed her tight for a moment, and then he started lowering her to the ground. But he did it slowly, groaning aloud at the sweet friction of their bodies sliding together.

The low sound excited her. She couldn't wait for her feet to be back on the ground before kissing him again, so she bent and captured his mouth with hers. That sped things up. He practically dropped her back on her feet so he could close both hands on her head to hold her in place while he kissed the hell out of her.

They kissed for long moments, standing there wrapped in each other's arms. Maree marveled at the power of the desire building in her veins, coiling in her belly. What a gift he'd given her, helping her get past all the ugliness and cruelty she'd known to reclaim her sexuality. This sweet yearning, this carnal wanting—it was her birthright. Every woman's birthright.

Then he pulled away from her suddenly. Her momentary confusion cleared when he tore his coat off and bent to spread it on the ground. He straightened and met her eyes.

"Lie down with me, Maree." His eyes were eloquent in the moonlight. "Let me love you."

Her throat threatened to close up again, so she decided to let her actions speak for her. Undoing the clasp at her neck, she removed her cloak and tossed it down with his coat. At the flare of heat in his eyes, a thrill shuddered up her spine.

"You're cold," he said, clearly having noticed the shudder. "We don't have to do this. I mean, not here. Not now. If it's too cold, I mean."

She smiled. "Kallem, I'm the opposite of cold."

"Oh, thank God!" He started pulling his own clothes off, and Maree did likewise. In short order, they were standing there, naked in the moonlight, in nothing but their socks, and in Kallem's case, his anklet and a compression bandage around his knee. And, dammit, it *was* cold. This time, the shiver that went through her owed everything to the tiny breeze that skated over her exposed skin. But Kallem had the answer. He bent and picked up her cloak.

"Here," he said, draping it around her naked body and fastening it. "You can keep us both warm with this."

"Perfect." And it was. Making love to Kallem in the moonlight, wearing her hag's cloak. She went up on tiptoes to kiss him again, and he slid his arms beneath the cloak and pulled her close. Close enough for her breasts to press against his chest and her belly to bump his erection. She leaned into him, thrilling at the feel of him.

"I want that inside me." She dug her fingernails into his shoulders. "Now."

He had her on the ground in seconds. "I hope you meant that, because I don't think I have much foreplay in me."

"I'm not going to need much." She rolled so she knelt astride him, being careful not to bump his knee, then reached for his cock. He seemed even bigger than she remembered. But the thought didn't frighten her. Not this time. She knew he'd fit perfectly. Because she couldn't help herself, she pumped his shaft a couple of times, delighting in the velvety feel of him and the way his breath hissed out.

"God, Maree, you're so beautiful. I missed you so much." He filled his hands with her breasts, dragging his thumbs over nipples already grown hard. A sharp stab of delight went straight to her center. *Now. She needed him now.*

She positioned his cock at her entrance and bore down on him, impaling herself, drawing a cry from both of them. But instead of pain, there was only bright, dazzling pleasure. Seeking more of it, she began to move on him, rising, sinking, grinding. Beneath her, he met her motions, his hands on her hips. Then he curled up to catch one of her nipples in his mouth and suckled hard.

Maree threw her head back and came apart, her orgasm rolling over her in the moonlight. When it was over, her thighs were trembling and Kallem's cock was still hard as stone inside her. She could feel every inch of him, clenched tight in the dying spasms of her ecstasy. He'd held still for her, she realized. Held still so she could focus on her own pleasure.

"Maree?" His voice was hoarse.

"Yes?"

"Do you think you'd be okay with me on top of you?"

The question took her by surprise. Would it be okay? Or would she panic?

"It's okay," he said, reading her delayed response as trepidation. "On our sides is good."

He pulled her down to his chest and she straightened her legs so they could roll with him still buried deep inside her. She knew then, knew it would be all right.

"Keep coming," she urged. "I want you on top."

He paused. "Are you sure?"

"Kallem, I'm sure. It's you and me. I know you won't hurt me."

"Okay. But if it feels bad, we'll shift. You might have to smack me or something, though."

She tugged him and they rolled over. Immediately, that old claustrophobic feeling roared to life, but she pushed it down. This was Kallem. And God help her, she loved him. Maybe she'd never stopped loving him. She refused to let Marcus Will Montag, that pathetic excuse for a man, take this from her.

Kallem propped himself on his arms and rocked into her. "Oh, Jesus, you feel so good," he said.

"Mmmm." Maree focused on Kallem's looming presence above her. His form blotted out the moon, and she couldn't see his face, so she touched it instead, shaping her hands to it. He turned his face into her right hand and kissed the palm. She felt something inside her let go. And with it, she felt that sweet tension start to rise again.

"Is this okay?" he asked, rocking into her again.

"Very okay."

As he thrust into her, she let her hands slide down his neck to his chest. Yes, definitely more ripped, she decided, delighting in the changing textures as her hands drifted from smooth skin to crisp hairs to nipples. She felt his thrusts quicken and smiled.

She slid her hands up to his sides, then down to his butt. She had a sudden vision of what they must look like in the moonlight, her legs spread beneath him, the impressive muscles of his back, the white gleam of his buttocks.... She remembered how fascinated she'd been by that part of his anatomy even before he'd bared it. Suddenly, she found herself right there again, her excitement coiling tighter and tighter.

She moved her hands higher on his back. She knew he was trying to minimize the contact between their torsos so she wouldn't feel so helplessly pinned, and she loved him for it. But she was ready for more. "Come down on me, Kallem." She urged him down with her hands.

He stilled, his arms remaining rigid. "Are you sure?"

"I'm sure. I want to feel you against me."

He complied, and the sensation of his cool chest meeting hers and squashing her breasts gave her a shock she hadn't anticipated. A good one, not a bad one. When he resumed moving, he felt even more amazing inside her.

"Kiss me, Maree."

She did, opening her mouth to him. The thrusts of his tongue echoing what he was doing with his cock made her excitement coil even tighter. God, how much she'd missed out on all these years. But she was reclaiming it now. Reclaiming *everything*.

She closed her hands around Kallem's face and broke the kiss. "My arms. I want you to pin them over my head."

He stilled as he processed her words. "But that's what the...."

"What the Reprobate did. I know. What the Prophet did, too. Now I need you to do it, with love. And with my full consent. There's no taking in that."

She lifted her arms away and he pressed them up above her head, pinning them there with one hand. He was supporting himself with one elbow now, and he'd had to move up higher on her body. The result changed the angle of their joining. When he resumed moving inside her, against her, Maree gasped. "Oh, that's good, that's good, that's good!"

For long moments, there was nothing but the sound of their harsh breathing and their bodies coming together. She felt her orgasm coming closer and closer. She could feel his own excitement peaking too, in the tempo of his movements and the deep tremble she felt building in him.

"Come for me, Maree," he urged hoarsely.

She didn't need much urging. A few more grinding thrusts and the ecstasy exploded again, sending shockwaves of pleasure rippling through her. Immediately, he gave a stifled shout and pumped into her until his own orgasm took him.

CHAPTER 43

KALLEM PULLED Maree on top of him and settled her cloak around them. The ground's coldness seeped up through the impromptu bed of his coat and their other clothing, but he didn't care. Maree was in his arms. Her head rested on his chest, her breath warm on his skin. Her body felt soft and boneless and sated. And so infinitely precious to him.

He felt pretty sated himself. Not to mention happier than he could remember being since...well, *ever*. She'd believed him. Believed and forgiven. It was more than he deserved, more than he'd dared hope for. She hadn't said the words, but no way would she have made love to him like that if she hadn't forgiven him.

Smiling, he kissed the top of her head. "I love you, Maree. I mean, in case you somehow missed that."

"No, I didn't miss that." She drew her hands up onto his chest and lifted her head so she could look at him. "I love you too."

His heart jolted in a combination of joy and terror, but he couldn't have said which emotion was uppermost. "You don't have to say that." Oh, crap, that didn't sound right. "I mean, I *do* want you to say it, but I need you to mean it. If you're not there yet, if you need more time, that's okay. As long as you're ready to give us a chance, let me earn your—"

She put a hand over his mouth to stop the flow of words.

"You think I don't know my own mind? Marcus Will Montag tried to force those words from me. He couldn't. That part of me—at least my soul—the bastard couldn't rape." Even in the dimness of the moonlight, he could see the dangerous glint in her eyes. "Kallem, I've had my family stripped from me. I've been disenfranchised, enslaved, used and abused. But I rose up and stabbed my tormentor with his very own knife. I escaped with Zophia and survived soldiers and Reprobates to reach this place where women are not just breeders or whores or slaves of some other kind. Where we are gifted in our own ways. This place where a woman is free to choose and make her own decisions. I'm a free woman, Kallem. And dammit, I *do* love you. Freely and by my own choice."

"Jesus, Maree." He crushed her against him, pressing her face into the hollow of his neck as he blinked furiously. "Thank you."

Her arms dropped down to hug his sides. They stayed like that until he felt a shiver go through her.

"We should get dressed, I guess."

"Yeah. I know."

He released her reluctantly and helped gather their clothes. He was dressed again in thirty seconds, pulling his jacket on while she was still contending with her first layer. He frowned as he watched her. Then he dropped his gaze to the rucksack. As she pulled her cloak back on over her clothing, he hefted the backpack and slung it on his shoulder, surprised at the weight of it.

It hit him then, like a slap in the face. "Oh, Christ, you're leaving!"

She lifted her face to meet his gaze. "Yes."

He fought down panic. Maree was her own woman. A *free* woman, as she'd said. She could go where she liked, with or without him. "Where? I mean, I thought this was your ultimate destination. Leola—Society Three—your sister…"

"It is." Her voice had thickened.

"Then why leave?"

"I have to go back."

His blood froze. "To the Prophet's compound."

"Yes. I need to go back for Liz."

Kallem knew the woman she spoke of. The Prophet had used her sometimes, particularly when his attentions had put Maree in the infirmary.

"He'll take it out on her," Maree said. "He knows we were friends. He's always used that against me. If I wouldn't go to him without having to be dragged there, he would call for her and take his fury out on her. That's what he'll have been doing, every day and every night since I left."

"Bastard!" Kallem realized his fingers were balled into fists and forced them to open. "But if that's the case, Maree, she may be dead already."

"Maybe," she allowed. "But I don't think so. She's a fighter, like me. A survivor. But either way, I need to know. I can't go on living here, knowing that she's paying the price."

Shit. He could understand that only too well. Her conscience—her honor—wouldn't let her leave Liz at the mercy of the Prophet's depravity.

"But that's not all I'm going for," Maree continued. "I'm going to fetch Zophia's young man back for her. I'm going to get John-Ryder, so he can be a father to his child, a husband to Zophia."

John-Ryder… Kallem saw the boy instantly in his mind's eye, handsome face, wildly curly hair, clear eyes, kind soul. Knowing Zophia, he could see why she had gravitated to him despite his utter lack of status. With that hopelessly crippled arm, he was treated little better than the women. He could also imagine how miserable the lad must be, his heart broken, his love not just lost to him, but hunted by the Holy Order...

Yes, he could understand her mission. But no way could she go tearing off alone.

"No," he said. "You're not going anywhere tonight."

She stepped back, and he knew the hand that went into the pocket of her robe was now wrapped around the hilt of a knife.

"Don't try to stop me, Kallem. I love you and I don't want to hurt you, but I'll use whatever force I need to if you try to prevent me from leaving."

He held her gaze in the moonlight. "Maree, just listen, I—"

"Forget it," she said. "You're not going to stop me, Kallem!"

"I don't want to stop you." He held up his right hand. "Swear to God, Maree. I just want to delay you. If I'm going to come with you, I need to go back to the village, pack some more supplies. And maybe more importantly, I have to tell Leola. Otherwise, before my ankle bracelet and I got very far, she'd send her warriors after me."

"You would come with me?"

How could she doubt it? "Of course I'm going with you. You need my help." She started to bristle, and he forged on quickly. "For instance, how were you planning to slip unnoticed past the fences? That's presuming you can even get there safely, through the roaming bands of Reprobates and past soldiers who are likely still out there looking for you. I know how they travel; I can think like them! I know all the strengths and weaknesses of the compound. The layout, the sentries, the passwords and protocols. I know the secret entrances through which contraband gets in." He moved close. "Maree, I'm your best chance to get in there and get back out alive. To get Liz out. And to get back here

289

to your sister, who'll be devastated if anything happens to you. She needs you. Your niece needs you."

He saw from the set of her face that she was considering his words, and he held his breath. Finally, she spoke. "It makes sense, everything you say. But if we go back and tell Leola, she might insist on coming along."

"That's not a bad idea," he murmured, thinking about the possibilities. "Our chances would be a lot better if we had some well-trained warriors with us. And Lord knows an empath would be a definite plus."

"But I don't want to endanger anyone else! That's why I was leaving tonight without telling anyone. Kallem, they've already risked so much to help me and Zophia. I just can't lead any one of them into harm's way."

He looked down at her steadily. "They've been in harm's way since the moment they decided to resist the Cursed New Order," he said gently. "Don't you think they should be allowed to make up their own minds, as free women and men? And you know, if we had a bigger party, we could probably get away with quite a cache of guns and ammo. It might make the difference in the Society's future, being able to defend itself."

She sagged. "Dammit. Are you always going to use reason against me when we argue?"

Laughing, he lifted her off her feet and kissed her. Then he put her back down, threaded his other arm through the rucksack's shoulder strap so it settled onto his back, and took her hand. "Come on. Let's go blow Leola's mind.

Chapter 44

Maree blended into the place as only one who'd lived there could. Her heart hammered crazily in her chest as she moved around the compound, following the path she'd been summoned along so many times as the Prophet's whore. But this night, she came as the enemy to Marcus Will Montag.

No, I come as his reckoning.

Kallem had led them to a secret entrance near the back of the compound. He'd lifted a trapdoor that Maree probably couldn't have found even if she'd known where to look. Moss covered the door, and tree roots had been glued to it in such a way as to make them seem to flow seamlessly over it. Leola had eyed him assessingly. "This had better not be a trap, Soldier."

He'd lifted his pant leg to remind her of the anklet he still wore. "Search my mind, Empath. It's no trap. This is an emergency evacuation route for the Prophet and his council, and is known to only a handful of senior officers in the Guard."

She'd nodded once. "Very well. Give me ten minutes to get back to the main gates." With a kiss and a fierce hug for

Xavier and another hug for Maree, she'd slipped off into the night. Her role would be to distract the guards, showing her hag scar, offering two quilts for the females, accepting the taunts and torments of the soldiers as though she were a meek, vulnerable and pitiful outcast.

Xavier had stared after her a moment before complying with her order and jumping down into the tunnel. He was a watcher. And it was a gift that Maree had come to respect. The man could sleep so lightly that the smallest noise, the slightest change of scent in the wind or flicker of light in the distance, could awaken him. He knew the terrain around Society Three—made it his job to. Knew the paths. And Maree knew his love for Leola. Where she went, he went. Which was why he was here this night.

Maree, Kallem and the two remaining members of their party had followed Xavier into the tunnel, waiting ten minutes before emerging near the Prophet's personal kitchen garden, dormant now until spring. They'd parted company there, Maree going after Liz while the others focused on their assigned tasks. But not before Kallem pulled her close for a quick, urgent kiss.

"Be careful," he'd commanded.

"You too," she'd replied.

Now, she pulled the long robe tighter around her. No snow had yet fallen, and it was bitterly cold, both strokes of good fortune. No snow meant that pursuers would have a harder time following them. And the cold meant she could bundle herself and swath her face, hiding her identity and her hag scar in the process, without raising any eyebrows. She'd wrapped the dark scarf around her head several times, until only her eyes peeked through. She wore heavy gloves. Long stockings beneath her knee-length dress. Everything to afford disguise, and to afford advantage. There would be a price on her head, no doubt. For she was the one who'd gotten away. With the breeder. And yes, with herself—her soul—intact!

And now there was another soul to be saved this night.

Every fiber in her body tensed as she approached the first guard at the door. Though her face was covered, his was not. The guard's name was Quaid. Attentive. Alert. Many times he'd escorted her to and from her own quarters. Into this hell and back. There'd never been an ounce of compassion in the man. Never. Despite the bruises, the burns, the screams he had to have heard...

"Who is it?" He snarled at her. "What do you want, woman?"

Woman. He spat the word as if it were poison on his tongue. As if it were a curse.

She lowered her voice, graveled it. He couldn't recognize her—not yet. Maree hunched over, lowered her eyes as she feigned feeble and fearful. "I've come from the medic, Soldier," she said. "He...he sends a special order...a special potion for the Prophet. One he requested specially."

"Why didn't the medic come himself?" Quaid barked.

Maree pretended to flinch. One quick slice from the blade she had strapped to her thigh and this fucker would be dead. Her skills had been honed to deadliness in these past few weeks. Kallem had taught her much; her sisters had taught her more. Like the power in pretending weakness until the moment was right to strike.

"He...he couldn't come," Maree said.

"Attending to someone else?" It was a test.

"No, never!" Maree cried out, careful to keep her voice hoarse. "There is none more important that the Prophet. None more worthy—so the testament reads! The medic continues his work. Since that whore injured him, the pain...the medic continues his task of trying to take that pain away."

It was a gamble. But one Maree could make comfortably. She knew the man within that chamber. Knew his addictions. His weaknesses. Her knife blow might not have killed him literally, but—and she'd thought about this long and hard—it would be killing him in another way.

Quaid hesitated. "Show me," he ordered, gesturing to the basket she carried. Oh, how she'd hoped he would.

Maree carefully pulled back the cloth.

Do it, you fucker!

Quaid picked up the first vial. He held it up to the moon's light.

That light is mine, Maree thought.

"These vials are empty!"

"I...I ..." Maree sputtered.

He tore the basket from her. "What kind of game is this? What else have you—"

"No, don't!" she cried. But her cry only spurred him on. Of course it did. She'd been counting on it.

Quaid lifted the black velvet covering upon which the vials had rested and dug his hand into the cradle of moss beneath.

"What the..." He pulled his hand out. "It's burning!"

She could see it burning. Right before her eyes—the hand didn't shoot up in flames, but swelled up in blisters. It doubled in size. Pain and shock widened Quaid's eyes. He opened his mouth to scream, but nothing came out.

Because Maree shoved a handful of the moss from the basket into his gaping mouth. The tiny poison-laden stems bent harmlessly in her gloved hands, but the plant didn't bend harmlessly in Quaid's mouth. Maree unwrapped the scarf from her face, stared at the startled soldier, at the dying man.

"Don't fight it, Quaid," she said, locking eyes with him. "Give in, you fool, you have no choice. You're as good as dead anyway. Isn't that what you always advise the young girls when they're brought to the Prophet?"

He swung—feebly and fearfully—at Maree. She ducked his swing easily and grabbed his jacket. He was about to collapse, and she'd just as soon he do it under cover of darkness so she didn't have to drag him there. Unsteady on his feet, he reeled in the direction she'd pulled him, then pitched forward on his face. Without remorse, she watched him die. Painfully.

She slipped into the quarters, down the hall and easily past the unsuspecting secondary guards. If she'd gotten past Quaid, they had no reason to stop her now. After all, she was just a woman.

She knocked on the Prophet's door. And her adrenaline spiked as she waited. She was at the gate of her hell again. At the door to the den of the rapist. But this time, it wasn't as a victim. Nor as one summoned.

The door creaked open.

Liz!

Maree dared a glance up, but her old friend—her beaten friend—did not meet her eyes. She glanced at the basket. "He's over there," she said, her voice emotionless. Even without Liz's prompting gesture, Maree knew where to direct her eyes to see the Prophet. Still, she was shocked when she saw him. The Prophet—Marcus Will Montag—lay on his bed, facing the ceiling as he moaned. He was covered in his robe, but it was belted so tightly around his frame, she could see how emaciated he'd grown. He was pale, too, as if he'd not seen daylight in weeks. Months even. Since she'd left. He looked bedraggled, like a beggar. Worse than a Reprobate. Like a man beaten down. "Leave the basket by his bedside."

Liz turned away from her. Maree grabbed her arm as she did. The other woman turned slowly to face her, as if by the very grip she knew. Maree lowered the covering from her face.

Liz's eyes shot wide. "Maree!" she mouthed the word, half in disbelief. Her eyes scanned the length of the hag scar, but Maree felt only pride as she did so.

"I've come to get you out of here. We have to hurry. Others are waiting. Others are here! We're getting you out of here."

Liz's eyes filled with tears. "I...I never thought I'd..." Emotion choked her words. "I'm not sure I can."

He'd beaten her. Body, mind, oh God, but not her soul. Surely there was some soul left, longing to escape. Strong enough to escape.

Hooking the basket on her arm, Maree grabbed Liz gently by the shoulders. "You can. You must! Look what that man did to you. Look what he took."

"He...he took everything."

"No. As long as you can run and you can fight, the fucker will never take everything. You're my friend. You're my *sister*. I can get you out of here. We can get out of here together. But we must go now."

"I'm scared to try...scared to believe there can be anything else."

"Oh, Liz, I know they keep hammering that fucking *thou shalt not disbelieve* refrain at us, but this time, it's true! Every damn one of us has been pounded with that Ending Testament. You have to believe in this, Liz—a future where you can be safe. A world where you can live with value. Don't disbelieve that."

The Prophet stirred on his bed. "Liz...Liz, who is that with you?"

Liz jumped, startled. "Go," she whispered. "Go before he—"

Maree pulled the scarf completely from her face and walked over to the bed.

The Prophet's eyes widened, and in them Maree saw a strange combination of fear and hope. "Maree," he whispered. "I knew you'd come back to me." Then his eyes fixed on her scar. "Who? Dammit, who...hurt you? I'll have them killed. No one...no one was to hurt you..."

She touched the scar. "It doesn't matter now. No one will hurt me again."

Suddenly, he turned angry. "You tried to kill me. And you ran! After all I gave you! All I offered you! You ran and took the breeder."

"I took my sister!" The comment didn't seem to register.

"You were mine alone!" he said. "I was...I was good to you, wasn't I? Never shared you."

"I was never yours," Maree snapped. "Not the way you wanted."

"He never got your soul," Liz said, her own voice a whisper. "That was what he always wanted. You never gave that up."

"Nor did you, Liz!" she said.

Liz blinked as though processing what Maree had said, as if being brave enough to allow it. "You're right. I never did!"

Maree sat down on the bed beside the Prophet, settling the basket of needles and poisoned moss beside him. As if knowing their deadly potential, he tried to move away. Even without him being in a weakened state, she could easily have bested him physically now. Liz aided her as they tied him up. His hands above his head, his feet to the bedposts at the bottom. Liz gagged him herself. Maree pulled her knife—the one she'd tried to kill him with so many months ago—from under her dark robe. She held it to his throat. He cried. Tears streamed down his face. He fought for breath.

"I could kill you," Maree said. "I know about such things now, how to kill a man and how to be sure he'd dead. I could end you right here and now with one slash of this blade. But I'm going to let you live, Montag. Going to let you live so you can tell them all—you have no choice. Tell everyone Society Three is no myth. Isn't a whisper. It's a truth. And that we're ready to fight for what we believe in—freedom for our sisters. I'll let you live to tell them—"

"Let him die! And we'll tell them ourselves!" Swiftly, Liz's arm shot out. She brought her fisted hand down hard on the Prophet's chest, driving both of the needles into his heart.

Air. That was all the syringes contained. And all she needed to kill him. She locked gazes with Montag as she pushed the needles' plungers, watching his terror and disbelief bloom in his eyes and slowly fade as he died.

They left the needles, the basket with the poisoned moss, and the dead 'prophet' on the bed as the two women covered themselves and left the chamber. But before they did, Maree left something behind. The Prophet's own knife—the one she'd injured him with.

After all, shouldn't a snake return to its pit? The Prophet had been so proud of that knife and everything it stood for. The handle was a cobra's head, wide, twisting, ruby eyes set within its silver skull. The blade was the beast's tail, pointed, sharp and deadly. Yet somehow it still managed to look phallic as she cradled it in her hand. Then she lifted her arm and struck, driving the blade deep into the wall above The Prophet's bed. There. Maree smiled viciously and victoriously. She'd returned the snake to its pit. This was how she'd show them all!

Let them know she had returned. Warn them of it. Let it be her promise.

Let her be the demon in the soldiers' nightmares.

"The medic's supply was insufficient," Liz said demurely to the first guard. "We will return within the half hour. Let the Prophet sleep. He's...he's in such pain when he awakens."

The guard grunted as he let them pass.

As soon as they were out of sight, the two women quickened their pace, hurrying through the dark compound to the rendezvous point near the Prophet's winter-dead garden. Liz nearly screamed when she saw Kallem step forward from the shadows, but Maree hushed her.

"It's a trap!" Liz hissed.

"No, Liz! He's one of us now," Maree said.

Kallem showed his scar-slashed tattoo to prove it.

"It's true, child. He's with us." Leola, who'd ghosted out of the dark, laid a calming hand on Liz's trembling arm.

Maree almost wilted with relief to see Leola back, safe. They had precious little time before the Prophet's body was discovered. She had to tell them.

"The Prophet is dead," Maree said. "I know that wasn't part of the plan, but it...well...happened."

Leola's teeth gleamed in the dark as her smile flashed. "It might not have been part of the plan, but I can't say I'm surprised."

"Good," Kallem said. "I'm glad to hear it."

Maree breathed a little bit easier. "Where are Xavier and the others?"

"Jarvis and Kai are already outside the compound," Kallem answered. "They're in the woods with the hounds, waiting for us. As for Xavier, he—"

"Xavier is here."

They glanced up to see Xavier coming with another male in tow.

"Where's...where's Zophia?" the young man panted, his eyes fixing on Kallem. "This man said you were taking me to see Zophia."

"Patience, John-Ryder," Kallem answered. "You'll see her soon."

The compound was quiet as Kallem located the trap door. The troupe followed him through the tunnel, then into the ruined city. They traveled quickly and silently over abandoned streets to the edge of the woods on the other side. The dogs were there, placid as could be with their new handlers. Initially, Xavier had proposed slaying the hounds to prevent a K9-assisted pursuit, but Kallem had persuaded them that they could be an asset to Society Three, protecting the encampment. It had been a bit of a risk, but one that looked like it would pay off.

Leola set a hard pace. All but Liz carried a heavy burden of guns or munitions in their backpacks. Two soldiers had been slain in the acquisition of the weaponry. Maree slid her arm around Liz and helped her hurry along. John-Ryder, seeing Liz's exhaustion, slid his shoulder under her other arm. Maree knew then that Zophia was right about this young man. He was a worthy choice for her.

At dawn's first light, they stopped on a hillside, one Maree recognized from her own first days of freedom. They were miles from the compound, but their rest would be short and the race would not stop until they were back at Society Three. Soldiers were no doubt on their trail even now. And there were signs of Reprobates all around, though Maree suspected they would steer clear of such a large party, particularly one with men and dogs. But tired as they were, and despite the dangers, they were also full of hope. Three days' travel and they'd be back at Society Three. John-Ryder, tired as he was, paced ceaselessly, a look of dazed wonder on his face. All these hours after being told he was a father, he was clearly still coming to grips with the idea.

Liz slept by a fallen tree beneath a single quilt, one Leola had not left behind. It was all she needed. She slept easily. Peacefully. Jarvis and Kai bedded down to rest with the bloodhounds, the better to bond with them. Leola and Xavier wandered off by themselves—not far, but far enough to be alone together. And Maree found her own easy peace in Kallem Marsh's arms.

"Killing the Prophet," she whispered. "It was an act of war." She turned in his arms to face him. "We are at war now."

"No, Maree," he said. "We've been at war since that first needle. The first lie by the corrupt government—the false prophet. We've just never been this ready to fight back." There was steel in his voice; hard and cold determination in his eyes. "But now, the warriors are rising. Resisting. And you are among them, Maree. You are first among them."

Maree knew—she knew it with all her heart—that Kallem Marsh was right.

EPILOGUE

Swagg Keenan stood by Marcus Will Montag's side, looking down more in disgust than in horror at the syringes protruding from his skeletal chest. Montag's pale face looked hollowed and craggy, more from the months of drug abuse than the dimness of his chamber. *What a waste. What a fool.*

The soldier, Gomez—the one who, thankfully, had known enough to beckon Swagg himself rather than his commanding officer when he'd discovered the murdered Prophet—stood by the door. A smarter than average young man. This one would be of use to him. This one he would keep close, reward well.

"You saw them leaving?"

"Yes, sir," Gomez answered nervously, yet again.

"Two women."

"The whore, Liz and the other. I assumed she was one of the medic's servants. Quaid had let her through and—"

"And you didn't see her face?"

"No, sir."

Swagg picked up the knife from where it had been stabbed into the headboard above the Prophet's bed. Though the blade was bloodless, he wiped it on the bed's coverlet, as if to rid the piece of all trace of its bearer. He then turned the ornate knife in his hand, looking at the glittering snake eyes. He looked again at the deeply-embedded needles. There was no need for forensics here. No need to second guess.

Oh Maree, the favor you've done me! You simple little whore...

Swagg turned, hid the edging smile, and addressed the young man sternly. "Private Gomez!" he snapped.

The soldier had been at ease, but now he stood at rigid attention. The boy was terrified, so he waited before he spoke.

"Tell no one what you witnessed here tonight," Swagg finally commanded. "Not that you saw the women leaving. Nor that you found the Prophet dead, nor of how you found him. It's crucial, and not just for your own well being. It is necessary for the survival of the Holy New Order that you follow my command. Do you understand? It's to your own benefit to understand, Private."

Gomez looked at Swagg, understanding slowly dawning in his dark eyes. Brightening there. "Yes, sir."

"And do you understand why it is important that the Holy New Order needs your cooperation? Your silence? Your loyalty?"

Gomez nodded. "Because thou shalt not disbelieve. No one can. We can't allow it."

Swagg was more than satisfied.

He nodded toward the door. "You will be rewarded, Gomez. From this night forward, know where your loyalties lie, and you'll be rewarded very handsomely."

Gomez nodded his agreement. All traces of nervousness were gone now; he stood straight as he anxiously awaited Swagg's next order.

302

Now that he'd dealt with the soldier, Swagg's mind twisted around the events that must have unfolded here this night. Kallem Marsh had to be involved, the way they'd gotten in and out of the compound undetected. Montag's favored soldier sent out alone after the breeder and the whore to avoid embarrassment to his fragile ego. And now, Kallem had turned. The whore Liz was gone and so was that crippled boy, John-Ryder—it had already been reported to him. And the dogs were being searched for within the compound gates, but Swagg already knew they wouldn't be found. Soon rumors and gossip and questions would be circulating throughout the compound. They'd grow if he didn't do something to stop it.

But he always did something to stop the whispers.

He had to spin this. He had to spin it not just perfectly, but to his perfect advantage. He turned and motioned Gomez to him. "In the northernmost pen, you will find a new-born calf. Take this." He handed Gomez the Prophet's knife. "Kill it. Kill it with this knife to the back of the neck. But don't bleed it."

That would be the sign.

"Let no one see you do this, Gomez. Let no one see you going. You're a soldier; use your stealth. Use your command. A command, young man, that will only grow if you are loyal to me."

Gomez took the knife from Swagg and saluted. "Yes, sir." It was the look in his determined eyes—Swagg knew he would not fail.

As Gomez closed the door behind him, Swagg sat. He lowered himself into the overstuffed chair set at the head of Montag's bed. His angry hand gripped around the intricately carved armrest as he looked around the room. The elaborate carvings. The paintings. The low lighting that Montag had felt made his appearance all the more majestic. Swagg's frustration grew.

"Idiot!" Swagg spat his curse toward Montag's corpse. He slammed his closed fist on the armrest of the pompous chair. "A throne doesn't make a Prophet. Nor a king. *Power* does. Resources. Fear! And most importantly, you fuck." He leaned forward as if Montag could actually hear his words. "*I do.*"

Swagg sat back in his chair. He pulled a slender communication device from his pocket, one of no more than a few dozen on the continent that still worked. And only because he allowed it to work. Technology. Communication. Security. Medicine. Food. Swagg controlled it all. Power—it was all about power and domination. Always would be. And with women as a virtual army of slaves, it would always be his.

When the pandemics had taken so many men, shifting the demographic so suddenly, Swagg alone had seen the opportunity. The women had to be kept under control. Kept down. The Ending Testament had been his idea. It had been so easy to put the words into Montag's vapid head! And people followed the tall and charismatic man he'd been. As the world crashed around them, fearful people followed their false prophet.

"And the only thing more powerful than a prophet born of man, is one born of legend," Swagg mumbled.

The phone in his hand was clicking through. There was an answer.

"It's time," Swagg said, clenching the small phone in his hand. "Come to the Principal Compound at once. Be at the gates at dawn. I'll have the zealots waiting. Tell them you saw signs. Formations of stars; visions from heaven. Warnings from hell. Tell them to look for a slaughtered calf—they'll find it. And then tell them you are their new savior. One to replace the Prophet murdered by those who disbelieved. Murdered by those who must suffer."

The dark voice answered back through the phone. "I understand."

"And one more thing," Swagg said. "Tell no one that we're brothers."

The line went dead in his hand.

OTHER BOOKS

Subscribe to Norah Wilson's newsletter so you never
miss a new release.
She frequently does giveaways for newsletter subscribers
only.

http://eepurl.com/or4IT

Available from Norah Wilson:
Romantic Suspense
Fatal Hearts, Montlake Romance
Every Breath She Takes, Montlake Romance
Guarding Suzannah, *Serve and Protect #1*
Saving Grace, *Serve and Protect #2*
Protecting Paige, *Serve and Protect #3*
Needing Nita, *Serve and Protect - free novella*
Serve and Protect Box Set
In Harm's Way (multi-author box set)
Paranormal Romance
The Merzetti Effect—A Vampire Romance, #1
Nightfall—A Vampire Romance, #2

Dix Dodd Mysteries by N.L. Wilson
The Case of the Flashing Fashion Queen (#1)
Family Jewels (#2)
Death by Cuddle Club (#3)
A Moment on the Lips (a Dix Dodd short story)
Covering Her Assets (#4)
Check out Dix Dodd's website: http://www.dixdodd.com

Other books by the writing team of Wilson/Doherty
Young Adult
Comes the Night *(Casters, #1)*
Enter the Night *(Casters, #2)*
Embrace the Night *(Casters, #3)*
Forever the Night *(Casters, #4)*
Casters Series Box Set *(#1-3)*
Read about the Casters series at
http://castersthebooks.com
Ashlyn's Radio
The Summoning (Gatekeepers, #1)

ABOUT THE AUTHORS

NORAH WILSON is a USA Today bestselling author of romantic suspense and paranormal romance. She lives in Fredericton, New Brunswick, Canada, with her husband, two adult children, beloved Rotti-Shepherd mix Chloe and tuxedo cat Ruckus.

HEATHER DOHERTY fell completely in love with writing while taking creative writing courses with Athabasca University. Motivated by her university success, and a life-long dream of becoming a novelist, she later enrolled in the Humber School for Writers. Her first literary novel was published in 2006. She writes in a number of genres with Norah (cozy mystery, YA paranormal, dystopian romance). Heather lives in Fredericton, New Brunswick with her family.

Connect with Norah Online:
Twitter: http://twitter.com/norah_wilson
Facebook: http://www.facebook.com/NorahWilsonWrites
Goodreads:
http://www.goodreads.com/author/show/1361508.Norah_Wilson
Norah's Website: http://www.norahwilsonwrites.com
Email: norahwilsonwrites@gmail.com

Connect with Heather Online:
Facebook: http://www.facebook.com/heather.doherty.5
Email: heatherjaned@hotmail.com

www.ingramcontent.com/pod-product-compliance
Lightning Source LLC
Chambersburg PA
CBHW021944170626
46808CB00001B/26